Guilty Gucci

D1051403

Guilty Gucci

Ashley Antoinette

www.urbanbooks.net

Urban Books, LLC
78 East Industry Court
Deer Park, NY 11729

ISBN 13: 978-1-60162-481-9
ISBN 10: 1-60162-481-6

First Trade Paperback Printing February 2012
Printed in the United States of America

10 9 8 7 6 5 4

Distributed by Kensington Publishing Corp.
Submit Wholesale Orders to:
Kensington Publishing Corp.
C/O Penguin Group (USA) Inc.
Attention: Order Processing
405 Murray Hill Parkway
East Rutherford, NJ 07073-2316
Phone: 1-800-526-0275
Fax: 1-800-227-9604

"Guilty Gucci . . . a Red Bottom Edition"

Another Ashley Antoinette Classic

I dedicate this novel to the two men who make my life worth living. To my husband and son. JaQuavis Jovan Coleman and Quaye Jovan Coleman. My every breathing moment I am thinking of the two of you. Our family bond is cemented by love that is blessed by GOD. Together we will weather any storm, accomplish every goal, and take over the world one day at a time. I'll always be with both of you. You give me purpose. You are my protectors. You are my soul mates and I live for the two of you. My Kings Forever.

Love Always Your Wife and Mommy

www.ashleyjaquavis.com

Chapter One

RIP!!

Chanel winced in pain as the hair from her vagina was removed while undergoing her monthly Brazilian wax. The sting was so great that it brought tears to her eyes. She bit into her bottom lip as her usual esthetician finished and applied a cool mist to her skin to hinder the raw feeling.

"I tell you, I've been doing these for twenty years and I have never had one myself. I don't know how you gals put up with so much pain!"

"It's all in the name of money," Chanel replied.

"Money? You mean beauty, sweetheart . . . it's all in the name of beauty. That's how the saying goes," the woman replied.

Chanel nodded, but she had meant it as she had said it the first time. She kept herself groomed because it kept her paid. Her men loved her bare assets and she gladly kept it that way because it led her to the money. Chanel was a girl who came from everything and had fallen from grace until she had nothing left. Growing up wealthy, Chanel was used to having it all. The best education, luxury clothing, stocks and bonds, vacation homes . . . she had been afforded everything. The Stocker women had always been beautiful. They were bred up with doe-shaped eyes, long legs, and slim waists. She was from the high society for sure and it had been inevitable that she live her life among the lucky elite . . . the wealthy. She had been spared nothing and in a family full of powerful women she was the next in line to inherit the throne of seduction and matriarch influence. She had learned to manipulate early in life, watching her mother charm her way through the world. Chanel learned to do the same with ease. No one, especially men, had ever told her no. It just wasn't a word that was meant for her. Hearing it burnt her ears like gonorrhea did a French whore. As a little girl she learned to bat her eyelashes . . . As a teen she perfected the art in swaying her hips . . . As a grown woman she learned to spread her legs; all of her tactics always led her down the same road . . . the road to riches. She always got her way, no matter what. Her mother and aunts ran the family because no male was ever quite man enough to take control of the affluent empire. Lavish living without regard for bank balances and an unexpected economic downturn caused the family money to dwindle substantially, but with looks that women would kill for, the Stocker women did not stay down for long.

It wasn't until Chanel's mother, Lidia, roped in the big fish . . . did their luxury lifestyle become cemented in stone. Faugner Scott, a high-profile attorney, was the greatest catch in Lidia's entire pool of men. He was the founding partner at Ryman, Lerner, and Scott . . . the District of Columbia's largest firm to be exact.

Before anyone ever noticed that her family was in dire straits, Lidia had married Faugner, under the terms of a very strict prenuptial agreement of course. Faugner was like a knight in shining armor, coming in on his white horse . . . more like his white Phantom . . . to save the day. His net worth was in the millions and as Mrs. Faugner Scott, Lidia no longer had to worry about her own finances. Chanel and her mother were moved into

Faugner's home immediately, and they took over the castle quickly, redesigning it from top to bottom and taking their places on their new throne.

At age sixteen, Chanel had a new father figure in her life. She took to him quickly because he treated her so well. She was sent to the best schools, drove the flyest whips, and literally wanted for nothing. Lidia was rarely around because she lived the life of a socialite and kept wife. She hosted charity events, threw dinner parties, and chatted it up at daily brunches with the other wives at the country club. Enjoying her secured spot at the top, she was never in the household. She was busy putting in work and making herself desirable in a network of wealthy men and women. That way if she ever fell off she could easily become the next man's trophy wife. Networking was all in the game. She left out in the morning and returned well after midnight on most days. Not to mention the various vacations that Faugner allowed her to indulge in. She was away more than she was home and her new family barely saw her. Chanel had been the one to do the laundry and cook the meals. Upon moving in with Faugner, Lidia immediately dismissed the notion of a housekeeper. "No woman, no matter how old, how fat, how ugly, needs to be around my husband that much. I am the only queen of this castle," she explained when Chanel asked why they couldn't hire help. "That's what I have you for, dear. I handle my part in the bedroom and you handle your part around the house. Between the two of us we will make sure that this power move will be our last," Lidia said. Chanel fell in line and played her part, doing all the things that her mother neglected to do. She made sure that her stepfather's briefcase was waiting at the front door and that his tie was adjusted neatly around his neck each morning. She had played her mother's role for so long that she began to take her place.

Faugner and his stepdaughter went to dinners and plays. They had a movie night every week and grew close quickly. He was good to her and Chanel loved him dearly. She thought that he was the perfect man. He was strong, extremely handsome, rich, and so supportive. He treated her like a princess. Her mother had already given her an unhealthy relationship with money. There was no limit as to what she would go through to get it. Chanel's happiness depended on her wealth and with Faugner spoiling her he only made it worse. She became accustomed to a certain lifestyle and she would eventually move mountains to maintain it.

As Chanel dressed herself she remembered how it had felt to be so well kept. To be taken care of and she remembered the day that it all was taken away.

"I can't believe Lidia isn't here to help me shop for a prom dress. She said she would be here," Chanel complained as disappointment laced her tone. "I'm not even surprised." Chanel's eyes pooled with tears of frustration. She couldn't even be mad at Lidia. Her mother had never been one to keep promises so Chanel felt like a silly kid for even allowing herself to look forward to the rare mother/daughter bonding excursion. It was foolish of her to get her hopes up and now that she had been let down she had no one to blame but herself. Lidia was only concerned about one person . . . Lidia.

Faugner stood off to the side on an important call, but he could see the sadness that took over Chanel's face. He adored her and hated to see the dismal look in her eyes.

"Hey, let me call you back," he said abruptly. He sat on the Parisian leather furniture that decorated his great room. He patted his lap, suggesting for her to come take a seat. Chanel sat down, her bottom lip inadvertently poking out, revealing her crushed feelings. "You know your mother wouldn't miss this unless it was very important," Faugner whispered, trying to put a temporary bandage on Chanel's scarred heart.

"Yeah, right," Chanel scoffed. "She never makes time for me. I don't even know why I expected her to take me in the first place." Chanel rolled her eyes toward the sky while shaking her head back and forth. She folded her arms tightly across her chest as it heaved up and down from stifled emotion. Anger pulsed through her as she thought of the constant disappointments that her life had been. Sure she had never been denied any material possession, but since the day she was born she had been going through an emotional famine. "She's such a joke. I can't wait until I'm eighteen so I can get from around her. You can't miss what you don't see."

She was noticeably upset, despite the fact that she was putting on her best poker face. Faugner hated to see sadness painted upon her face. "You're too beautiful to look so angry," he said as he arose from his seat and headed toward the door. "Let's go."

"Go where?" she asked.

"You have a prom dress to buy, right?" he asked. He held up the keys to his Phantom, the one car that he never allowed her to drive. "And you're driving."

Her eyes lit up and her frown melted away, giving way to a smile. "Seriously? You're going to come with me? You hate shopping," she said.

"I hate shopping with Lidia. You're much better company. Let's go," he replied as he gave her a wink. She joined him and he wrapped his arm around her shoulder, pulling her close before escorting her out of the house.

Faugner was a young success story. He had started his own law firm right out of college after setting a precedent and attaining a perfect score on the bar exam. He was now the city's most sought after attorney and at forty-two he was the youngest partner at his firm.

Chanel drove all the way into New York City, knowing that Faugner would never protest. He smirked at her as he watched the sly smile she displayed. She was dying to roll down the window so that she could cruise the streets with her pretty face on full display. "You came all the way to the city you might as well go on a shopping spree," he said.

She beamed and replied, "I was going to anyway. You spoil me too much to tell me no."

Chanel ripped up and down the streets of Manhattan like a young socialite with bags galore. The handsome gentleman whose arm she clung to looked more like her sponsor than her stepfather. He had only been in her life for a year and a half, but he contributed so much. They were friends and he understood her. He made her feel special and made time for her; things that her own mother was too busy to do. She loved Faugner's attentive nature and she reveled in his presence because when she talked to him he spoke to her not at her. He treated her like an adult and listened when she opened her mouth. Her respect for him was immeasurable. Chanel wrapped her arm through Faugner's and clung to him as they maneuvered through the city blocks. "I love it here. As soon as I graduate I'm moving here. Can't you just see me in New York City? It's where I belong. A loft apartment in Midtown . . . midnight walks through Central Park. . . ."

"I can see it. It's a fitting choice," he replied as he admired the stars in her young eyes. He remembered what it felt like to have big dreams; to be young with the world at your feet and optimism in your heart. The reality didn't always live up to one that was plotted out in your head, however. Life had a cruel way of beating you up no matter how much success one attained. There were so many other factors, so many things that could happen that could change things for the worse. Faugner wouldn't tell Chanel that though. How could he? It was her right to fantasize about how grand her life would be. It was a part of her rite of passage into adulthood. He refused to kill that illusion of a perfect life. "I'm going to miss you though. It won't be the same without you around, but if it's really what you want to do I'm behind you. In fact, I know a Realtor up here who can help you find something. I'll foot the bill and all," Faugner said. "Just promise you won't let some young Harlem nigga steal your heart and turn you sour."

Chanel knew that the only man who had her heart was Faugner. She was infatuated with him and no boy could measure up to him in her eyes. She wanted a husband just like him one day and some knucklehead from New York shouting, "Yo, son!" wasn't going to cut it.

"I promise," she replied. "I'm not thinking about no dudes."

After shopping they hung out in Times Square and dined at Faugner's favorite upscale restaurant. By the time they were done half the night had passed.

"We may as well stay the night and drive back in the morning," Faugner suggested, knowing that he had consumed too much wine to drive safely back to D.C.

"What about the firm?" Chanel asked, knowing that Faugner never called off work. He was all business all the time . . . hardworking; something that she admired.

"I make my own rules at the firm. That's why I'm the boss," he replied. "They will survive one day without me. You need my undivided attention right now so that's all I'm focusing on. I never want you to get lost in the chaos. Lidia and I can handle it, you shouldn't have to."

Chanel nodded her head, his words warming her because it was exactly what she needed; someone whose world revolved around her. She knew that Faugner couldn't cater to her every day, but today he had been thoughtful and it had made her feel wanted.

They checked into a five-star hotel and Faugner handed her the key to her room. "I'll see you in the morning." He kissed her forehead and then retired to his own sleeping quarters to call it a night.

Chanel looked at all the shopping bags feeling overjoyed that Faugner never gave her a limit. Even Lidia would have limited her shopping and told her no at some point, but Faugner never did. He whipped out his black card effortlessly and without a second thought to cover her elaborate and expensive purchases. He didn't treat her like a child. Seventeen-year-old Chanel always felt grown up in his presence. Looking around the luxury room she relished in the lifestyle that she was living. She wasn't quite ready for the night to end, and as she walked over to the mini-bar mischief filled her mind. Faugner had already let her indulge in a glass of merlot at dinner; surely he wouldn't mind if she kept the party going on her own. Chanel didn't even particularly like the taste of alcohol, but she loved the way the slight buzz of the red wine was making her feel. She pulled a small single-serve bottle of chardonnay from the fridge and didn't bother with a glass. She popped the top and drank it quickly as she made her way to the claw-foot tub to draw herself a bath. Picking up the cordless phone she ordered room service and then grabbed another small bottle of wine, this time pouring it in a glass, before she stepped into the warm, bubbly water. A long sigh eased out of her pursed lips as she enjoyed the heat while perspiration built on her face. She enjoyed the bath as she laid her head against the back of the tub while sipping on the wine. She couldn't wait to get this type of freedom. She wanted to live by her own rules on her own time . . . be responsible for her own life. She was ready to discover the world. Chanel had yearned for her mother to show her the ropes of womanhood, but she was too busy living her own life to give any direction to Chanel. Chanel's only life lessons had been learnt by being observant. Her eyes and ears had taken in all that Lidia had done over the years and she interpreted her mother's actions in her own naïve way. Lidia had neither the interest nor time to teach her daughter anything. So Chanel was determined to get out on her own and find the love that her mother failed to give her.

A knock at the door interrupted her relaxation and she quickly stood to her feet. The wine hit her all at once and her head spun slightly, reminding her that she was a lightweight. The buzz made her entire body tingle, hardening her nipples as the cold air hit them. She got out of the tub and wrapped herself in the plush hotel robe.

KNOCK KNOCK!

"I'm coming, I'm coming," she called out. Chanel opened the door to greet room service, but was hit with the unexpected when Faugner stood sternly before her. He looked at the glass in her hand and removed it before walking inside. "The front desk called me to let me know that the mini-bar was being used," he said.

"I thought I would have a drink," she said as she closed the door and took her glass back from him. "You let me drink at dinner tonight."

"I let you have one glass," he corrected. "It's attractive for a woman to know her limits. I don't ever want you to become a lush. Drunk women make foolish decisions."

Chanel walked toward Faugner, the robe hanging loosely off of her shoulders. Her wet skin glistened and Faugner noticed the tautness of her breasts as they sat upright, perky from youth and inexperience. He quickly diverted his eyes back where they belonged . . . on Chanel's face.

"I won't become one. I have you to look after me. You always take care of me," she said before she took the glass to her lips and finished the entire drink. Her head spun slightly as the premium wine took its effect. Enjoying the way that it was making her feel, Chanel waltzed over to the mini-bar to retrieve another bottle.

"Chanel, stop while you're ahead," Faugner warned as he approached her. Chanel chuckled softly and opened the bottle.

"Relax, you don't have to act so parental. *You* are not my father," she reminded. "We can have a little fun."

She tilted the bottle to her lips and wrapped her entire mouth around the nozzle as she let her tongue lap up the wine. She was feeling it and the liquor had made her bold. Releasing her of her inhibitions and making her feel sexy, powerful, in control.

Faugner reached for the bottle, but she quickly put it behind her back. "If you want it you'll have to get it," she said mischievously. She had always found her stepfather attractive. His good looks appealed to her, but now that she was partially drunk she grew the guts to flirt openly with him.

"You're drunk, Chanel . . . Just give me the bottle so that we can call it a night," Faugner said with impatience as he stepped closer to her to reach behind her back. His body pressed against hers, pinning her against the small desk. She sat her bottom down on top of it and he stood between her thighs.

"You want it?" she asked as she pulled it from behind her back. She removed the robe, exposing her bare body. "Come and get it." Chanel poured a small amount of wine on her bare breasts and spread her legs seductively. The wine had her flower budding and she was ready for it to be plucked. Her clit throbbed and she heard Faugner's breath catch in his throat as the wine dripped from her perky breasts, down her stomach, and ended in a puddle between her legs.

He reached for the robe and pulled it back over her shoulders.

"What are you doing? You're seventeen," he hissed harshly.

Chanel smiled because she knew that he was trying to do the right thing, but the imprint of his hard dick showed through his slacks. For the first time she felt how much power her womanhood gave her and it turned her on to know that she had caused the swell in his pants. She pulled the robe back down and rubbed his swollen package through his slacks. "I want you to fuck me, daddy," she said.

She stood and began to kiss his neck as she wrapped her arms around him. He dodged her advances, moving his face from side to side. "Chanel, wait. . . stop," he said as he wrestled with her, trying to keep her from touching him in his most sensitive of places.

"I would but you don't want me to," she replied. She stuck her tongue in Faugner's mouth and pressed her pussy against him as she grinded into him. She was so wet that she left his pants slick. A guttural moan escaped his lips . . . betraying his protesting position.

"I feel good don't I?"

"Chanel . . . I'm flattered, but you're my daughter," he said. "You have to stop. This isn't right. Stop, stop!" He grabbed her roughly as if he could shake the sense back into her, but Chanel was persistent. Lust had taken over her and she desperately wanted to feel him inside of her. Her clit was throbbing with so much intensity she was sure it had its own erotic pulse.

"I'm your wife's daughter and I do everything that she should be doing for you except fuck you," she replied. "I cook for you . . . I clean for you . . . I wash your clothes and rub your shoulders after work . . . but at the end of the night you fuck her. I go to sleep with my hands in my panties at night while I listen to you grunting and her moaning through the walls. We both know you should be fucking me. Her old pussy isn't what you want. You see my face when you fuck her don't you?"

Hearing Chanel say such dirty things only made Faugner's dick brick more. It was true that he had fantasized about her many times before but he had never intended to act on it. Now that she was here spread out in front of him like a beautiful buffet, his most carnal instincts urged him to have his way with her. His dick throbbed as she gyrated against him, making him feel as if he would bust at any moment. "Stop," he protested.

"Okay," she said as her fingers fiddled with his belt. "I'll stop but this is my room. If you really want me to stop all you have to do is leave." Chanel paused and looked up at Faugner. "You leaving?" she asked.

Faugner knew that this situation was dead wrong, but his feet were frozen in place. He didn't move and Chanel smiled as she removed his manhood from his

Polo drawers. "Fuck me," she whispered. "Oohhh fuck me. Teach me not to give your pussy away."

Plagued with passion, Faugner couldn't resist her and he grabbed her waist, lifting her in one swift motion onto his dick.

He backed her up until her back hit the wall and then he put a pounding on her young wetness. She sucked him in like a vacuum and he clenched his ass cheeks as he moved with skill, in and out of her. It felt wrong, but Faugner didn't care. It was too late to turn back and the sex was better than anything he had ever felt because the way that her pussy was absorbing his dick made it all right. His chocolate stick was swallowed by her gushiness as he grunted in her ear. Chanel was in heaven and she matched him stroke for stroke, thrusting her hips forward as she took the dick like a pro. The girth and size of him was more then she had ever experienced and she was loving his grown-man stroke as they fucked to a silent rhythm. "I love you. I love you . . . ooooh I love this dick. This feels so good."

Chanel had never had grown-man dick before and it was nothing like the little teenybopper boy toy who she had let take her virginity. Her body was being worked over by a seasoned lover and she melted at his touch. He carried her to the bed, not even coming out of her to walk, and then placed her down atop the stark white duvet. He dug deeper into her, digging out her guts as she moaned loudly, crying out in pleasure . . . in ecstasy. It was overwhelming to her young body and most certainly overwhelming to her young mind. The orgasm that overcame her body caused involuntary tears to fall down her cheeks. Their bodies intertwined, twisting from one position to the next without ever losing their rhythm and when they reached their climax they both groaned while holding each other tightly.

Faugner pulled out of her and released himself on her stomach as his head fell back in utter ecstasy.

Faugner looked down at Chanel and a thousand guilty bricks brought him back to reality. "This should have never happened. You know that right?"

Chanel nodded her head, unsure of what to say. She was speechless . . . He had left her breathless.

He looked down at her and shook his head. Chanel was the most beautiful young girl he had ever met and the last thing he wanted to do was to take advantage of her. He had fallen head over heels for her from the moment he laid eyes on her. It wasn't until she opened Pandora's box did he realize that there was more to his attraction than familial affection. Chanel was everything he would ever want in a woman. Ambitious, wild, witty, submissive to a man, beautiful . . . her only flaw was her youth. They belonged to two completely different generations and no one would ever understand. He was taking statutory risks by even being in her room. Chanel expected him to leave, but instead he crawled into her bed and pulled her into his arms.

"You're young," he whispered solemnly.

"I know," she replied. She reached behind her and found his manhood and massaged it gently, feeling it grow in her hands.

"I care for you, Chanel. I do and I will do anything for you. No one can know about this . . . about us," he said as he held her from behind while whispering the words in her ear.

"Us?" she asked as she turned around to face him. Her eyes were glazed slightly but they were hopeful, as if he held the key to her happiness in his hands.

"This . . . no one can know about this," he corrected. "I will always take care of you, Chanel . . . but Lidia is my wife, whether I like it or not. This thing with you doesn't change that. This has to be between us."

"I just want you to myself anyway. I won't say anything to anyone," she whispered. She positioned herself on top of his hard body and slid down onto his girth. Its thickness parted her walls as she mounted him. He put his hands on her hips and watched her as she rode him slowly, her mouth falling open in an O of satisfaction. They sexed all night until the sun came up and they finally collapsed from exhaustion. Chanel talked Faugner into extending their trip to New York one more day and the beginning of a love affair was forged right there amid the chaos of the city streets. They had everything in common but age. Nothing could have prepared Chanel for the hold that Faugner put on her. It was the greatest love she had ever felt . . . and the greatest one she would ever lose.

Temptation and lust made it hard for Chanel to stay away from Faugner. Even after they returned to their home in D.C. their sexual trysts continued. As their relationship flourished, her mother's relationship with Faugner diminished and Lidia was beginning to notice the change.

Months passed and Lidia was slowly losing her husband to her daughter. She could no longer satisfy him in bed . . . in fact her body turned him off. Chanel's breasts stood firm and round without the assistance of an underwire. Her hips and thighs had no cellulite; her stomach bore no stretch marks. She had none of the imperfections that came along with being a grown woman. She was still flawless and youth was on her side. Time had betrayed Lidia and her husband was drawn to a younger woman . . . to her daughter.

"Good morning," Faugner said as he walked up behind Chanel as she poured herself a cup of hot tea. "I miss you."

Chanel smiled. "I miss you too," she whispered back as she craned her neck to make sure that Lidia was nowhere in sight. "Your wife has been taking up a lot of your time lately." It had been an entire month since the last time they had been intimate with one another. Lidia had been keeping close tabs on Faugner, which made it extremely hard for him to ever get too close to Chanel. "Are you having sex with her?" Chanel asked with a tone of resentment in her voice. She knew that she had no right to pose such a question, but her young heart was involved. She couldn't help but to be jealous.

Before he could respond the sound of stiletto heels against marble tile floors interrupted them as Lidia descended the stairs. Faugner put some distance between himself and Chanel as they both went about their morning routine normally.

"If I don't get out of here soon I'm going to be late for brunch with the ladies . . . I swear I don't know why I even entertain these gossiping-ass floozies . . . I should just cancel," she fussed as she applied her earrings and sighed in exasperation. She grabbed her clutch and turned toward Faugner. "Will you be home when I return this evening?" she asked.

"Depends on how things go at the office. I'll call you if I'm going to be late," he responded as he sat down to the meal that Chanel had made him.

"You own the firm. I don't know why you just can't leave when you want to leave," Lidia complained.

"I leave exactly when I want to leave," he responded as he sipped his coffee as he absently pretended to read the morning paper.

Lidia walked behind her husband and wrapped her arms around his neck as she bent over to kiss his neck. She had known him long enough to know that if she wanted to get her way she needed to use sugar not shit.

"I love you, baby. I had a sexy surprise for you tonight. I wish you'd come home early," she crooned.

Chanel's hands shook as her eyes misted. She was glad that her back was toward them because they couldn't see her tears. She hated that she had to share the man she loved with another woman . . . her mother at that! She wiped her face and took her own plate to the table. She sat across from Faugner and her bottom lip curled in contempt as she eyed the couple. Faugner could feel the tension coming from Chanel and he removed Lidia's hands from his body. "I'll call if I'm going to be late," he said shortly.

The sound of the house phone was a quick escape for Chanel, who jumped at the opportunity to answer it.

"Don't even pick it up!" Lidia shouted. "It's nobody but Trisha Hamilton calling to rush me. As a matter of fact . . . answer it and tell her I already left. I've got to go, honey, but I'll see you tonight!"

Lidia was out the door before she even finished the sentence and Chanel picked up the phone and hung it right back up.

She walked back into the kitchen and sat back down at the table; her eyes never left her plate as she gave Faugner the silent treatment.

"Chanel," he called as he watched her. Her feelings were obviously shattered and he hated to see her hurting. A man of his prestige, wealth, and good looks could have any woman in the world, but instead he had fallen for this young girl. He did not know how it had occurred, but he was too deep in to climb out of the messy bed he had made.

She didn't respond.

Faugner stood and walked around to her side of the table. He reached for her hand but she snatched it away.

"You're still fucking her," she said. "You said that—"

"And I meant it. I haven't touched your mother since we went to New York," he stated sincerely, cutting her off. "She senses that something has changed between us but I don't want her, Chanel."

He grabbed her hand and pulled her to her feet, forcing her into his body. His strong arms wrapped around her small waist but she pulled back in resistance.

"Don't," she whispered as she pulled her face away from his as he tried to kiss her. "Is this what it's going to be like forever? Do you know how I feel sitting here watching her fall all over you?"

"I'm sorry, Chanel. I really am but you know my situation. You're not even eighteen yet. I'm risking my career and my freedom doing this with you. I love you and you're worth it, but your mother is my wife for the time being."

Chanel knew that she looked young and sounded immature but she didn't care. "I just want you to be mine," she whined sadly. Her young heart couldn't handle the circumstances that she had gotten herself into. Chanel didn't want to share her man with anyone else. It was torture. "She doesn't even deserve you. You should be mine."

"I am yours," Faugner replied as he reached underneath her dress and palmed her pussy, creating friction against her clit. "And this is mine right?" he asked.

She nodded her head and bit her bottom lip as she felt her wetness saturate his fingers. "You haven't even been coming to my room at night. I've been waiting on you, daddy," she admitted.

"I wanted to, baby girl, but your mother has been on my back. It's been wet for me?" he asked as he lifted her from the floor and placed her on the kitchen table.

He placed a hand on her neck and pushed her down, forcing her to lie flat on the table, then he spread her legs. Her young flesh smelled fresh and was waxed clean the way that he liked it. He personally paid for her Brazilian wax services once a month. It was a painful ritual that she was becoming accustomed to. He lowered his head and devoured her juicy clit.

"Aghh!" she moaned loudly as her back arched and her thighs tensed in pleasure.

Faugner circled his tongue on her love button, enjoying the taste of her pink flesh as she humped his face in heat.

"Oooh, daddy," she moaned. He reached up and rolled her hard nipples between his fingers as he simultaneously pleasured her.

His dick was solid and stood at attention but he wanted to let her get off before he ever entered her. Their chemistry heated the room and all bygones were forgotten as she screamed out as her orgasm came raining down.

Chanel squeezed her thighs around his head and her fingertips rubbed his head as she came in his mouth. Her eyes snapped shut as her body shuddered.

"Aghhh, daddy!"

Both of them were too caught up in their rapture to notice that Lidia had doubled back for the wallet she had left on her nightstand.

"You son of a bitch!" she shouted as tears filled her eyes. Her voice roared through the foyer and like a lioness that had suddenly been forced to protect her home front she attacked. "This is why you haven't been interested in me?"

Faugner and Chanel were completely caught off guard. He stood with Chanel's juices covering his mustache while Chanel scrambled off of the table, pulling her dress down over her thighs.

"Ma!" she exclaimed as she frantically adjusted her clothes.

"And you!" Lidia screamed. She lunged toward Chanel but Faugner stepped in front of her to shield her from her mother's attack.

"You're protecting her? Defending her! Fucking my daughter, you bastard!" Lidia was on a rampage. "I will ruin you, motherfucker! You will get out of my way or your statutory-raping ass will be all over the afternoon news!"

Lidia stormed past Faugner and slapped the taste from Chanel's mouth.

"Ma, I'm sorry!" she cried.

"No, bitch, you're not sorry, but you will be," Lidia warned. She dragged Chanel out of the house and tossed her on the front porch. "You get the fuck out of my house! You are no longer welcome here. If you ever come back I will kill you dead. You want to sleep with my husband? You just bit the hand that feeds you. You're a disgrace and a whore! I'm not letting you come between my marriage and I'm not leaving my husband over you. Now get off my property!"

Chanel sobbed uncontrollably as she went to reason with her mother, but before she could step one foot over the threshold the door was slammed in her face.

"Ma!" she shouted as she hit the door with the palm of her hand. "Mama, please! Open the door! Ma!" she cried, but neither Faugner nor her mother ever answered it.

Faugner was stuck between a rock and a hard place because he knew that Lidia would make good on her threat and expose his relationship with a minor for the world to judge. No one would ever understand that the emotions he felt for Chanel were genuine and he would lose everything. So despite the sincerity of his feelings for Chanel, he couldn't come to her defense. He ached inside as he listened to her cry desperately through the door.

"I will destroy your entire existence if you ever disrespect me again. You want to embarrass me and betray me, you bastard? You have messed with the wrong one, dear love. A woman scorned is nothing compared to what this scorned bitch will do," Lidia warned before stalking up the stairs and out of sight. Faugner was stuck in the nightmare that had become his reality. He had jeopardized so much over Chanel and even in the aftermath of being caught up he still couldn't harbor his feelings for her. He didn't regret his affair with her, but he was not foolish enough to think that Lidia was making idle threats.

Chanel's entire world changed drastically from that moment forth. She was all mixed up in the head because her young emotions were running rampant. It was like she could see her heart broken into little pieces before her, but she couldn't quite put it back together. Chanel had no friends so she couldn't bum even one night's sleep on anyone's couch cushions. She was on her own at a tender age and as she walked away from the plush estate that she called home, she felt lost. Day turned to afternoon, which eventually gave way to nightfall and Chanel found herself in a city diner eating a meal she couldn't afford. Her tear-streaked face was set in anguish as she allowed her heart to bleed from its very first heartbreak.

"He didn't even stand up for me. He just stood there," she sobbed to herself as the salt from her tears seasoned her plate. As she leaned her head against the diner window she wished that her head was as clear as the night sky. She could see straight to the full moon that illuminated above her head. It was full and bright, enticing her to leave her problems on this sinful earth and take it straight to the stars. She wanted nothing more than to just be free of the mess that her life had suddenly become. Chanel had never felt so lonely. Loving a man was like giving him all the power and until that very moment Faugner had cuffed her nicely, making the creases of her mouth turn upward simply by being around her. But now she was experiencing the flip side. Their underground love affair had been exposed and she was tasting the bitter flavor that the whirlwind romance had left behind. *I have to talk to him,* she thought. *He can't just leave me. We were supposed to be together. He doesn't love her!* The frantic thoughts raced through her mind one after another as she silently waged a verbal war against her mother. Chanel didn't care that it was she who had done the betraying. In her eyes her man had been stolen. Fuck the logistics.

In the haste of the madness, she had been unable to grab her belongings. She closed her eyes and shook her head in deep regret, knowing that her cell phone had been left on the bureau beside her bed. She couldn't recall his number by heart. *I know I know his number. Why can't I remember it?* she asked herself, stressing to the point of insanity. Knowing that Faugner's contact information was unlisted, the only thing she could do was call his office to leave a message. She knew that he would get it the next morning, she just had to bide her time and pray that he reciprocated her need for communication. She used her shirt to wipe the snot from her nose and clear the streams of wetness that had run down both sides of her face. Although no one was worried about Chanel, it felt like the entire restaurant was staring . . . as if they knew the predicament she was in. She felt judgment as she rose from her seat and walked swiftly to the back of the restaurant where the payphones were located. Her mouth twisted in a grimace as her privileged ear touched the grimy plastic of the telephone receiver. She pressed zero and waited for the operator to greet her.

"Faugner Scott's office . . . I need to be connected to attorney Faugner Scott," Chanel blubbered into the phone. She couldn't even control her voice long enough to speak clearly, but somehow the operator connected the call. This would probably be the only chance for her to reach out to Faugner so she pleaded with the machine shamelessly for him to come to her rescue.

"Faugner, it's me. I need you right now. I have nowhere to go. Why are you doing this to me? I love you. You didn't even take my side? Please come and get me . . . I need somebody. I don't have anyone but you. I thought you loved me," she ranted repeatedly, while sobbing. The voice mail system cut her off right after she left the details of her location.

She returned to her table and sat all night, hoping with all of her might that Faugner would come for her. Hours passed and the diner began to fill with the club hoppers who were looking to parlay the after party into the small establishment. There wasn't an available table in the spot, which only brought attention to the fact that she had loitered for too long.

"Look, honey, you've been here all night. This ain't no shelter, sweetheart. You can't sleep here. We have too many people and not enough tables to let you just linger around like this a motel," the waitress said as she tapped a long red fingernail against the steel tabletop, waking Chanel up from the brief nod she had fallen into.

Chanel opened her eyes and immediately protested because she really had nowhere to go. "Look can't I just stay for a little while? I'm waiting on someone. He's meeting me here soon," she said in a low tone so that the group of people standing behind her wouldn't overhear. "He'll be here any minute."

"Listen, honey, you've been singing that same song all night—"

Before the lady could continue a dark-skinned guy stepped out of the crowd and said, "Don't worry about it . . . she can keep the table. I see some of my peoples across the room. We'll gang up with them."

The waitress looked skeptically at Chanel as if to say, *he just saved your ass.* "Yeah, okay, but if someone else comes in you will have to give them your table. And I need to take your bill up now," she said rudely. The implication that Chanel was going to stiff her was evident in her tone of voice.

Chanel wanted to snap back from embarrassment. *How dare this broad try to play me? Putting me on the spot, you funky, diner-working bitch,* she thought, ready to go in.

The guy frowned slightly in curiosity but from the deer-in-headlights expression on Chanel's face he knew that she didn't have the money. He pulled out a fifty-dollar bill and handed it to the waitress.

"This should cover her food and the rest is for you. Just let her keep the table," he said sympathetically.

Chanel smiled graciously. "Thank you," she said.

One of the girls from the group popped her gum loudly and stepped in front of the guy. "Are we going to eat or what?"

"Y'all go ahead. I'll be over there in a minute," the guy said, without ever taking his eyes off of Chanel.

He sat down across from her. "You a'ight? Looks like you're having a rough night," he said.

"I'm fine. I'm waiting for my . . . my . . ."

"Pimp?" he asked.

"Excuse me?" she shot back, highly offended.

The guy held his hands up in his own defense, hearing the anger in her voice as she explained. "Whoa . . . I did not mean to offend you, baby. You just look . . ."

Chanel covered her face with her hands as she remembered her appearance. "Like shit," she finished. She tried to tame her hair and wipe the runny mascara from her cheeks, but it was use. The usual teenage beauty queen was out in the most popular after-hours spot in the city looking like a bum broad. She hadn't realized how foolish she looked until the guy had sat across from her.

"I'm waiting for my boyfriend," she corrected. "We had a fight. I needed to clear my head. . . ."

"You're good. I didn't mean nothing by it. You just look like you could use some help. I just assumed . . ." the guy offered.

"Well you know what they say about making assumptions!" she shot back. "And even if I needed help, I don't even know you and you don't know one thing about me," she said.

"You're right . . . I'm Corey Banker . . . My friends call me Banks," he introduced.

"So we're friends?" she asked with a slight smirk.

"Not yet, but I'm hoping we could be. Even with your eyes all puffy and your makeup a mess you still kinda fly," he admitted with a laugh.

She had to laugh too and as she exhaled she had to admit that the laughter felt good. He had definitely lifted her spirits even if it was only for a fleeting moment.

"So what's up . . . you got a number where I can reach you?" he asked.

"Not really. My situation is complicated right now. I'm with somebody and besides I don't mess with dope boys," she said. "I'm a lady. I'm not impressed by your chain and your flashy old-school whip. I prefer my men more seasoned." She was teasing lightly but behind the fun and games she was serious. Faugner had spoiled her and she was used to living the champagne life. There was nothing that this young boy could do for her with his beer money.

"Oh now who is the one making assumptions? Huh? What, you like old men or something?" he asked. He knew plenty of chicks who played in the league of sugar daddies. The nasty old-head niggas was making it hard on young'uns like himself who were hoping to score a date with one of the city's pretty young things. These new-school divas didn't respect anything but money and that was something that Banks didn't have at the moment. A young man on a football scholarship at Morgan State, he only had ambition to offer. He wanted a chick who could jump on board and help him bring his dream into reality, not one who wanted to benefit off of his hard work after every brick was laid and cemented. Banks wanted a Bonnie to his Clyde, a woman who could see that it got greater later and one who was willing to put in some work to help build a lucrative future.

"No, not old men, just old money," Chanel said, confirming his suspicions.

At that moment Faugner walked up to the table and cleared his throat, interrupting their conversation. His appearance was scruffy as if he had gone through hell just to get there and there were red scratch marks on his face and neck.

"You came?" she said in shock as Faugner eyed the young man before him.

"Of course I came."

"Umm . . . Faugner, this is . . . Banks. He paid the bill for me. He was just leaving," she explained.

Banks stood up and reached out his hand but Faugner simply looked at it.

"Let's go, Chanel," he said sternly as he walked toward the exit. Chanel hesitated.

"So that's your name," Banks said.

"Yeah," she answered with a smile. For some reason she didn't want to leave because she knew that their paths wouldn't cross anytime soon. "Hey, thanks for everything."

"Yeah, I'll be seeing you around. My money won't be young forever. It'll grow up one day," he said with a wink.

She smiled and left him standing where he stood, intrigued by her essence.

"Who is he?" Faugner asked.

"Oh? You can speak now? But earlier when my mother was dragging me out of her house you didn't have anything to say? How could you?" she asked as she turned toward him entering the front seat of his luxury car.

"She's threatening to kill my career, Chanel. You wouldn't understand," he shouted. He had never raised his voice at her or spoken down to her before. The fact that he felt that she couldn't relate stung.

"Why? I'm young not dumb!" she argued. "You hung me out to dry! I've been out here all day and all night without a dime. I have nowhere to go!" Her anger dissipated into sadness as the weight of her dilemma caused her shoulders to sag forward. Wrecked with sobs she poured out her soul to him. "I can't do this anymore, Faugner. You have to leave her. I love you and I want you to choose."

Faugner sighed. He had forgotten how fragile a young girl's heart could be. He had enjoyed the immaturity of her body. With Chanel he was the best lover she knew because she hadn't experienced many before him. That was to his advantage and now as he sat listening to the rawness of her pain he realized that his was the disadvantage of it all. The young girl had invested everything into him. In him she saw her hopes and dreams, her future . . . but in her Faugner only saw the present. Their affection for one another was unbalanced. She loved him more and everybody knows that the one who loves the most always loses. It was true that Faugner did care for Chanel. He would even go so far as to say that he loved her, but he was a realist, also. Their relationship could never become public knowledge. There would be no long strolls through the park or movie dates after dark. They would always be confined within the four walls of some hotel room and no matter how expensive the sheets were, it would never be what Chanel deserved. He couldn't love her openly or freely because his colleagues would never understand. Unbeknownst to everyone else, his firm was slowly drowning in debt. He was wealthy but not even he was immune to a sick economic system. His firm was seeing the effects of a bad recession and just like any other businessman he had to be careful how he handled this financial downturn. He couldn't afford to go out on that love-struck limb with Chanel, especially when he knew that it was bound to break.

"I do love you, Chanel. I do," he replied.

"Then leave her!" Chanel cried. "Just leave her."

"I can't do that, sweetheart," he whispered. Chanel leaned her head against the passenger side window and cried as Faugner drove her to the Four Seasons. He went inside and purchased the penthouse suite for two weeks. He would never see Chanel out on the street and figured that it would be enough time for things to cool off at home. He retrieved her from the car and wrapped his long tan raincoat around her shoulders, pulling up the collar to shield her face as he escorted her up to the room. She was distraught . . . shattered by the thought of being without him. Her young heart was in such tangles that she didn't even look at the situation through her mother's eyes. She hated her. Secretly she felt that they had always hated each other.

She wrapped her arms around herself and sat on the edge of the bed. Faugner wiped his beard and sighed, then sat beside her, placing one hand on her knee. The last thing he had ever meant to do was mislead her to this point. If life were a fairy tale she would be his happy ending. She made him feel things that he never had before but life wasn't an illusion, but yet an ugly reality full of responsibilities and expectations. Life was full of disappointment. A foolish man would love her despite the age difference, despite the taboo surrounding their illicit affair, but he had never been a risk taker. He had gone with the odds his entire life and with his financial stability on the rocks he could not afford to be with her. Choosing Chanel over Lidia would bankrupt him and possibly imprison him.

"You know we have to end this," he whispered.

Chanel looked up at him, eyes cloudy, chest pounding. "No . . . no! I can't let you go," she pleaded shamelessly as she tried to crawl onto his lap. "Please, daddy, I don't want to let you go," she whispered, tearing at his clothes as he turned his head to avoid her kisses.

"We have to, Chanel. I could get into a lot of trouble. Your mother will never let this happen," he said sternly. "Even if I leave her I can't be with you. She knows too much. She will use it against me. You won't want me when I can't take care of you . . . buy you the things you like."

"Daddy, no. Don't, baby. Don't say that. I love you. I'll do anything for you. You don't need her," she whispered as she struggled against him, finally pushing her tongue down his throat. The warm wetness of her mouth caused him to groan as she used her body weight to push him backward on the bed. His hands roamed her body, his touch electric as she mashed her body against his.

"I love you," she whispered. "I thought you loved me."

Faugner didn't know what it was about this young girl but she drove him insane. "I love you too," he replied as he grabbed the back of her neck while passionately savoring the juices on her tongue. "I won't let you go. You're mine. Please tell me you won't let her take you away from me. Make love to me, Faugner. Put your mouth on me," she whined. His touch had lit her fuse and she was ready to explode.

Caught up in the lust the bulge in his pants was doing the thinking for him as he pulled Chanel's shirt over her head and released her beautiful, perky breasts. He suckled them, licking her nipples into erection, making her lips part as gasps of air came out. Sheer pleasure was what she felt. Faugner was always so gentle, so patient, so skilled with her. The cream coating the walls of her pussy and wetting her inner thighs was proof that he was doing something right. Using his strength he lifted her until she sat on his face and he was parting her southern lips with his tongue. She melted like a Popsicle on a hot summer day as she rotated her hips until she came, long and hard. Faugner fucked Chanel like it was the very last time and brought her to an orgasmic high so many times that she lost count.

"I want this forever," Chanel whispered as she lay under him, a sheen of perspiration cooling her down after the heated session they had just had. "I don't want you to be with her."

"Even if I left your mother it wouldn't be enough. She would still be a thorn in my side. Nothing less than death will stop her from outing us," Faugner explained as he stroked her head.

That was the only seed needed to grow the idea of murder in Chanel's head.

"So why don't we make that happen?" Chanel asked.

Silence filled the room as Faugner lifted his head to look at Chanel. "What are you talking about? Don't say things like that," he said.

"I don't want you with her. I don't care what it takes," she admitted. "If she's out of the picture you wouldn't have to worry about her destroying your career or stopping us from seeing one another. I know we couldn't just come out as a couple, but at least we could still see one another."

Chanel was desperate and she was ranting like a madwoman as she sat up, trying to convince Faugner to see things her way. Yes, she was plotting on her own mother, but they had never been a team. Chanel was more an inconvenient accessory . . . her mother's biggest regret. Chanel wasn't crazy . . . she was crazy in love. As insane as it sounded Faugner couldn't help but to bounce the idea around in his head. Chanel's motivation was love, but Faugner was straight thinking about the money. Tossing the numbers around in his head he knew that he had two insurance policies of $1 million each taken out on his wife. Her untimely death was just what he needed to make him financially stable again. His money problems were an issue that he kept a secret. Neither Lidia nor Chanel knew of the sensitive matter, but each time they went on an elaborate shopping spree, he dreaded the total outcome. This sounded the like the perfect out. He could kill two birds with one stone.

"Are you serious?" he asked.

"I can tell that you're thinking about it. Are *you* serious?" she answered, to see just how far they were going to take this conversation.

"I know a guy," Faugner said hesistantly, thinking of one of his notorious clients. "This is your mother, Chanel."

"You're my man," she replied matter-of-factly. Her response was so concise that Faugner felt the hair on the back of his neck rise.

"This is murder we're talking about, Chanel," he whispered urgently to ensure that she understood.

She nodded her head nervously but didn't speak as she brushed a tear off her cheek.

Since Lidia was forcing her to choose, she was following her heart.

"Once I press play there is no taking it back. I just want you to understand," he explained.

"I do. This is what I want if it'll get me you," she replied.

Lidia's life hung in the wings and she wasn't even aware of it. She never saw the shots coming a few weeks later when a "burglar" broke into their home. Lidia was there alone because her husband was at work and her daughter was in school . . . the perfect alibis. When the intruder shot her at point-blank range in the face her entire world went black. The phone call came to Faugner at 11:28 A.M. and he quickly picked Chanel up from school as they rushed to the hospital, feigning worry and fear. The role of distraught daughter and horrified husband were played to a tee. They each were deserving of Academy Awards. It wasn't until they learned that the bullet didn't kill her did they realize just how much had gone wrong. Lidia survived and the guilt of what they had done forced them apart more than Lidia could have ever done. Tormented by what they had done, they grew uncomfortable around one another. The secret that bonded them also destroyed them. They couldn't look at one another without the devil occupying the space between their gaze. No amount of love could have sustained under those circumstances. Their relationship had been poisoned and there was an unspoken awkwardness between them.

Chanel moved away as soon as she was legally able to do so because she couldn't bear to look into her mother's scarred face. The once beautiful, mature woman now looked like something Frankenstein had put together. The scars from her surgery made her face look like puzzle pieces that didn't quite fit. She was hideous now and Chanel couldn't help but to think that now her mother's outsides reflected her insides. Ugly. Faugner stayed with Lidia, miserable but feeling obligated after the role he had played in her shooting. Their love had driven them both to madness and although Faugner snuck away every once in awhile to check on Chanel, they both knew that he would never stay.

"It will be seventy-five dollars," the lady said, snapping Chanel out of her daydream. Thinking of the past haunted her, sending chills down her spine.

Chanel shook her head from side to side as she focused on the woman in front of her. "What?" she asked.

"The wax is seventy-five dollars," the lady repeated.

Chanel smiled unsurely, knowing that she had zoned out momentarily as she took a stroll down memory lane. She laid a crispy hundred-dollar bill on the counter. "Keep the change." She pulled out her cell phone and scrolled through her list of favorite people. She smiled when she got to his name. She hadn't spoken to him in years but she was sure that the number had not changed. He always kept it the same so that she could reach him. He was no longer married to her mother. After years of staying out of guilt, Faugner finally left Lidia. They both were living in hell as a couple and decided to part ways so that they could each find inner peace. The $5 million that Faugner gave Lidia was the only reason she ever agreed to leave her posh marriage. Parting with the money nearly broke Faugner, but he knew that his firm would see better days and eventually dig him out of the hole that Lidia had left him in. Although Chanel knew of the divorce she didn't have any expectations of commitment from Faugner. The only thing they had was memories . . . some were the greatest of her life and others the worst. They went months, sometimes years without speaking but Faugner had always made sure she was okay. He had sent her money and would sneak off to spend long weekends with her on some exotic island, until she started to see other men. It was at that point that his jealousy caused him to stop his dealings with her. He wanted her to himself, but Chanel knew that the two of them would never be a real couple. Their relationship would always be taboo . . . too complicated for others to understand. She didn't hold her breath waiting around for Faugner to make an honest woman out of her. Even if he married her today the karma from setting up Lidia would surely make their union fail. She did her own thing and as she matured into a young woman she began to explore her options in men. The moment she began sleeping with another man was the moment that Faugner gave her an ultimatum. "Don't give away my pussy. Respect me or we're done," he told her.

"Respect you? Respect *you?* When you start claiming this relationship, you can start putting chains on this," she snapped, pointing to her womanhood. "Until then, you fall in line. I fuck who I want to fuck and if it's not you on a particular night then so be it." Chanel called herself trying to make him jealous. She had young dudes her age lined up around the block to make her their girl, but her interests were elsewhere. She wanted Faugner, but he wouldn't admit that he wanted her too . . . at least not openly. Chanel refused to be an exclusive secret and as a result Faugner walked out of her life. Chanel had never felt heartbreak so tough. The void he had left in her life was too huge to fill. No other caress felt like his, no one else's compliments could elicit such smiles out of her. No one could give her what Faugner had and losing him scarred her forever.

Chanel walked out of the full-service salon, headed toward home. She pulled down her car visor and admired her beautiful face. "Your loss," she said, referring to Faugner. He had left a bitter taste in her mouth. She had seduced, manipulated, and trained man after man, but Faugner was the only one who was able to do the same to her. He had gotten inside of her head at an early age. She had been mind fucked and it had been quite some time since she had last seen him, she was still so in love . . . although she would never admit it aloud.

She cleared her head of her past ghosts and put her mind in the right place for what she needed to do. No longer blessed with a silver spoon in her mouth she relied on her good looks to pull petty capers on thirsty niggas looking for a one-night stand. They wanted fast pussy and she wanted fast money. They never expected for her to lift their pockets by the end of the rendezvous. Chanel always kept herself well groomed, not only for herself, but to attract her prey with ease. From her freshly waxed love zone to her professional hair and nail job, even her biweekly facials . . . it all contributed to her money-making cause. She didn't have time to play wifey in order to get the things her pretty heart desired. Chanel was into working for hers . . . just the only job she had ever had was working men. That was her game of expertise. Like mother like daughter.

Chapter Two

"Get him out of me now!" Raegan shouted as she pushed with all of her might. "Now . . . get him out!" At twenty-two, Sunny Raegan was about to give birth to a baby . . . a boy . . . a son who she planned to name Micah II. Her heart pounded with the intensity of stampeding horses as she gripped the hand of the nurse who stood near her bedside. She had been in labor for ten hours and it was nothing like the fairy tale day she had made up in her head. It was her first child and she had been distracted by the ideal of having a baby. She had imagined children's birthday gatherings, adorable blue outfits, and nursery rhymes. She was inexperienced in motherhood and knew nothing about the labor pains, stretch marks, and the unending turmoil that came along with giving birth. After ten months, forty weeks, and countless hours of bloated feet, morning sickness, and a huge, uncomfortable belly, the day had finally come for her to meet her baby.

"Okay, Raegan, breathe, sweetheart . . . You have a few seconds before the next contraction comes," Dr. McEwen announced as she looked up at Raegan through her blood-stained thighs.

Raegan collapsed her head against the pillow and gasped for air as she looked around the room. It was full of people . . . nurses and doctors and orderlies . . . all there to help bring life into the world, but their presence wasn't enough. She was surrounded by a roomful of people, yet she had never felt so alone. None of them mattered to her; none of them could offer the type of support and love that she needed. The one person who was missing . . . the one person who had promised he would be there, was nowhere to be found. Micah had left her to bring their son into the world on her own.

"I need my phone . . . I need to call his father. He can't come yet. Micah has to be here," she pleaded as her emotions took over and tears emerged in her young eyes.

"You don't have time to make a call, Raegan. This baby is crowning and it's time to push," the doctor said.

"Please . . . just one call," Raegan begged.

The doctor nodded and a nurse handed her the hospital phone. She felt intense pressure between her legs and fought the urge to push as she dialed Micah's number. Whatever bit of strength she had left abandoned her when she heard a female voice answer the phone.

"Hello?"

The air deflated from Raegan's lungs. "Who is this?" she questioned weakly.

"Who is this?" the girl asked with a slight laugh.

A vice grip of anger squeezed tight at Raegan's heart, making it feel as if it would burst as she replied, "Who am I? Who are you? And why you answering my boyfriend's phone, bitch?"

Raegan was asking questions she already knew the answers to. *He's fucking around on me,* she thought as she gasped for air. *I'm lying here giving him a baby and he's with some other bitch! I knew he would do this to us.*

"Raegan, it's time. Put down the phone. Your baby needs you to be strong," Dr. McEwen said sympathetically, sensing that the best day of Raegan's life was turning out to be the worst day of her life.

Reluctantly, Raegan hung up the phone and gripped behind her knees as she pulled them to her chest. With a broken heart it took every single ounce of her being to push out her son. This was not how she had expected it to be. The joy of her first child was overshadowed by the humiliation and utter devastation that consumed her. The circumstances made it hard for her to be happy on this day. Affliction and hatred plagued her as she experienced the most satisfying pain she had ever felt. She didn't know how to feel. She was up and down all at the same time and Micah had taken away her fighter's spirit. Everything in her wanted to give up, but with her legs stretched wide open and her child depending on her for life that was the last thing she could do. She gritted her teeth and bore down as she took her anger out on her labor process. Every time a contraction hit her she growled like a lioness as she pushed relentlessly. Intense pressure built between her thighs as she struggled and closed her eyes . . . push . . . push . . . push . . . The word replayed through her mind repeatedly as flashes of Micah's face popped in and out of her thoughts. Finally, she felt her child come into the world and the moment she saw him, he became the love of her life. His subtle cry broke through the air like the scent of soul cooking on a Sunday morning. He was the spitting image of his father and she couldn't wait to show Micah what a beautiful combination the two of them had created. She was young and naïve. Raegan was sure that her newfound love for her child would be shared by his father. So positive that this baby would keep him faithful, she couldn't wait to get home to start her new life as a mother. She had given Micah a family, a seed to call his own . . . She was sure that this cemented her spot in his life. As she looked down at her baby she smiled and pulled him to her as she kissed his forehead. "I love you, baby boy," she whispered. As she sat alone in the cold, sterile room she had never felt so alone. There were no cards, no family members around to give their unwanted advice, and no father doting over his newborn child. It was just the two of them and as Raegan fell asleep with her child in her arms her joy quickly transformed to sadness.

As Raegan watched the city streets pass her by she felt a calm that she never knew existed. Her baby lay sleeping on her lap as she made her way home. She couldn't believe that the man who had fathered her child had missed the birth, but she told herself that it didn't matter because once he laid eyes on their son he would be smitten. Other chicks wouldn't be able to compete now that she had given him an heir. He would choose her, he would wife her . . . he had to. Right? After all of the things he had promised her and all of the people she had defied to be with him . . . it was time for him to return her loyalty. As the cab crept up to Micah's home butterflies filled her stomach. "We're home, baby boy," she cooed as she grabbed the bag of baby products she had accumulated from the hospital. She looked at the meter and said, "I have to go get some money out of the house. I'll be right back."

The driver nodded and Raegan exited the vehicle. She shielded her son from the cold winter wind as it bit at her exhausted limbs, almost knocking her off her feet.

She stepped inside and the heat instantly melted away the stiffness that clung to her bones. Afraid that she would awaken her baby, she didn't announce her presence. Instead she crept inside as she made her way to their bedroom. Everything in her wanted to cuss Micah out for not being there for her but she contained her anger. No matter how much she showed her displeasure she couldn't change the fact that he had missed the most important day in her life. *Just be cool, Raegan. It doesn't matter. As long as he is here for us now, just let it go,* she told herself.

When she entered the bedroom she lost all composure and her knees became so weak that she had to reach out, gripping the wall just to steady her balance. Her breaths became so shallow that it felt as if she would suffocate. The empty feeling she felt in her chest hurt worse than anything she had ever felt. Before her eyes, lying in the very bed in which they had conceived their son, lay Micah sleeping beside another bitch. She had only been gone for two days and already he had replaced her. She never thought he would have the audacity to bring another girl into their home, but the proof was in the pudding. He couldn't lie his way out of this one. Her eyes scanned the room and the evidence of his night of passion gave away his indiscretions. The condom wrapper on the bedspread, the black panties on the floor, the ruffled bed sheets beneath them, the way the girl's legs were intertwined with his . . . They painted a perfect picture of what had gone on the night before. Her heartbreak turned to rage as she walked out of the room, careful not to wake the sleeping couple up. *This nigga want to play games with me,* she thought. *He got this bitch in my house . . . in our bed.* She went to the spare closet and grabbed a suitcase as she began to fill it with some of her possessions. She took some of his as well, grabbing his Rolex and diamond chain. Micah wasn't a huge player in the game. He was getting little money . . . bill money and usually had some spare change to floss with so when she hit his stash she only pulled out ten stacks. It wasn't much but it was enough to give her the confidence to leave a no-good nigga with no-good intentions. Raegan put on a pot of boiling water as she walked outside to return to the cab. She put her baby's blanket on the seat, then placed him gently on top of it and then put her bag inside.

"Give me five minutes. I need to handle something real fast," she said as she handed the cab driver a hundred-dollar bill. She walked back inside with the determination of a woman scorned. Her insides rattled with every step she took, but she shook off the pain and made her way back to the pot she had prepared on the stove. As she grabbed the potholders and lifted it from the blue fire that danced beneath the steel, she halted as she looked out of the window at her awaiting cab. Her heart beat with intensity as adrenaline pumped through her. She headed up the steps and into the bedroom. She pulled back the covers and poured the scalding water right onto Micah's crotch.

"Aghh! Shit!" Micah screamed as he awoke in tremendous pain and the girl beside him scrambled to get out of the bed. He jumped up grabbing his manhood as he looked at Raegan in surprise. "Fuck is you doing?"

"Fuck am I doing?" she shot back. "What the fuck are you doing, Micah? I just had your son yesterday and you were laid up in this bitch with her?"

"Bitch, I should kill you," he shot as he lunged toward her and pinned her to the wall. Raegan's head hit the drywall hard, cracking it as Micah choked her.

"Fuck you," she said with teary eyes.

"Micah, stop," the random girl said as she tried to pull him off of Raegan. "Let her go."

"Bitch, nobody's talking to you," he seethed as he slapped her hand off of him.

"I give you a son and you give me an ass whooping. Is that how this works?" Raegan asked. Micah grabbed

Raegan's vagina roughly, threatening to rip the stitches that kept her insides from falling out and causing her to cry out in pain.

"Say you're sorry, bitch!" he demanded as he tightened the grip on her neck, cutting off her air supply. For a fleeting moment Raegan wondered if Micah would truly kill her and in that instant she realized that he was all talk. His actions never backed up his words of affection. He didn't love her. There was no way that this was what love was supposed to feel like. She fixed her lips to concede, but before the words could leave her mouth, the girl behind him lifted the steel pot and hit Micah upside the head with all of her might.

The hit barely fazed Micah as he turned to react, but Raegan grabbed the lamp off of the dresser and swung it at the back of his head. It shattered over him as glass stuck in the back of his neck and blood dripped from his open skull. She had split him open down to the white meat and felt no remorse as her emotions cheered her on.

Raegan and the girl attacked him simultaneously as he tried to shield himself from the blows. Raegan was swinging with all of her might while the girl was using her stiletto heels to pound out his face.

"You dirty dick-ass nigga. Fuck you!" Raegan shouted as she backed up from him. "Stay away from me and my son!" She backed out of the room as the other girl frantically slipped into her dress. Micah lay crumpled on the floor, bleeding as Raegan walked out, disgusted at herself for ever loving his bum ass.

When she finally made it outside she almost cried when she saw her suitcase sitting on the curb and her baby lying on top of it. The cab was long gone and her son was crying at the top of his lungs. "Oh my God. I'm so sorry . . . Mommy's so sorry," she whispered as she rushed to pick him up. She noticed that her bag was open slightly and her stomach sank as she knelt to examine the contents of her bag. The money was gone. She was broke and she had just burnt the only bridge that led to her stability. Hopeless, she knew that she couldn't go back inside. It was official. She and Micah were over. She had no choice but to start walking. She cradled her baby, trying to warm him in one arm as she carried her suitcase in the other. As she walked her tears froze on her face and her baby's cries broke her heart. "We don't need him, boo. We've got each other."

BEEP! BEEP!

The sound of a car horn caught her attention. The girl who had just fucked her man pulled up beside her. Raegan didn't hate her. Micah was a dog and she had known it all along. She had chosen to ignore the obvious in hopes that she would be the lucky lady to change his ways.

"Hey get in," she said.

Raegan kept walking and didn't look the girl's way.

"Look I can give you a ride. It's cold out here and you're walking with a baby. He's going to get sick," the girl reasoned. "I can take you wherever you need to go."

Raegan hesitated, knowing that she had no real destination. As much as she wanted to turn down the ride . . . the thought of warm heat lured her to the car.

"I didn't know he had a girl," the girl said as she drove off. The heat instantly settled the baby down. "I didn't even like that nigga. I was gonna rob him. I just wanted to find out where he kept the safe."

"What safe? That small balling–ass mu'fucka didn't have no safe. He had shoebox money," Raegan scoffed as she shook her head from side to side.

"Look. I apologize. I hope you don't have any ill will toward me," the girl said. "I'm Chanel."

Raegan wanted to beef out with the girl, but inside she knew that she had set herself up. She had invested her all into a man who had invested nothing. His disloyalty was inevitable. If it had not been this girl it would have been the next.

"Raegan," she replied.

"Where can I drop you off at?" Chanel asked.

Exhausted, Raegan sighed and responded, "There's a shelter on—"

"You're gonna stay at a shelter with your baby?" Chanel asked judgmentally. "You don't have any family?"

"No," Raegan said shortly. "The shelter will be fine."

Chanel shook her head and headed toward her own house. "A shelter isn't fine. What you gonna do, have your baby around crackheads and dirty homeless people?" Chanel shook her head back and forth. "You can stay with me for a few nights until you make arrangements."

Raegan wanted to protest but knew that she didn't have many other options. "You don't even know me."

"I know but I feel bad just dropping you at a shelter with a newborn. I have a roommate, but we live in a four bedroom so we have plenty of extra space," she answered. "I know you have to be exhausted. Once you rest up you can decide what your next move is. Besides I feel kind of guilty. I feel like if it wasn't for me you would be at home with your man."

"Highly unlikely," Raegan said.

"Well I hope you burned his dick off . . . Broke nigga don't deserve to ever get any pussy," Chanel uttered with a sneaky smile.

The girls broke out in laughter as Chanel headed home. As soon as Raegan stepped foot inside Chanel's home she could tell that the girl was getting a little bit of money. "My girl Lisa stays here, but you'll hardly ever see her. She's a good girl . . . a college student. Her head is always in the books so she won't even know you're here," Chanel said as she showed Raegan to one of the spare bedrooms.

"Thanks for this," Raegan said gratefully as she held on to her sleeping baby.

"Thanks for what?" Chanel replied as if it was nothing and to her it was no big deal. Real bitches did real shit and there was no way that she could see herself leaving Raegan and her son out in the cold. She invited Raegan to her home partly out of guilt, but mostly out of sympathy. She knew what it was like putting your trust into a no-good-ass nigga. Men had a way of selling women dreams of love and happiness. She remembered how it felt to have the rug suddenly pulled from under your feet. Her head had once been in the clouds and the long fall back down to earth had been hard one. Chanel had been burnt one too many times, so she felt Raegan's pain.

"Get you some rest, girl. I'll watch your baby so you can catch a few hours of sleep. You look like you're about to pass out," Chanel offered, her eyebrows dipping low in concern.

Raegan reluctantly handed Chanel her son. She didn't want to give him to her, but she was so damn tired. Chanel could see the lioness in Raegan coming out over her baby cub.

"I'm not on no petty shit," Chanel said to ease Raegan's concerns. "I'm just trying to help. I don't think with my heart . . . I think with my pocketbook. After I pulled off I didn't think a second thought about your man and I don't judge you for fucking him up. I'm just glad you didn't fuck me up."

Raegan chuckled as she handed Chanel her son. "Thank you."

"You're welcome. What's his name?"

"Micah . . . Micah II," Raegan replied.

Chanel brought the swaddled baby up to her face and kissed his nose. "Come on, Micah . . . let's go talk shit about your bullshit-ass daddy," she cooed. She gave Raegan a knowing look and Raegan chuckled as she shook her head and retreated to her room. She didn't know that she had just made a lasting friend. In fact she didn't know Chanel from the next bitch on the street, but she appreciated her. In the short time that they had known each other Chanel had been God sent.

Chapter Three

KNOCK! KNOCK! KNOCK!

"I swear to fucking God if that knocking wake this baby up I'ma slap the black off of somebody," Chanel whispered as she looked at the sleeping infant who slept beside her. It had taken her hours to get baby Micah to go to sleep and her irritation was at an all-time high.

Lisa appeared at Chanel's door. Her headscarf covered her short, tapered haircut, and she folded her arms in annoyance.

"You expecting somebody? It's three o'clock in the morning," Lisa complained. She didn't notice the baby in the room until she walked in. Her eyebrows rose in confusion. "Whose baby?"

"A friend of mine. She is in the spare room. Can you answer the door before he wakes up?" Chanel asked. "You know I don't let niggas know where I live so that has to be for you."

Lisa walked out of the room, her slender, long legs leading the way. Snatching the door open, she was ready to go off, but the sight of D.C.'s finest caused her spark to fizzle out.

"Can I help you officers?" she asked, her displeasure apparent.

"We are looking for a Sunny Raegan," one of the officers stated.

"Who?" Lisa asked.

"Ma'am, does a Chanel Rodgers live here? We need to speak with her. She was with the young woman we are looking for," the officer informed, with an impatient tone.

"Hold on. I'll be right back," Lisa said defensively as she began to close the front door. One of the officers placed his foot over the threshold to stop it from closing completely.

"Can we come in, ma'am?" he asked.

"Do you have a warrant?" she shot back. She didn't know what kind of trouble Chanel was in but she wasn't about to just feed her girl to the wolves.

"No. . . ."

"Then no, you cannot come in. I'll be right back," she snapped as she closed the door. She sprinted upstairs and into Chanel's room.

"Fuck is wrong with you? Why are you running?" Chanel asked.

"The police are at the door asking about you and a girl named Sunny Raegan," Lisa informed as she shrugged her shoulders.

"The police?"

The voice came from the hallway and both girls looked up as Raegan walked into the room.

"I take it you're Raegan," Lisa concluded.

"Yeah," she replied.

"Well the police are here for you," Lisa said.

"Lisa, you have to tell them she's not here," Chanel said.

"No, it's okay. I'll see what they want," Raegan said. Chanel gently grabbed the baby and followed Raegan down the stairs and to the front door.

She opened the door with a pounding heart and stared the officers directly in the face, while both Chanel and Lisa stood behind her.

"Are you Sunny Raegan?"

"Yeah, that's me," she answered unsurely.

"You are under arrest for kidnapping and assault . . . Turn around please, ma'am."

"What?" Chanel exclaimed as Raegan was put in handcuffs.

"Wait . . . I didn't kidnap anybody. He's my son!" she shouted as they pulled her out of the house against her will. "Wait!" she protested.

"I was there . . . Hold up! You guys are making a mistake!" Chanel shouted. The sound of commotion awoke baby Micah and his screams mixed in with the confusion to create chaos. Chanel handed the baby off to Lisa as she followed behind the officers as they carted Raegan away. Her bare feet froze from the snow-covered ground but she marched behind them, throwing insults and objections at their backs.

"Please . . . don't do this. I can't go to jail. I just had a baby. He needs me. This is wrong. It's a misunderstanding," Raegan pleaded.

Chanel stood pissed off and shaking her head in disgust as she marched back into the house.

"What was that all about?" Lisa asked.

"Some bullshit. Her whack-ass baby daddy playing games and telling lies. Can you watch him while I go downtown to see about getting her out?" Chanel asked.

Lisa nodded her head. "Yeah, of course. Go ahead."

Lisa stood rocking baby Micah in her arms as Chanel stormed out of the house and disappeared into the night.

Raegan sat with her face in her hands as the silence tormented her. She sat in the tiny holding cell, worried sick over her newborn son and shivering as an eerie cold set into her weak bones. She had just given birth and instead of bonding with her new child, she was fighting to keep him. Stressed beyond belief, Raegan hadn't even had the chance to recuperate from her delivery and it felt as if she would break down at any moment. *I just want to get out of here and back to my son,* she thought as she stood timidly, gripping her abdomen as she felt blood leaking between her legs. She was a mess. Every move she made seemed to send bolts of painful shock waves through her uterus, making it feel as if she were giving birth all over again.

She gripped the grimy metal bars and looked at the female officer who was processing her arrest paperwork.

"Excuse me, miss, can you tell me what's going on? I just had a baby. I shouldn't be here," Raegan said.

The officer didn't respond. She didn't even look Raegan's way. Completely ignoring her, the cop kept her eyes focused on the sheets of paper on her desk.

"Lady, please! I'm just trying to get out of here and get back to my son," Raegan said angrily. "This is some bullshit."

Without even looking up the cop responded, "You might as well sit down and get comfortable. You have to go before a judge to be arraigned and there are no judges available until Monday morning. You'll be in here for the entire weekend."

Eyes misty out of pure rage, Raegan jerked against the bars as if she wished she could break through them. "Agh! I hate him!" she screamed, as she slumped against the concrete wall and slid to the floor.

Frustration, fear, and worry consumed her, eating away at her like a moth to old clothing. Helplessness took over her and the utter failure she felt caused her to cry. She hated to be weak, but being disconnected from her child so soon after meeting him was terrorizing her. Her motherly instincts were on overdrive and she wanted to move mountains to get back to her son, but the steel and concrete held her captive. Raegan sobbed for two days. There were no clocks or windows so she had no sense of time. Forty-eight hours felt like forty-eight months. It was as if she were on death row; the anticipation was murder. She refused to eat and quickly lost all of her energy. Her body was fighting to recuperate itself and lack of sleep mixed with starvation only made things worse. The shift of officers changed every eight hours and none of them were sympathetic enough to offer her any assistance. It wasn't until they opened the cell Monday morning to take her to court did they realize that she needed medical attention. Raegan lay deathly still on the steel bench. She was in so much pain that she couldn't speak. She lay grimacing as she hugged herself tightly, feeling as though her insides had been ripped apart.

"Ms. Raegan, we need you to get up now," the officer said as he pulled her to her feet, only to have her legs give out immediately.

"I . . . I can't," she whispered. "I need my son . . . I need my baby. Why are you trying to keep me away from him?" she asked, her voice barely audible.

"On your feet, Ms. Raegan," the officer said persistently. He pulled her up again and forced her to her feet. It was then that he noticed the blood stains that covered the back of her pants. The floor felt as if it were giving out beneath her and Raegan reached out for support but found nothing but air. Raegan didn't take two complete steps before she passed out.

***

Raegan awoke to Chanel and Lisa standing near her bedside.

"Hey, hon, how are you feeling?" Chanel asked.

"Where is my baby?" Raegan asked.

"He's with his dad, sweetie," Lisa stepped up and said. "He came with the police and I had to give them the baby. I'm so sorry." Lisa didn't know Raegan, but she felt extreme empathy for her situation.

"There's an officer outside of your door, Raegan. You still have to be arraigned, but I've got the bail money put up and we have already contacted a lawyer," Lisa said.

Raegan closed her eyes and laid her head back on the bed. "I can't do this right now. . . ." she said.

"You don't have to. Just lay back and rest. You lost a lot of blood, Raegan. You can't help your kid if you are unhealthy. The doctor said that you had a setback. You were doing way too much, hon. You have to take care of yourself. Everything is going to work itself out. Just concentrate on getting better and we'll tackle your bitch-ass baby daddy together."

Raegan looked quizzically at Chanel and Lisa as they stood on the sides of her bed. "You two barely even know me. You've already done enough. I can't ask you to—"

"Girl, bye. We're not leaving you on stuck. It is fucked up what's happening to you. Not to mention Chanel told me she screwed the nigga and then left empty-handed," Lisa scoffed.

"We've got your back, girl . . . through all of this," Chanel reassured. "Friendships are made under the most unlikely circumstances and besides you didn't ask, we offered."

Raegan was astonished at the code of loyalty that these two girls held, and she felt so grateful to have them suddenly appear in her life at a time when she needed them most. She would need a few allies to go up against the bullshit that Micah was throwing her way.

Being held up in family court, arguing against a man with a wounded ego and a thirst for revenge was the worst experience of Raegan's life. The picture that Micah's lawyers were painting of her made her look extremely unfit and through it all Raegan feared that she would ultimately lose her son. She went through so many ups and downs that her hair began to fall out from the stress of it all. Until the conclusion of the custody battle, Raegan was able to keep baby Micah with her and she showered him with so much love. She never knew when their time would be cut short so she made the most of every day with him. Chanel and Lisa had become like her sisters. They kept their word and never turned their backs on her. They were the support system that she needed. Raegan had been on her own for so long that the feeling of belonging to a family was foreign. Chanel and Lisa would forever have her in their corner because they had picked her up and given her strength when she had lost all hope. Their faith and support never wavered. Her friends stayed by her side through the entire battle. Even the day she received the judge's decision they were there without having to be asked.

"I'm not giving Micah full custody! Fuck that! He wasn't even there when my baby was born. Now all of a sudden he wants to be there full time!" Raegan shouted as she ice grilled her attorney. Livid, her foot tapped against the floor and her sharp breaths could be heard across the room.

"You don't have a choice. The judge has already ordered that your son be turned over to his father. He made you look extremely violent to the judge. You can always appeal to the family court later, once this has died down. You're lucky that the kidnapping charges were dropped and that you only received community service for the assault. This could have gone an entirely different way," the state-assigned attorney said with little patience. "You're unemployed and you attacked your child's father. You don't have a place to live because you are no longer living with the child's father. When your situation has improved we can revisit the idea of you regaining custody."

Raegan dropped her head and allowed her tears to surface as her heart broke in half. "Everything's going to be okay, Raegan. You have us," Chanel said as she reached over and hugged Raegan. Lisa gripped Raegan's hand in support and gave her a weak smile as she held on to baby Micah. The threesome had become extremely close. Two months had passed since the day that life had introduced them to one another. What had started out as an awkward situation had blossomed into an unlikely yet valued friendship. Chanel and Lisa had accepted Raegan and her son into their lives without hesitation. Micah had pressed full charges against Raegan out of spite and had tied her up in the legal system. The girls had taken good care of baby Micah while his parents battled it out, but the fight was over and they all had to say their good-byes to her son. Raegan had lost and it felt as if she were handing her child over to a stranger.

Lisa handed Micah over to Raegan. She cradled him in her arms and kissed his forehead before she got up and reluctantly walked out of the room.

Micah stood with a smirk on his face as he reached out for the baby. "Give me my son," he spat.

"Why are you doing this? Because I caught *you* cheating? You didn't even want him. Why are you taking him from me?" she asked.

"Bitch, you took from me so now I'm taking from you. You should've left my paper where you found it," he seethed as he stared at her in contempt. "You give me my money I might give you your brat back."

Raegan shook her head in disgust. "You doing all of this over ten thousand dollars?" she asked. "You bitter, broke bastard!"

Micah put the baby in a car seat and then turned away from Raegan.

"I want my baby!"

"I wanted my money! We can't always have the things we want," he mocked as he left the lawyer's office feeling as though he had gotten the last laugh.

Chapter Four

Nahvid sat behind his cherry oak desk as he leaned back in his executive chair and focused on the man speaking before him. He only half listened as exhaustion plagued him. He was a man who wore many hats. His many businesses occupied much of his time, but it was his dealings in the street that caused the bags to form beneath his eyes and made his heart heavy. He had planned to give the streets up a long time ago, but they always pulled him back in. The game had chosen him back when he was a young kid coming up in Baltimore and they had a hold on him. He couldn't let go. He had a strange fear of going broke despite the millions of dollars he had in the bank. He feared poverty . . . It was his only fear. He had been down skid row and he refused to go back. He was addicted to it all.

The Money.

The Power.

The Prestige.

"I swear, Nah, the cops took that shit out of the trunk of my car and kept it moving. They robbed me."

Nahvid folded his hands on top of his desk and stared the man in his eyes. *This stupid mu'fucka,* he thought in frustration. Sometimes it felt as if he were a scholar surrounded by idiots. Niggas just didn't move the way that he did. Nahvid was a different breed. They didn't make them like him anymore. Nahvid didn't care to hear the tune the guy was singing. He wasn't interested in hearing sob stories. Nahvid was about his paper and if the nigga didn't have it, a conversation was not going to be the consequence. Nahvid wasn't about talk and his silence put fear in the young hustler's heart. Nahvid had been in the game long enough to know guilty men couldn't handle silence . . . they needed the noise to distract from the lies they told. Silence intimidated liars and they dominated the conversation so that others didn't have time to dispute their stories. So as the hustler went on and on he dug his grave deeper and deeper.

"Yo, my man . . . all that you're talking sounds good, but it is irrelevant. Do you have my money?" Nahvid asked sternly.

"That's what I'm trying to tell you. I got pulled over and the cops took the weight out of my car," the guy rambled.

"And yet you sit in front of me," Nahvid responded sarcastically.

"Man, I swear on my moms . . . those pigs were dirty. They just took the weight and let me go. If you hit me with something I can flip it and work off my debt to you, fam," the guy promised. He tried to put on a brave front but the quivering in his voice gave him away. "Come on, Nahvid man. I've known you since the sandbox, fam. I know how you get down. I didn't steal from you. I'm good for it, Nah. Just let me pay you back a little at a time."

Nahvid's brow bent low as if he were highly offended. "Did I hit you with the work a little at a time?" he asked.

At a loss for words, the man didn't respond.

"Then I don't want my money a little at a time. Nigga, how you goin' to spoon-feed me my own dough? Now I'ma ask you again. Do you have my money?"

The hustler shook his head and lowered his eyes to the floor as if he were a little boy being scolded by his father.

"Then you know who you need to go see. Right now this is about you. You go see my man Reason and I'll keep it about you. If you run then I'ma make it about that wife and those two kids you got out there in Southeast," Nahvid threatened. He didn't need to make eye contact or even raise his voice for his point to hit home. He simply picked up his phone and proceeded to handle the day's business as the hustler stood to his feet. The color left the man's face as he stared at Nahvid in desperation.

"You can see yourself out, fam," Nahvid dismissed shortly as he nodded toward the door.

Nahvid put the call in to his right-hand man, Reese "Reason" Grimes, and with the snap of a finger a man's life was on a countdown. "Make it clean . . . no headshots. I've known the nigga awhile. Let his wife have an open casket," Nahvid instructed before hanging up the phone. Nahvid yielded so much power in the streets that niggas delivered themselves to the execution block.

The sound of glass breaking caused him to stand to his feet as he pulled his .45 out of his desk drawer and made his way toward the noise. When he entered his kitchen he lowered his pistol and leaned against the wall as a shallow pit filled his stomach. He knew it was her without even seeing her face. Her slender frame and long jet-black hair were embedded in his memory. Even through the stench that covered her body, he recognized her natural scent. His eyes watered as he watched his mother rummage through his refrigerator, desperately shoving anything into her mouth that she could find.

He wanted to be disappointed in her, but this had become a routine long ago. Crack binges, clean binges, crack binges, clean binges. She never stuck to one thing for too long. Her crack addiction was too much for her to handle. She had a monkey on her back like none he had ever seen. She was part of the reason he entered the dope game in the first place. Being born to a drug-addicted mother he knew that the taste of crack had already been introduced to him. He was born hooked, a crack baby in fact and he knew that crack cocaine was destined to be a part of his life. Instead of smoking it, he chose the lesser evil and sold it. It was either one or the other. His mother had introduced him to it too early for him to ever be completely free of it. He walked up behind her and wrapped his arms around her waist, holding tightly as he hugged her from behind.

"Hey, Nita," he said, calling her by her first name as he always had. His mother had always treated him like a friend. She was his homegirl and they had come up on the mean streets as a two-man team, until Nahvid reached the age where her addiction was an embarrassment to him.

Nita stopped scrambling and calmed down. Her son always soothed her soul. She rested her head on his strong chest and replied, "Hey, baby."

"When did you get out?" he asked. "I thought you were going to try this time."

"I did try! Those mu'fuckas kicked me out the program," Nita shouted.

"Kicked you out for what?" he questioned. He took her hand and turned her toward him. "Don't lie to me, Nita. What did they kick you out for?"

Nita lowered her eyes and shuffled her feet nervously. "I brought a little something into the center with me. . . ."

"Ma . . ." Nahvid sighed in disappointment.

"Just a little bit. To hold me over you know. . . ." she explained.

"No, Nita. I don't know," he countered. "You got to get off of this shit. You're killing yourself."

"We all got to go sometime," she said as she pulled a cigarette from her bra and put it in her mouth. She lit it and only took one pull before Nahvid snatched it from her lips and broke it in half.

"You're pushing it, old lady," he said with a smile.

"Old lady? Who you calling old? Huh? I remember back in the day when I was the finest thing walking these streets. I was on the scene let me tell you . . ."

"Yeah, yeah, yeah. I've heard it all before," he teased as he put his arm around his mother's shoulder and pulled her close.

"Let's go take a hot bath and then I'll take you out to eat," he said.

He escorted his mother upstairs, his heart delighted by her presence. He sat on the toilet as she bathed herself. He wanted to give her privacy, but he was afraid that she would hop out of the window and disappear like a thief in the night. They reminisced about the good ol' days. When she spoke of her past . . . before the drugs . . . before the shame . . . her eyes sparkled clear and vibrant. He had no memory of her before crack. All of his stories were filled with dark times so he didn't share them. He simply listened to her and let her talk until her heart was content. He enjoyed her presence. It wasn't often that he got to indulge in her and he cherished every fleeting moment that they shared. He told himself that he was going to get his mother clean. The day she kicked her habit would be the day he gave up the game. *She's going right back to rehab in the morning,* he thought. As he held out a towel for her she stepped out of the tub and he wrapped her up, ensuring that she was warm. Despite her flaws, his mother was his world. He adored her and it tortured him to see her in pain.

"You getting skinny, girl, you need to put some meat on those bones," Nahvid cracked as he escorted her into his bedroom. He pulled out a drawer where he kept a few things for her and dressed her as if he were the parent and she was the child.

"Meals aren't always easy to come by, baby boy. Yo' mama ain't never been desperate enough to eat out of no trash bin. If I can't eat at a table then I would rather go without. Lately I've been coming across more trash bins then dining tables. I feel like I'm all skin and bones," Nita stated.

Nahvid wanted to tell his mother that she couldn't play both diva and addict. The two didn't match, but he never wanted to embarrass her or belittle her. When she stayed away Nahvid was slightly grateful. Out of sight, out of mind was how he regarded her . . . but here she was, standing in front of him and he felt obligated to help her change.

"You never have to go without, Nita. As long as there is air in my lungs I will make sure you have whatever you need, but I can't put money in your hands right now. You and I both already know where it'll go. I can feed you but I can't supply your habit," he said openly.

"It's recreational with your mama, boy. Don't worry about me. Just worry about yourself. I got this," Nita said as she rubbed the top of her son's head as he knelt before her, placing socks on her feet.

Nahvid sighed deeply, knowing that there was no such thing as a recreational user. In his mind if you smoked crack you smoked crack. It wasn't a party drug that could be experimented with lightly. She was hooked and obviously in denial about her dependency. He hated to burst her bubble, but he could not sugar-coat things for Nita. "You're a crackhead, ma. It's a problem. I've been on my own since the day I was born because you can't leave that shit alone. I don't hate you for it. I never have, but I can't let you sit in my face and act like you have everything in control. Things have been out of control and if you don't get off of that shit it will kill you. Then what I'm supposed to do? Huh?" he asked as he stood to his feet. He stared at her intensely, but she couldn't look him in the eyes. Tears threatened to fall down her face. "It hurts thinking about all that you've done to me, doesn't it? How you think I feel? I'm in the streets, Nita. I hear the stories. You sucking dick, robbing, conning, doing whatever you got to do to get high. Do you even know how many fights I got into coming up defending you? I held you down, no matter who spoke badly about you, but I'm still waiting for you to return the love. When are you going to beat the odds and fight for me? I love you, Nita. You're my favorite girl in the world but you don't make it easy on me. You show up and then you leave me. You hurt my heart, Nita. Every time you leave it kills me. Stop running. You've got to get clean," he whispered.

"I know, Nahvid," Nita whispered as she wiped the snot from her nose. His words cut deeply because she knew that he was speaking the truth. It had never been her intention to be a horrible mother. She had got-ten lost along the way and now she felt like it was too late to turn things around. So she smoked herself into oblivion where none of her mistakes mattered. But her son was standing before her, pouring out his heart like he never had before. It did matter . . . her actions did hurt him. "I'ma get clean, baby. Mama will. I promise. I will."

***

Nahvid pulled his grey Range Rover up to the rehab center as his mother cowered in her seat beside him.

"You can do this, Nita. I'm going to be behind you every step of the way. This time I'll be here every day to visit. Twice a day if they let me. I'll do whatever it takes to help you get right," he said.

He noticed that his mother was silent. He could see through her . . . she was intimidated by the inevitable hard journey to come. He got out and helped Nita from the car before accompanying her inside.

"They're not going to let me back in here, Nahvid," Nita said shamefully.

"Don't worry about it. They will let you in. You wait right here," he replied as he motioned to one of the seats in the reception area. He knew that the rules to the rehabilitation center were strict, but the $25,000 knot in his pocket ensured Nita's readmission. Nahvid walked in and made the arrangements with the director. Hopeful that this time would be different he went to retrieve Nita, but when he saw the empty chair she had been sitting in, he knew that she was long gone. His heart sank into his stomach as disappointment filled him. He should have known that she wouldn't go through with it. She wasn't ready to let go of her pipe dreams and there was nothing he could do to change that fact.

Raegan walked into the rehab center, her attitude at an all-time high. She couldn't believe Micah had taken their son from her. *Now I have to go in here and deal with these people,* she thought as she snatched the door open. She was so pissed off that she didn't realize that someone was coming out at the exact same time and she collided into him with full force. She lost her footing on the ice beneath her and went flying to the ground. Her head smashed against the pavement, sending a blinding pain shooting through her.

She sat up as she winced in pain, instinctively reaching for the back of her head.

"Are you okay?" Nahvid asked as he knelt down beside her.

"Umm yeah . . . I'm sorry I didn't see . . . oww," she moaned as she stopped midsentence to touch her tender head.

"Let me help you up," he offered as he scooped her legs and lifted her from the ground before setting her on her feet.

Raegan cleared her hair from her face and he was taken by surprise at how beautiful she was.

Damn, what is she doing sucking on a pipe? he asked himself, instantly assuming that she was an addict. He shook his head in disgrace. "You a'ight?" he checked once more.

She nodded as she brushed herself off. "Yeah, I'm fine. Thanks."

She walked inside of the building and he made his way to his car, each dismissing the other without a second thought.

Raegan sighed as she shifted her weight from foot to foot. Chanel was late and Raegan was more than ready to go. Her first day of community service had left a bad taste in her mouth and she wanted nothing more than to get home and scrub the smell of crack off of her. The door opened and a chocolate girl exited the building. Her grey eyes mesmerized Raegan . . . she was taken aback by how pretty the girl was. She caught herself staring and turned her head.

"I wish this bitch would hurry up . . . it's cold as hell out here," Raegan uttered to herself.

"You ain't lying," the girl whispered back. "You're the new girl right?"

"Oh no, I'm not a patient here. I'm just volunteering," she said.

"Do I look like a crackhead to you?" the girl asked with a laugh. "Damn that's fucked up. I need to put myself together a little better if I'm coming off like that."

Raegan laughed and replied, "My fault, girl. I'm bugging. You just kinda assume that everybody in this place have problems bigger than your own, you know?"

"Problems I've got . . . an addiction, not hardly," the girl replied. "I'm Gucci."

"Raegan," she introduced.

A car horn honked and Raegan looked up hoping it was Chanel.

"That's me . . . I'll see you tomorrow though, Raegan," Gucci said.

Raegan nodded as she watched the girl step into the black Mercedes that was waiting curbside. It was sitting right with all-black everything and she shook her head as she thought, *damn wish it were me.*

HONK HONK!

Chanel pulled up just as Gucci rolled off.

"Hurry up, bitch . . . We're going out tonight. It's time to cheer you up!"

Raegan rolled her eyes and lowered her body to get into the car. "I'm not feeling it, Chanel. I just want to go home and wash the smell of cigarettes out of my hair. I feel so dirty. The people in that place are a mess," Raegan said as she silently wondered how some of the rehab participants had even let themselves get to such a dark place.

"No, not trying to hear it. You're coming out tonight! We're leaving at nine o'clock. You've been depressed, walking around like a zombie for months. I know it's hard being away from your son, but tonight we are going to go out and you're going to get your mind off of it for a while," Chanel insisted.

"How the hell you get tickets at this concert? K. West has been sold out for weeks!" Lisa yelled as she made her way to the center of the front row.

"One of my niggas got 'em for me," Chanel replied.

"You don't need to rob this nigga then, he's a keeper," Raegan said with laughter. The girls were laced thanks to Chanel's latest sponsor. He was so friendly with the paper that she didn't have to rob him. He kept her pockets full of money. He had plenty of it and didn't mind sharing. Raegan's black Prada dress looked as if it were painted on and red-bottom Louboutins made her shine like a star in a crowd full of duds. Fashion was not an issue for the girls. Chanel's boosting skills were A-1 and she never stepped out of the house unless she was proper from head to toe. Any chick associated with her had to be up to par. There was no bad apple in their bunch. Her circle of friends was official. Bad bitches for sure. Raegan's hair was pulled high off of her face in a genie ponytail. Everything from her eyebrows to her manicure was on point and the attention she was getting let her know she had put herself together right.

The entire front row was full of D.C.'s finest and the crowd went crazy when the soulful rapper hit the stage. The concert was nice but it was the intermission that was the real show. Everybody was dressed in their best as they walked around the Verizon Center trying to be seen.

"It's so much potential in here," Chanel said, eyeing potential victims for her latest scam.

"Damn, girl, take a night off. Ain't your pussy tired?" Lisa asked seriously as her face twisted in contempt.

"Ain't your third of the rent late, bitch?" Chanel shot back. "You need to let me put you up on game so you can get your paper up."

Lisa stuck up her middle finger as Raegan shook her head. A crowd of girls crowded around a group of guys standing against the wall and as Raegan walked by she noticed the guy who had knocked her off her feet earlier that day. Their eyes locked and she slyly looked away and turned up her sexy as she walked subtly, precisely . . . knowing that he was looking at her ass. She glanced back and to her dismay the guy wasn't watching. She peered at him curiously and smiled as she kept walking. Raegan had never been one to play her cards too closely. She wasn't obvious or desperate and there were plenty niggas in the building showing her mad love. *His loss,* she thought as she kept it moving with her girls.

Nahvid smirked as he sipped his Remy and stood among his circle, shutting down the event as usual. It never mattered who came to town. In D.C. Nahvid was the celebrity. This was his city.

"Shorty bad as hell. That's you?" Reason asked as he leaned into his man curiously.

"Nah," Nahvid replied. "I saw her earlier at the rehab center when I was fucking with my moms."

"Bitch a piper?" Reason asked in disbelief. "They making 'em like that now?"

"I don't know. I ain't never seen none like her," Nahvid stated. "She probably works there or something."

"You don't mind if I get on that?" Reason asked.

Nahvid wanted to tell him to fall back because Raegan definitely had him curious but he didn't want to rain on his man's parade. Pussy was on a regular rotation for Nahvid so he wasn't sweating over one chick. There were enough women at the event to go around so he nodded toward her. "Go ahead, fam . . . do you."

Nahvid watched as his man approached Raegan. He silently hoped that she turned Reason down. Nahvid didn't want a chick who was easy to get so this was the perfect test to see what type of lady she actually was. Reason had women standing in line to deal with him so he was a catch around the city. If she turned him down it wouldn't be for his looks, and Nahvid was eager to see how she handled herself against a hood legend. He played the cut as his man went fishing.

"Yo, can I talk to you ladies for a minute?" Reason asked as he approached them, while looking Raegan up and down. "What's your name, ma?" he asked.

"Raegan, we're going to keep walking; we'll be at the little girl's room," Chanel shouted.

"Okay, I'm coming right behind you," Raegan responded. She looked at the guy in front of her. "My name's Raegan," she responded.

"Raegan and Reason goes well together," he said with a charming smile.

"It's corny," she shot back with a smirk.

He laughed at her blunt nature, his ego slightly bruised as he rubbed his goatee. "You hard on a nigga huh? I'm just trying to get to know you, beautiful," he said as he put a hand to his heart as if she were breaking it.

Raegan rolled her eyes and shook her head. She could tell that Reason's lines were well rehearsed. "How many chicks have you come at like that tonight?" she asked.

Her question caught him off guard because he suddenly became dumbfounded. The look on his face gave him away.

"That many?" she asked. "Listen, brother, let me give you some game. Women don't like being a part of a herd. It's not good to hear when it's not meant exclusively for you."

She walked away leaving him staring at her backside as she entered the bathroom.

Nahvid chuckled as he watched his man throw up the white flag in surrender. "Was it that bad?" he asked, still laughing when Reason approached.

"Bitch was cold," he replied as he shook his head. "She's a crackhead."

"Why she got to be on crack, fam?" Nahvid asked playfully.

"Cuz the ho got to be high to turn me down," Reason replied. His feelings seemed genuinely hurt for all of ten seconds until his trained eye sought out another lady from the crowd.

Nahvid's interest in Raegan doubled just from the way she had handled herself. *I'll see her around,* he thought.

The after party was jumping. The parking lot of the Park Hyatt Hotel looked like a foreign dealership as the East Coast's biggest players came out for a night on the town. D.C. wasn't the only city in the building. New Yitty, Baltimore, Richmond, even Norfolk had come out to play. The girls parked their cars a block away from the hotel, along with the other ordinary folks with ordinary cars and made their way to the party. The entire hotel had been reserved for the after partiers with the famous rapper promising to make an appearance.

As Raegan walked through the parking lot she noticed Gucci standing near the black Benz she had gotten picked up in earlier that day. She was stunning from head to toe, dipped in gold. Gold dress, gold doorknocker earrings with the matching thick rope chain, gold stiletto pumps with the beautiful red bottoms . . . The bitch was gold everything, reminding Raegan of a hot girl from the '80s. Raegan had to admit that Gucci's man kept her fly. She was the epitome of a dopeman's wife. The girls waved to each other as Raegan passed by and made her way inside.

As soon as they entered the building Chanel found her victim for the night. "I'll probably meet you guys at home. Here are my keys. I see something I like over there," she said before making her way across the room.

"Want to get a drink?" Lisa asked.

Raegan was about to say yes until she saw Micah walk into the hotel. Her stomach instantly went hollow and her heart fell as she turned to Lisa. "No, I'm not feeling that well," she lied. "I think I'm going to just catch a cab home."

"You sure?" Lisa asked, unaware of why Raegan's mood had suddenly run cold.

"Yeah, I'm sure. It stinks in here all of a sudden. Too many grimy niggas," Raegan responded. She felt sick as she tried to remain inconspicuous while heading toward the door, but it was inevitable for Micah to see her. When he laid eyes on Raegan she could see the idea of revenge in his stare. He blocked her path.

"Fuck you going?" he asked harshly as he gripped the top of her arm. "What you rushing off for?" His tone was taunting as if he dared her to pop off.

"Let me go, Micah!" she said between clenched teeth as she pulled her arm away from him. "Where is my son?"

"I should fuck you up for that little stunt you pulled," he threatened as he backed her into a corner. His hostility was evident. He stood so close to her that it appeared as though they were an intimate couple, but behind the visage his hand was wrapped tightly around her small neck. She struggled against him. "Stop," she whispered as he put one hand up her dress. She pulled at his hand, desperately. "Stop, Micah!"

Her voice was loud but the music was louder and her protests were swallowed up in the sea of chatter.

No one would have even noticed how he was handling her if Nahvid hadn't been watching. He had spotted her from across the room and as he made his way over, his temperature rose in anger. He could see the look of concern on Raegan's face and although he did not know her, he wanted to.

"Is there a problem, my man?" he asked.

Micah turned and looked at Nahvid, but didn't loosen his grip.

"Nothing that concerns you," he shot.

"Yo, you don't know me and I think you want to keep it that way. I'm not on no rah rah shit, fam. I don't do that. So I'm gon' say this one time and how the rest of your night plays out is up to you. Walk away," he said with malice in his tone.

"Didn't I tell you, mu'fucka . . ." Micah got loud and turned toward Nahvid, which proved to be the biggest mistake of his life. Nahvid never traveled without his goon squad and they were waiting, more than willing to put in work.

Out of nowhere his li'l niggas mauled Micah, causing Raegan to turn her head. "No, please . . . make them stop," she said, thinking that Micah might harm their son just to get even with her.

Nahvid frowned in confusion. He wasn't beat for the drama. "Just a minute ago the mu'fucka was choking you out. Now you saving him?" He was about to dismiss her as a birdbrain, until she explained.

"He has my son. He's petty and is keeping him away from me out of spite. I don't want him to do anything to my baby just to get back at me," she pleaded softly.

Nahvid looked across the room at Reason and nodded toward the mob. He knew that was his cue to stop the commotion.

"Carry him out," Nahvid instructed as he led Raegan out of the building.

"Thank you," she said gratefully.

"You're welcome."

As Nahvid looked down at her, he had a million questions he wanted to ask . . . but he barely knew her and he didn't want to pry into her personal life too soon. She had just told him she had a kid . . . that he could deal with, but he wondered what other skeletons she had in her closet.

"I need to find my girls. I'm just trying to get out of here," she whispered as she wrapped her arms around herself, shivering from the winter cold.

He removed his Armani jacket and placed it around her shoulders. "Don't let my man mess up your night, ma."

"My night? Ha! That's funny. Try my life," she exclaimed as she shook her head. "I can't believe I ever fucked with him."

"I saw you. I kind of bumped into you earlier . . ."

"Oh yeah, that was you! I have a knot the size of a baseball on the back of my head thanks to you," she said half joking. She smiled at him and his heart fluttered. He was never a sucker for women, but Raegan was interesting. She was something different . . . new.

"My fault, ma. You got to let me make that up to you sometime," he replied.

"Anytime," she answered. "I'm Raegan by the way."

"Like Ronald?"

"Like Sunny," she said with a chuckle. "My last name's Raegan, but I've gone by that since I was a kid," she explained.

"Sunny Rae. I like that. I'm Nahvid," he introduced.

"It's very nice to meet you, Nahvid," she said. She discreetly looked him up and down, admiring his almond-colored skin, slanted Chinese eyes, and full lips. He was the most handsome man she had ever seen. It was more his style than anything that attracted her. He had a grown-man vibe to him that made her cream her panties.

"I'm about to shake this shit though. It's not my type of scene," he said. "Here's my business card," he said. "You let me know when I can take you out for dinner. You know? To apologize for knocking you off your feet."

"I will. Have a good night, Nahvid," she said. She stood on her tiptoes to kiss his cheek and whispered, "Thank you for handling that mess for me earlier. You didn't have to but I'm glad you did."

Raegan hopped into the first cab she saw and this time when she looked back at Nahvid, he was watching.

Chapter Five

Chanel looked around the hotel room as her eyes adjusted to the dark. The sound of snoring beside her let her know that her victim was asleep and it was time for her to make her move. She slid from underneath him, slowly, carefully so that he didn't awaken. She wanted to wash the smell of sex from her body, but there was no time. *I'll do that when I get home. Right now I just need to get the money and get out of here,* she thought. Locating her clothes she slid into her dress and heels quickly, then rifled through the LRG jeans that were strewn on the floor. *Bingo,* she thought as withdrew a large knot of money. Chanel flicked through it, seeing that it was all big faces. She threw the dough into her clutch bag then headed for the door. She cracked it slightly, not wanting to allow any light into the room. Before she could step one foot outside the door, a forearm came from behind her and slammed it shut.

"Bitch, where you going?"

She turned around to face the man she had just slept with hoping that he hadn't seen her rob him. "Empty that bag, bitch," he said as he put the chain lock on the top of the hotel door.

Chanel held on to the clutch and lunged for the door, but was pulled back by her weave. The guy violently dragged her back to the bed.

"You want to rob me, bitch? You can keep it, but you about to earn that paper. Get on your fucking knees," he ordered.

"Look you can have it back. Just let me go," she begged.

The dude grabbed his gun off his nightstand and without warning pistol-whipped her until she fell to her knees. Blood seeped from her mouth as she cried. "Grimy-ass bitch . . . You gon' take that paper with you, but you gonna work for every dollar. Open your mouth."

Chanel sobbed and keeled over as she begged him. "Please don't."

"Don't cry now, ho. Get up!" he shouted as he kicked her in the ribs.

Chanel crawled to her knees and reluctantly opened her mouth as the guy removed his dick. Urine filled her mouth as he ignorantly aimed his dick at her face, disrespecting her in the worst way. She spit it out while turning her face, but he wanted to shower her with every drop. He grabbed her hair roughly and shoved himself down her throat, choking her as he fucked her face. "Swallow that dick, slut," he seethed. He grinded so hard that it felt as though he would take her head off. There was nothing gentle about his stroke. He was punishing her. Chanel had been hustling and scamming men for a long time but never had she been caught. By the time her victims had even realized that she had run their pockets, she was always long gone. If she had known that this would be the repercussion to her actions she would have never done it. Chanel gagged and scratched at his abdomen, but his grip on the back of her head was so tight that she couldn't move. After releasing in her mouth he slapped her across the face, the gun cutting into her cheek as her head snapped to the right.

"Please . . ." she cried as she spit out a combination of semen, blood, and urine.

"Please what, bitch?" he asked. "Say you're sorry."

"I'm sorry!" she cried, still on her knees. She tried to climb to her feet, but he knocked her back down.

"Sit the fuck back down. I didn't tell you to get your ass up!" he shouted as he pointed the gun in her face, daring her to move. The guy retrieved his money out of her bag and peeled it off, flicking at her, making it rain all over her. After degrading and defiling her, he was letting her keep the cash. It was never about that. He had punished her because of her disrespect.

"You can have that little paper, bitch," he shouted. "Now get the fuck out."

Her greed wouldn't allow her to leave the money on the ground. She hadn't gone through this pain and humiliation for nothing. She came there for the dough and she planned on leaving with the dough. She picked up every bill and then scrambled from the room, grateful to leave there with her life.

Chanel stumbled into the house. She was barely able to keep her balance as the room spun wildly. Her head pounded to the beat of a faraway drum as she reached for the light switch. She was too embarrassed to awaken her roommates. She didn't want Raegan and Lisa to see her at her lowest point, but when the stairway light illuminated she knew that she would have to face them.

"Chanel, is that you?" Lisa called out from the top of the stairs.

"Y . . . y . . . yeah, it's me. I need help," she replied back, her voice trembling.

Raegan and Lisa rushed down the steps and stopped in shock when they say Chanel bleeding all over their hardwood floors.

"Oh my God. Who did this to you?" Raegan asked as she ran to her side. The strong stench of urine filled her nostrils as she led Chanel to the couch. "Sit down."

"What happened?" Lisa grilled.

"The nigga I was trying to hustle caught me," Chanel admitted.

"I told your ass this would happen," Lisa said. "You should have stopped while you were ahead. You wasn't getting big money from those niggas. You're risking your life for chump change and shopping money."

"Money is money and no matter what you say I needed it. This is all I know. This is my hustle," Chanel defended.

"Then you need a new hustle, hon," Raegan said sincerely.

Chanel looked at Raegan in disbelief. "So now you jumping on the knock my hustle train too?" she asked, not trying to hear what they were saying at the moment.

"No, love. I'm not knocking you. I feel you chasing the American dream. You want your piece of the pie. I understand that, but if you gonna do it why not go all out? Why the nickel and diming?"

"What do you mean?" Chanel asked. "What, I'm supposed to strong-arm niggas? I'm only one bitch."

"And I'm one bitch and that makes two," Raegan added. It was something that she had thought about for a long time. She had seen Chanel getting money and knew that she could help her take her hustle to an all-new level. Chanel was in it for materialistic gain, but Raegan needed this money. She had so much more at stake. Lisa looked at Raegan like she was crazy dumb. "What, Lisa? I'm dead ass. Niggas do it all the time. Sticking mu'fuckas for they paper. If we can hit just one good lick then we can all be set for a while," Raegan said. She couldn't even believe the words that were coming from her mouth, but her motivation was her child. She wanted to give Micah his money back so that he would return her son.

"I'm for that and that bitch-ass nigga who fucked me up is first on my list," Chanel said as she wiped her eyes.

Lisa stood with her hands on her hips, shaking her head. "Are you two fucking serious? Raegan . . . look at her. She in here smelling like piss, her mouth all busted up and you want to get in on that scheming bullshit?"

"All we have to do is do it once and do it right. I see those school loan bills that's piling up on your dresser, Lis. One good robbery will catch you up," Raegan said convincingly.

"So what you bitches are bank robbers now? Y'all gonna take a bank?" Lisa asked incredulously.

"Not a bank. A stash house," Raegan concluded.

"Niggas be having at least a hundred thousand in they stash spots. Not to mention the coke that be lying around," Chanel said, growing excited. This was the payday she had been looking for . . . the one that she needed to leave the game alone for good.

"You bitches are crazy. I don't want a damn thing to do with this one. Good night," Lisa said as she walked away from the conversation. She didn't even want to know too much about it. She couldn't tell what she didn't know.

"We can do this, Raegan," Chanel said.

"I know . . . I need this money too, Chanel. You know that's the only way Micah is going to let this beef with me go," Raegan replied. Her eyes bugged out as she thought of who they would target. "I know a nigga too. He picks up this girl from the rehab center all the time."

"How you know he papered up? Just because he's hustling doesn't mean he's doing it right. He could be an ol' hustling backward-ass nigga," Chanel asked.

"Trust me he's not just doing it for the lifestyle. He drives a Benz, keeps his girl laced . . . I saw them tonight at the after party. He's getting it. I know it," Raegan said surely.

"Then let's do it," Chanel said as she lifted her hand to give her girl some play.

Raegan cringed and said, "I'll give you a high five *after* you take a shower. You kinda stink."

Despite her pain, Chanel burst into laughter as Raegan chuckled too. In the back of her mind Chanel vowed that she would get revenge on the guy who had fucked her up. She would make sure that their paths crossed again one day, but in the meantime they were about to get money.

Chapter Six

For the next few days, Raegan made friends with Gucci. She made it a point to find out something new about her boyfriend each day. Raegan's suspicions were right. According to Gucci, her boyfriend, Jamie, was the perfect lick. Raegan felt bad because she genuinely liked the girl, but her boyfriend had to get it.

"Hey, is everything okay?" Gucci asked as they sat at the reception desk filing patient forms.

"Yeah, why do you ask?" Raegan responded, hoping she wasn't acting suspicious. It was awkward sitting next to the girl when Raegan knew in the back of her head that she was plotting on her man.

"I saw what happened the other night . . . at the after party. Dude was way out of line," Gucci commented.

"He's my child's father," Raegan admitted.

"What? And he fooling on you like that?" she asked.

"We have a lot of issues with one another. I'm not fucking with him. He took my son away from me," Raegan said. She didn't know what possessed her to tell Gucci her business. She kicked herself for being so loose at the lips. She wished that she could take back the words as soon as she spoke them.

"That's foul," Gucci replied.

"The messed up part is he wants me to pay ten thousand dollars to get my own baby back," Raegan said.

Gucci was silent. She could hear the yearning in Raegan's voice. She couldn't pretend to empathize with

Raegan. Gucci didn't have children. In fact she didn't want them. She was too afraid of what her mother's genes might do to her own kids.

"For what it's worth I can tell you love your baby. Don't let him beat you, girl," Gucci stated as she stood from her seat. Raegan half smiled as she watched her walk away. Her conscience nagged at her to change her plans but it was too late. Chanel was already in place. She had followed him around for days until he led them straight to his stash house. Today was the day that Raegan gave the go ahead and there was no turning back. With their finances in dire circumstance, it was now or never. They had watched his every move and had his routine down to a science. It was time to set their nerves aside and make this money.

At the end of the day Raegan left fifteen minutes early so that she and Chanel could already be in place when Gucci's man came to get her. They watched as Gucci came out of the building and got inside his car and when he pulled off, he never even suspected to check his rearview mirror. He had no idea what was about to take place.

Gucci sat back in the leather seat and sighed.

"What's good, baby girl? You don't got no love for your man?" Jamie asked as he reached over and palmed her thigh tightly. Gucci leaned over and kissed his cheek, but he turned his head and dodged her.

"You know what I'm talking about, ma. I just rode all the way across town to pick you up. Come put in some work," Jamie said as he lifted out of his seat slightly and grabbed his crotch suggestively.

Gucci wanted to tell him to kiss her ass. That maybe she would *want* to please him if he approached her differently, but what could she say. She needed him. He may not have treated her the best, but he kept her stable. The cash and gifts her threw her way made life bearable. Without him she would be on stuck. He was her man and she wanted to show him she appreciated the things he did for her, no matter how small. She slid her head between his legs and took him into her mouth, tears filling her eyes. Gucci would have gladly done what it took to please him if he didn't constantly make her feel as if she had to. With him, it wasn't a choice; it was a requirement that he had made clear from day one. He held her head and she finished the job as they pulled into her driveway.

"Go grab you an overnight bag. You're coming over tonight. I'll take you shopping in the morning," he promised. To most girls the offer would be romantic, exciting, but to Gucci it felt like a demand. But instead of standing up for herself she told him to wait a quick minute and ran into the house to retrieve a few items. She was labeled weak minded, not because she wanted to be but because she didn't know how to be anyway else.

Gucci avoided his stare and got out of the car with a short good-bye. She was halfway up the walkway when he called her name.

"Guch!"

She turned around and walked back to him, standing outside his window. He put his hand out the window and placed ten hundred-dollar bills in her hand. "Pay a bill or something, make sure your moms is straight," he told her.

She nodded her head.

"What do you say?" he asked.

"Thanks, daddy," she said as she backpedaled into the house.

She quickly peeked in on her mother and nodded to the nurse who was on duty.

"How you doing today, Ma?" she asked as she bent and kissed her on the forehead.

Her mother turned her head away and peered at the nurse. "She mean, Gucci."

Gucci arched her eyebrows and glared at the nurse. "What did you do to her? Did you hurt her?" she asked directly.

"No . . . no. I just helped her get dressed for the day. She was upset and crying about it, but I would never . . ."

Gucci put her hand up already knowing that her mother was giving the nurse a hard time. She didn't like to be undressed by strangers. Past ghosts made her wary of everyone but Gucci. "It's okay, Ma. I'm home now. Don't worry. Nobody's going to hurt you." She was used to taking care of things. Gucci's mother had relied on her ever since she was a young kid. Significantly disabled, her mother didn't function well mentally. Southern born she was labeled slow, even the most minute tasks seemed impossible for her to learn and Gucci had always been the glue that held everything together. Gucci was a product of her mother's rape. A male nurse who had been hired to take care of her mother had molested her for years. The crime wasn't even discovered until she went into labor with Gucci. There was no way that the sex could have been consensual. Gucci was a product of rape and had been born to a mentally challenged mother. Now here she was at twenty-three, burdened with the task of caring for a woman who had never wanted her in the first place. The man who raped her would whisper in her ear.

"Ooh this is some good coochie," he would say.

So when she gave birth to her baby all she could say was the word coochie, but she was so slow that she mispronounced the word.

"Gucci . . . Gucci," she said repeatedly. She said the word so much that the nurses put it down on the birth certificate. No, Gucci's name had nothing to do with fashion. It was a direct reflection of her mother's rape and it was a ghost that haunted her even to this day.

If Gucci had the money she would put her mother in an adult facility to make things easier. A professional home could take better care of her mother than Gucci ever could, but with her minimum-wage job at the rehab center she was going nowhere fast. With genetics like hers life wasn't easy. She inherited an empty head disguised by a beautiful exterior. Her body and face were magnificent, but they were of no value to her. She was simply living, trying to get by as best as she could. Her looks attracted men left and right, but the ones who caught her only took advantage of her. Although she wasn't labeled mentally challenged, she knew that she wasn't ever the smartest girl in the room. She knew other girls who looked like she did. They used their assets to get what they wanted. They had established hustles, pulled capers, and put a price tag on their pussies, all of which made life a little easier. Gucci was afraid to grind it out because she knew that she was easily outwitted. So instead she played the back, her confidence too low to ever take the lead.

"Gucci! Gucci!" her mother shouted from her room. Gucci sighed as she closed her eyes, overwhelmed by the abundance of responsibility that was placed on her. *I can't wait to get out of here. This shit is just too much,* she thought. She grabbed her bag and rushed out of the door. She was desperate for a way out and when she finally did escape she would never look back.

***

"What is she doing? She never goes home with him," Raegan exclaimed as they watched Gucci get back in Jamie's car. "She would pick today of all days." Raegan looked at Chanel and said, "Let's just do it another day."

"We're doing it today," Chanel concluded.

"Chanel, I work with her every day. She's cool people. I don't want—"

"Nobody's gonna get hurt, Raegan. We're just after the money. It'll be fine," Chanel said.

They followed Jamie until he arrived home. He wasn't smart enough to have a separate stash spot. He broke the number one rule . . . DON'T SHIT WHERE YOU EAT . . . and although he hustled hard, he was accessible. Now Raegan and Chanel were about to test him. Chanel pulled out two .45s and handed one to Raegan.

"Where did you get these from?" she asked.

"A friend of mine hooked me up. I told him I needed them for protection. They're dirty so if we have to pop a nigga they can't be traced back to us," Chanel assured. "You ready?" she asked.

Raegan nodded as she eyed the house. Her eyes never left it, not even for a second. She hawked it, wanting to make sure she knew exactly what she was getting herself into. When night fell and the shadows of the evening took over the street, the girls got out of the car.

"Pop the hood to the car," Raegan said as they got out. "She'll recognize me. You take the front and I'll be at the back." The girls split and as Chanel approached the house she turned the doorknob to see if it was locked. When it didn't budge, she had no choice but to ring the doorbell. She wore a winter hat and a cashmere scarf that she had wrapped around her face. She looked harmless. Like an around-the-way girl who had gotten herself stranded and was wrapped up to stay warm, despite the Louboutin hooker heels and short designer dress she wore beneath her short trench coat.

"Who is it?" she heard him yell through the door.

"Hi . . . I was wondering if I could use your phone. My car broke down and I don't have any cell reception," she replied.

Just as she suspected Jamie was soft on a bitch. If a man had come to his doorstep with the exact same problem he would have turned him away, but when he saw the pair of long legs glistening on his doorstep he opened up without hesitation.

"Thank you sooo much," she said as she stepped into the house. The only thing that they could see was her eyes.

Gucci came from out a back room to make her presence known. Scantily clad in her bra and panties she walked into the living room.

"Who is this?" she asked.

"Oh my car broke down. I'm just using the phone," Chanel said. "Oh yeah, and can I ask one more thing? I promise after this I'll be out of your hair," she said sweetly as she looked at Jamie seductively.

"What's that, ma?"

"Where's the money?" Chanel asked as she aimed her gun directly at him.

Jamie grabbed Gucci and pushed her toward Chanel, then took off for his back door. Thinking he had gotten away, he pushed the door open and ran right into Raegan's gun.

"Get in the house," she ordered as she eased him back inside. He backed up slowly, his eyes searching the kitchen for something he could use to defend himself.

"Don't even think about it," Raegan said. "By the time you make your move, your brains will be all over your kitchen floor."

Raegan walked him back into the living room.

"Fuck." He grimaced as he shook his head, realizing that it was a setup.

When Raegan saw Gucci sitting on the couch shaking in fear as Chanel held her at gunpoint she immediately felt bad. She was ready to get this over with.

"Where's the money?" she asked.

"I don't know what you talking about! What money?" he asked, feigning innocence.

"You don't know what we talking about huh?" Chanel asked. She bitch smacked him with the gun. "Don't play me, Jamie. Where's the money?"

"Just tell them!" Gucci shouted.

Jamie spit blood from his mouth. "Fuck you, bitch."

"Go search the house," Chanel said.

Raegan ran through the house searching for the bedroom. She tore it up from top to bottom and found nothing.

"I can't find it," Raegan mumbled to herself. She moved from room to room in less than five minutes, but came up short. "Think, Raegan, think," she said. She ran inside the kitchen and opened up his cabinets. Condiments and jars filled them. She pulled one of the cereal boxes down and opened it up. "Got it."

She didn't give a fuck. She grabbed every cereal box in sight, stuffing it into the empty black duffel bag she carried.

"Let's go," she told Chanel as she rushed back into the living room.

"Get your ass on the floor and turn around," Chanel ordered. Jamie didn't protest and did as he was told, all the while making threats.

"I'ma find you bitches," he stated bitterly.

"Yeah, yeah," Chanel replied. She bound his wrists with zip ties and then his feet, hogtying him so that he couldn't move. "Tie her up," she told Raegan.

Gucci watched in horror as Raegan approached her and when she saw the tattoo on her wrist her eyes bugged out in disbelief. She recognized it instantly and when she looked Raegan in the eyes they both knew that Gucci was aware of her identity.

"Let's go," Raegan said as she applied that last zip tie. The girls left out of the front door, ran to their car, and closed the hood before pulling off into the night.

Chapter Seven

"Oh my God, I can't believe we just did that!" Chanel yelled in disbelief as she flew down the interstate.

Raegan laughed, but nervous jitters filled her stomach. She knew that she had a problem. Gucci knew that she was behind the robbery. Nervous butterflies filled her stomach. "I think she recognized me."

"What?" Chanel shot out.

"There was something about the way she looked at me. Like she couldn't believe it was me," Raegan said. "What if she goes to the police?"

"She won't," Chanel said.

"But what if she does?" Raegan said. "What if she tells ol' boy it was me?"

"Now that she might do," Chanel responded.

"I have to cut her in," Raegan concluded.

"Fuck that. If you cut her in, it'll be from your own half," Chanel said seriously. "And there's no way she can prove it was you. She doesn't know anything. Don't get paranoid, girl . . . just chill out and think about all that money in that bag. That'll take all your worries away."

The girls sat in the middle of the kitchen floor emptying the cereal boxes. By the time they were done they were $40,000 richer and had a quarter brick in their pockets.

"That's twenty each," Chanel said happily. Instead of scraping and stealing her dough a few hundred at a time, she had just come up nicely by putting in less than ten minutes worth of work. "This is chump change compared to the bigger dealers in town."

"I know. I think we need to keep it to a minimum though. I'm willing to do it again, but we have to be smart about it. We should only do one lick a month. The hood gets paid on the first and fifteenth of the month. That's when niggas get big money because all of the smokers have that government check in their pockets. We need to do it on those days from here on out. This money is good money, but I guarantee we would have come out a lot nicer if we had hit ol' boy on the right day," Raegan said.

"What do we do with the coke?" Chanel asked.

"We definitely can't sell that to anyone around here. That'll be a dead giveaway. You try to meet some out-of-town hustlers and make some connections with them. This little bit ain't worth selling right now, but I'm sure we'll come across more. When we get our weight up we will wholesale it," Raegan said. "You just work on finding buyers for it."

The girls split the pot, but Raegan's money was already spent. After paying Micah the $10,000 she owed him she would only have $10,000 left. No matter what Chanel said, she knew that Gucci was a threat and she planned on paying her off to keep her silent.

Raegan picked up the phone to call Micah. She was eager to see her baby. She had his money and now all she wanted was for him to give her baby back and stay out of her life.

"We're sorry. The number you have dialed has been changed. No new number is listed."

When Raegan heard the operator's voice she was livid. *This nigga thinks I'm playing about my son,* she thought as she stood up. She grabbed the keys to Chanel's car and headed out the door. She was tired of the back and forth charade Micah was playing. It was tit for tat with him. As she sped over to Micah's house her blood pressure rose as she cussed him out in her head the entire way. She pulled up to the house and hopped out of the car. Everything in her was tired of him. His spiteful ways turned her off completely. Raegan would never regret her son, but she regretted the fact that she had made him with a man like Micah. Her fists pounded his door repeatedly, knocking so persistently that he didn't have a choice but to answer her.

"Where's my son?" she asked as soon as he opened the door.

His face was bruised from the once-over that Nahvid's goons had given him. She threw the stack of money she had for him directly in his face. His tall frame blocked the door so she was unable to enter his home.

"Give me my baby. You got your money."

"You can have him back when I say you can have him back," Micah said.

Tears filled her eyes. "Micah!" she cried out in frustration. "What is this really about? How can you keep him from me? I'm his mother."

"And I'm his father. Get the fuck off my doorstep before I blow your fucking head off," Micah said hatefully. "Don't come back. You wanted to leave so stay the fuck gone, but my son is staying right here."

He pushed her away from his door and slammed the door shut in her face.

"Micah," she yelled as tears trailed her cheeks. She pleaded on his doorstep until she had nothing left in her. When the lights went out she peeled herself off

of the ground. Feeling hopeless she left, not knowing
what else to do.

Nahvid spotted Raegan from behind the bar at his
soul food restaurant. *Everywhere I go I'm seeing this
girl,* he thought. The two of them together were kis-
met in his eyes. He had never wanted to know more
about a person. She sat in the corner of his bustling
establishment, drinking a glass of wine as she stared
out the window at the falling snowflakes. He thought
that she was playing hard to get. He had no idea that
she was preoccupied with other things. Starting something with him was the furthest thing from her mind.
The fact that she didn't seem to want him made him
want her more. As if his energy had tapped her on the
shoulder she turned her face toward his. The chandelier lights reflected off of the tears on her face and as he
walked from behind his bar toward her, she gathered
her things to leave.

"Sunny Rae," he said as he walked up behind her and
whispered in her ear. "Let me find out that bum nigga
of a baby daddy got you crying your eyes out."

"I'm sorry. I've gotta go," she said as she tried to leave.
She couldn't focus on him right now. She was too distracted. Her emotions were all over the place. She was
distraught and a little tipsy from the wine she had been
sipping on.

"You can't drive like this. Stay for a while until you
calm down. Have you eaten?" he asked.

She shook her head no and he snapped his finger to
get one of the waitresses' attention.

"Yes, sir?"

"Please set up a private table on the second floor for
me and my guest," he instructed.

He led her up to their table and then pulled out her chair as she sat down.

"Everything okay?" he asked.

"I'm fine, it's just been a long day for me," she replied. "I'm sorry I didn't call. Things have been crazy for me."

"I've been running into you a lot lately," he said.

"That's a good thing right?" she asked.

"I'm not sure just yet," he replied. "I find myself thinking a lot about you . . . wondering how you are and I don't even know you."

She looked up at him in surprise. A man like Nahvid could have anyone he wanted, but he was stuck on her. Flattered was an understatement.

"There's not much to know," she replied with a shy smile. "I'm like most girls."

"I highly doubt that," he responded. "What do you spend most of your time doing?"

Raegan thought about it and instantly became ashamed of her answer. She had been with Micah for three years and ever since meeting him her days and nights had revolved around him. "I've wasted a lot of time pleasing a man. I haven't taken much time for myself."

"We're going to have to change that," he responded. "A man is supposed to make you his center of gravity . . . not the other way around."

"So what do you do?" she asked.

"So she feigns ignorance huh?" he asked with a smirk, knowing that she was aware of his street status.

She shook her head and laughed slightly at his blunt nature. "No, I've heard about you . . . but I want to hear it from you. The streets say you are a scary guy, but the man I'm sitting across from seems so different."

"I'm a businessman. I like to involve myself in anything profitable. I don't like to take losses . . . I guess over the years I've had to make a few examples out of people, but that's not all that I am. I take care of the people I love," he admitted.

"I can tell. You seem very loyal," she said.

"Is that a trait that you possess?" he countered as he stared at her intensely.

"Depends on the person," she replied. "I'm loyal to a fault sometimes. I was loyal to my kid's father and look where that got me." Her voice cracked as fresh emotion seeped out into her tone. She smiled half-heartedly in an attempt to hide her distress.

"He's a dummy," Nahvid said, sincerely. "His trash just may be my treasure."

Raegan smirked and rolled her eyes. "Here you go," she scoffed with laughter.

"You're laughing but I'm not telling any jokes, ma. I'm a man who can recognize a good woman when she's right in front of me. I know what I want and when I see something I'm interested in, I usually get it," he answered.

"Is that so?" she asked sweetly as she folded her hands beneath her chin, her eyes dancing with flattery.

"That's so, shorty," he responded. "I don't like to be told no."

The two conversed over dinner and wine as if they had known each other their entire lives. Their chemistry was off the charts and as they learned a little bit about one another their attractions grew.

They talked and laughed for hours, the wine loosening lips that were usually so airtight. Raegan had never felt an attraction like this before. He had a way of making her feel better about life as if nothing could break her, not even Micah.

As the sun came up she yawned. "I have to get back home. I have my roommate's car and I have to be somewhere in a few hours. I had a good time with you. You don't even know how you turned my night around."

"Can I see you again?" he asked.

"The way that our paths have been intertwined I'm sure that you will," she replied. She stood and he escorted her to her car.

"Am I going to have to kidnap you in order to take you out on a formal date?" he asked. He put his hand behind her head and massaged the nape of her neck gently with his fingers. His touch electrified her body, making her eyes flutter and her clit throb. She was beautiful and sexy and classy and innocent and mischievous all at the same time.

"I don't want you to think I'm playing games," she whispered. "I'm just . . ."

"Playing games," he said, finishing her sentence. He stepped closer to her, trapping her against the car and whispering in her ear as his body pressed against hers. "It's okay though. I enjoy the chase, ma. I'm just wondering if I'm ever going to catch you."

Her nipples stuck out at full attention as her pussy rained her wanting onto her thigh. Her clit bloomed like a springtime flower and she gasped because he was making her hurt in a good way. The sexual tension between them was high and a thousand sensations shot through her body.

"I'm caught," she whispered as she took his lips into her mouth and kissed him seductively. His hands roamed her body until he reached her ass, squeezing tightly as he aligned his throbbing dick with her middle. He was hard and she could feel it through his jeans that he was thick and didn't come with any shorts below the waistline. They were in pure heat as he lifted one of her legs and slid his hand up her dress, ripping the thong she wore. The street was deserted but the possibility of being caught by a passerby made it even better for Raegan. It heightened her pleasure. She wanted to tell him to stop and that they barely knew each other, but he was making her feel too good and the only thing that came out was sighs of pleasure as he played with her clit. He rolled it, smashed it, tugged at it . . . pleasing her without ever sticking his dick inside of her.

"Let's go back inside," she whispered. She was fien'in' for the dick and could no longer contain herself.

Nahvid picked up her, holding her voluptuous ass in his palms as her legs wrapped around his waist and they kissed all the way back to the door. He pressed her against the glass, their grunts and moans filling the early morning streets. He would have made love to her right there but their moment was ruined when a car came down the street, the driver blaring his horn at them.

Raegan and Nahvid were on cloud nine, but quickly came back down to earth when reality set in. He put her down and rested his forehead against hers.

"You think I'm a ho now right?" she asked insecurely as she fixed her dress. "What the hell am I doing? This ain't me . . . I don't move like this . . ." she stammered as she spoke, feeling mortified at the way she was putting herself out to Nahvid. *I'm playing myself right now,* she thought. "I would pay to know what you're thinking right now." She shook her head in disappointment as she tried to brush past him.

Nahvid stopped her and put a finger to her lips, silencing her nonsense. "I think that you're beautiful and I want to see you again."

Her embarrassment was evident by the shade of red her cheeks had turned. She couldn't even look him in the eye. He put his finger underneath her chin and lifted her face. "Don't be embarrassed. I've smashed chicks who have made me wait forever and they still turned around and did me dirty. That means nothing to me, Raegan. We're two grown individuals so whenever we decide to take it there it will be because we made the decision together . . . responsibly. I don't have expectations of you, only standards of myself and you meet every one of them. I respect loyalty. I caught you, now I got to trap your heart, ma. Spend tomorrow with me."

"I can't. I have community service at the rehab center tomorrow. I have to complete two hundred fifty hours so that I can go back to the judge and try to fight for custody of my son again," she said.

"The director owes me a favor. You're done with that. He'll let the judge know you fulfilled your time. Now what's your excuse?" he asked.

She shook her head, unable to hide her smile. She was smitten with Nahvid. Whatever she needed he could make happen and it felt good to be handled with such care for a change. "I guess I don't have one. Can you pick me up from the center? I have to stop in for a second in the morning to handle something," she said.

"Done, just text me when you're ready" he replied.

Raegan nodded and he kissed her lips as he admired her beauty, noticing the way her eyes glistened with insecurity when she was unsure. He grabbed her hand and walked her back to the car, tucking her safely inside before she pulled away.

Chapter Eight

Raegan walked into the rehab center paranoid that the police or, better yet, Gucci's man, would come for her at any moment. Nahvid had made good on his promise by getting her out of the community service. *As soon as I clear the air with Gucci, I'm blowing this joint,* she thought. She quickly located Gucci and walked up behind her, grabbing her hand to drag her into the ladies' single-stall bathroom. Raegan locked the door and took a deep breath as she turned around, preparing herself for a confrontation.

"Look, Gucci . . . I know you recognized me last night, but I want you to know that we were never going to hurt you. You were never in any danger," Raegan said honestly. She reached into her purse and pulled out five stacks, handing them to Gucci. "This is half of what I earned last night," she offered.

Gucci was hesitant to take it. She felt betrayed by Raegan. "What's this? Hush money?" Gucci asked.

"It's my way of saying I'm sorry," Raegan responded.

"So what? You pretended to be cool with me so you could get to Jamie? That was your plan all along?" she asked.

"No. It wasn't like that really," Raegan replied.

Gucci shook her head and said, "I don't want the money. I want in."

"What?" Raegan exclaimed in surprise. She had not pegged Gucci as a hustler. She didn't seem like the type.

Gucci wasn't cut from the same cloth as Raegan . . . if she were, the two of them wouldn't even be having a conversation. If the shoe were on the other foot, Raegan would have popped off on sight. Gucci was too nice . . . too trusting . . . and too understanding. As Raegan thought about how naïve and innocent Gucci really was, a light bulb went off in her head. *She's perfect,* Raegan thought. *They will never see her coming.*

"I want in. I need a come-up, Raegan. This job is a dead end for me. Me and my mom are barely making it at home. I have to put up with bullshit from dudes like Jamie because without them I would be starving. I'm tired of it and I want in. I just want to get enough to set my mom up and send me on the first thing smoking out of this city," Gucci said with a faraway look in her eyes.

"I'm not in this by myself. I'll have to run it by my girl. Can we meet you somewhere? Tomorrow night?" Raegan asked.

"We can meet at my place. Maybe then you will see why I need y'all to put me on," Gucci stated. Raegan was surprised that Gucci was singing this tale of poverty. She would have bet her bottom dollar on it that Gucci was living the champagne life, but from the look of desperation in her eye, Raegan knew that this wasn't the case. Looks could be deceiving and Gucci had the world fooled. She was down bad and ready to climb her way to the top. Tired of watching other women get it . . . envying chicks who had the world in the palms of their hands, she wanted to become a part of the big-girl club.

As Chanel sat in Gucci's driveway, anxiety filled her gut. "I don't know about this, Raegan. We just robbed her boyfriend," Chanel said skeptically.

"I'm not advocating either way. If she's in that's cool and if she ain't that's fine too. Just meet her. See what type of vibe you get and then we'll decide from there."

When the three of them got together they clicked instantly. Their interactions were so natural that they appeared to be old friends. Gucci was so easygoing that she endeared herself to Chanel and Raegan. Her spirit was infectious and now that they had an additional set of eyes and ears, they were ready to take it to the next level.

Gucci sat inside the crack house, her eyes discreetly roaming the room as she counted the number of people in the room. She had become a regular over the past month. Playing her part and getting as much information on their victims as she possibly could. The dirty clothes she wore and her ruffled hair made her almost fit in with the fiends around her. She stood and went to cop from one of the d-boys in the kitchen. Their operation was all the way sloppy. They allowed their customers to get high in the basement so that when their highs came down they didn't miss the second helping sell. It was this tactic that allowed the girls to catch them slipping.

Gucci kept her head low as she approached one of the young hustlers, "Can I get two twinky's?" she asked. She handed him the twenty-dollar bill and took the beige-colored rocks out of his hand before scrambling back into the basement. She carefully searched the room until she found a young girl sitting idly in the corner. Eyes wide and shaking she was in need of a hit. She had been lingering in the dope spot all day trying to hit a lick on one of the other fiends. With no luck, she had the shakes and was irritated beyond belief.

So when Gucci approached her with a proposition she jumped at the opportunity.

"Hey you trying to hit this with me," Gucci said as she sat down next to the girl.

The girl eyed her suspiciously but all doubt was erased when she saw the twinky sitting in the palm of Gucci's hand. She reached for it as if she were about to touch a precious art exhibit, but Gucci snapped her hand shut quickly . . . right before the girl got to it.

"What you playing games for? You not even a smoker," the girl snapped.

"You don't know what I am," Gucci responded harshly.

"Look I might be down bad but I'm not out. I've seen you in here trying to blend in but you never smoke nothing," the girl said.

"I've seen you in here too . . . too broke to smoke anything. Now you want this or not?" Gucci asked.

"What I got to do for it?" the girl asked.

The girl was so transfixed on Gucci's closed palm that she couldn't focus.

Gucci snapped her fingers. "Hey . . . you want it?" she asked.

"What I got to do?"

"I need you to go upstairs and cause a distraction," Gucci whispered as she looked around to make sure no one else was listening. Despite her convincing appearance she felt naked, as if everybody in the room knew that she was present with ill intent.

"What kind of distraction?" the girl asked with a frown.

"I don't care what you do. Just distract the niggas upstairs. A girl is going to knock on the front door. When you hear the knock . . . you start," she said.

The girl couldn't have been a day older than eighteen. She had a bad addiction but hadn't put enough years in on the street to realize that this was a fool's mission. As Gucci watched her walk up the stairs she picked up her phone to let her girls know that her part of the plan had been fulfilled. Now it was up to them.

Ten smokers in basement and six guys upstairs cooking up. Guns all over the kitchen table. Money under floorboard in kitchen. Girl about to cause distraction. Come in NOW!

When Raegan read the text she relayed the message to Chanel and with adrenaline on high, they made their move. Their disguises never changed. Trench coats and high Louboutins was the getup; that way if they ever had to switch roles they could easily play the damsel in distress card.

Gucci crept up the stairs and saw the girl she had bribed approach the hustlers. Out of nowhere she fell out on the floor, knocking the boiling pots off of the stove.

"Fuck is this fiended-out bitch doing up here? Get her ass out!" one of the hustlers said irritably. "I told y'all about letting these mu'fuckas smoke in the spot anyway."

"I think the bitch dying or something," one of them observed.

"I don't give a fuck . . . just get the seizing-ass bitch out the kitchen. Throw her ass back in the basement and get up here and bag up this batch," the block lieutenant ordered.

Gucci smirked knowing that the girl was putting on. She had gone all out. Gucci hurried to the back door and unlocked it, turning it quietly as she let Chanel and Raegan inside. They passed her a pistol and tied a scarf around her face.

"Don't blow this, Guch. Just point your gun and get the money. Any nigga get stupid you pop off. We'll ask questions later," Raegan schooled before making her way up the landing that led to the kitchen.

"Nigga, get that bitch out of here!" the dude said, losing his patience. Raegan and the girls met him on his way down the steps and she clicked off her safety, placing the chrome .45 dead center in his forehead.

"Back the fuck up," she ordered.

The young girl screamed out in surprise and raised her hands as Raegan and Chanel backpedaled them into the kitchen.

"Let me see them hands, gentleman! You cooperate and we leave quietly!" Raegan shouted out as Chanel and Gucci came up behind her, guns pointed. They followed her lead as they quickly gained control of the room.

"Get on the floor," Raegan shouted.

"You know whose money you fucking with?" one of the hustlers asked as he complied, getting on his knees.

"Yeah . . . mine, now get your ass down," Raegan spat as she kicked him in the back, digging her heel into his neck as he lay helpless beneath her. She turned to the young fiend and nodded her head. "You too. Get down."

Chanel and Gucci let their girl star in the show . . . they alternated so that no one voice would become recognizable. Each one did things differently and it made them less predictable. Today was the Raegan show . . . her girls were just the guest stars.

Making the men lie belly down in a circle, Raegan watched them all at once. She wasn't stupid. She knew that their brute strength could easily overpower them. She had to depend on her pistol in order to give her the advantage. Gucci went around binding their feet and hands. Her nervous energy caused her hands to tremble, but she moved diligently, not wanting to misstep.

Chanel quickly located the floorboard and a smile spread across her face as she saw the pot. It was definitely bigger than their last hit and in her mind the money was already spent as she helped herself to their stash. She put the money and uncooked cocaine in the bag, then moved to the table and stuffed the guns inside as well.

In less than five minutes they were in and out. As they left the young girl came running out of the house behind them. They hadn't tied her up because she didn't pose a threat, but as Chanel turned on her heels, her finger wrapped around the trigger.

"Yo!" she shouted.

When she saw Chanel's gun her hands went up in fear. "I just wanted my dope. She forgot to give me what she promised," the girl said.

Raegan reached into the bag and pulled out a stack of money then tossed it to the girl. "Let's go," she said, knowing that it was only a matter of time before the niggas figured out a way to get loose.

"Your fingernails weren't dirty!" the girl shouted as Raegan, Gucci, and Chanel climbed into the rental car. "That's how I knew you weren't a fiend! Your fingernails were too on point."

Chanel knew that the girl was right. They would have to pay more attention to detail next time. Luckily the hustlers they had just robbed hadn't noticed. The girls left the scene, thinking of the riches in the bag and the lovely capers to come.

Chapter Nine

"Nah, hey, baby, it's me. It's Mama."

Nahvid looked at the number that had appeared on his cell's caller ID when he recognized her voice.

"Where are you, Nita?" he asked concerned.

"I'm staying with a friend in Baltimore," she said back. "Mama miss you, baby. I'm ready to come home now, Nah. I need help, baby. I'm ready to get clean. I just need some money, baby. I need a little bit of money so I can fix myself up before I see you."

As soon as she asked for it he knew that she wasn't serious. She was gaming him, trying to use him to get her next high. He didn't want her out their tricking and selling her soul to the devil in order to get high. "I'll give you some money, Nita. Just come stay with me. We'll work on your habit, Nita. Wean you off of that shit," he whispered.

The line was silent as if she was seriously thinking of his offer.

"I'm ready, baby. I'ma come," she promised.

"I'll come get you," Nahvid said. "Where exactly are you?"

"I don't want you coming here, Nah . . . coming over here causing havoc to my friends . . . like they the ones got me hooked on this shit. I did this to myself, baby. But I'ma come. I'll be there next week. As soon as I get back in town I'm coming to you," Nita promised.

"Is this the number I can reach you at?" he asked.

"Yeah, this my cell phone, Nah. Look at your mama with a cell phone," she bragged with a laugh.

"I see you, old lady," he said as he chuckled. "I love you, Nita. Keep this phone on so I can reach you. I'll pay the bill. Who's the carrier?" he asked. He knew that Nita would blow with the wind in a heartbeat and he wanted to be able to reach her no matter what.

"Verizon," Nita replied.

"Promise me you're coming," Nahvid said seriously.

"I promise, baby. I'll be there," she said.

Chapter Ten

The first thing that Raegan did was attain her own lawyer to fight against Micah's pricey, experienced attorney in family court. She knew that if she wanted her son back she couldn't take any shorts so she contacted the best, and then moved into her own place to prove to a judge that she could take care of the two of them. As she stood in her large three-bedroom luxury apartment she became sad. It was empty just like her heart and because she couldn't fill the void within her she decided to fill the space within the four walls.

Raegan laced her home with every comfort and modern design that she could find as she ordered exclusive furniture. Her tastes were exquisite and she didn't hold back. She purchased without thinking . . . without negotiating . . . without a budget. She threw caution to the wind, ignoring price tags . . . partly because she wanted to see what it felt like to be a rich bitch, but mostly because it was a lovely distraction from the absence of her son. As she chose things to fill her son's room she felt a pair of hands squeeze her shoulders. The touch was so comforting that it made the stress melt from her tense body. She spun on her heels and smiled when she saw Nahvid's face.

"Hey, how are you?" she asked as she reached up to hug him.

"How are you?" he asked. "You're the toughest woman in the world to keep in touch with. You making me feel like an ugly nigga."

She blushed, surprised that he hadn't given up on her yet. It had been a few weeks since their last encounter and even though he took her absence as disinterest, she thought of him all the time. But the lifestyle she had picked up and the robberies she was committing left her with little free time. She was in grind mode and a man was the last of her concerns.

"Stop, you're making me feel so bad. I've just been busy that's all," she replied. "You shopping?"

"Yeah, for a new bedroom set," he said. "Can you help me out? My mom is coming to stay with me for awhile and I need a woman's touch to make her feel at home."

"Of course," she agreed. Raegan thought that she was doing it big until she watched how Nahvid lived. She picked out things from store to store and he purchased without even looking up from his cell phone. He handled his business while she worked with his personal sales associates at each store. She picked out everything from furniture and clothing to toiletries and jewelry, sparing no expense. They ripped through the entire shopping center and when she was done, Nahvid whipped out a black card and totaled out the bill. Impressed by his status in the game but more importantly she was surprised by his legitimacy in the corporate world. She listened as he talked Wall Street language, speaking of stocks and shares. He was a dream man. He came from the hood . . . from nothing and had made quite the businessman of himself . . . all without losing his connections to the streets.

"Sorry about that," he said as he finally hung up the phone.

"That's okay. I live to shop. I haven't done it in a long time and I've never done it like that before. I didn't even notice," she replied.

"You should visit Paris then. If you like to shop you would love it there," he said nonchalantly as if he weren't speaking of a place halfway around the world.

"I don't know what world you live in but in mine, Paris might as well be another planet," she said, slightly offended.

"Let me take you," he said.

She scoffed and laughed.

"I'm serious," he concluded. "I need to get you all to myself. Show you my world. Maybe convince you to be a part of it for awhile."

"Are you for real?" she asked.

The dudes who she was used to dealing with thought dinner and a movie was the crème de la crème. Nahvid was on a completely different level.

"I don't put things out there that I don't mean. I can rent a private jet and have it waiting on the tarmac in a couple of hours," he said.

"A couple hours?" she exclaimed, overwhelmed at his generosity and hypnotized by his power. She shook her head in disbelief and said, "Okay. Let's do it. I have to go pack. I have so much to do."

"It's a shopping trip. Everything is on me. We'll buy it all when we get there," he said. Nahvid was really blowing her mind.

They dropped her car off at her place and then she stayed the night at a hotel near the airport.

Raegan expected for Nahvid to push up on her that night. She was waiting for him to make his move, thinking that she had to reciprocate the trip with sexual favors. To her surprise he got her a separate room. The move was unexpected but she definitely appreciated it. After calling her girls and letting them know where she would be, she fell asleep, anxious and excited all at the same time.

Chapter Eleven

Paris was beautiful in the wintertime. The crisp, clean, glittering city lent an ambiance for romance and Nahvid and Raegan seemed to get seduced by it all. They appeared to be a couple who had known each other for years as they spent all of their time confined to the opulent five-star hotel. They were so into each other that they hadn't yet explored the Parisian culture, instead they learned each other . . . their likes . . . their dislikes . . . their memories . . . their fears. They shared everything as they enjoyed the seclusion halfway around the world. They did everything that lovers do and spared each other of nothing. Nahvid had come fully prepared to lavish Raegan with whatever her heart desired, but he found it refreshing that she hadn't asked for a single thing. He was used to chicks who wanted to get next to him for material reasons and Raegan was like a breath of cold, fresh winter air. She matched his wit and intellect, stroked his ego just right, and ravished him without inhibitions in the bedroom at night. All of those rare qualities on top of her beautiful exterior had Nahvid thinking that she had to be a dream. Their conversations were so deep that sometimes they became heated as they argued their points to one another, but she never backed down and stood firmly for the things that she believed to be true. She was an independent thinker. A lot of men would have called her headstrong or stubborn, but Nahvid loved a challenge and found Raegan extremely sexy. Many women would stick by his side because his paper was stacked high, but Raegan was the type of woman who would stay around when the chips were down. They argued like adversaries, but they never took it personally though. Makeup sex was the remedy to everything and they enjoyed the fights because they knew the pleasure that was to follow. Together they were incredible. Their chemistry was amazing and as they soaked together in the antique tub Nahvid had an overwhelming desire to keep her as his own. The sunrise peeked through the shutters as it illuminated the room with a soft amber glow.

"Once we leave here I don't want to have to chase you anymore, ma. You good for pulling disappearing acts," he whispered in her ear as she leaned against his chest while playing with the bubbles that surrounded them. She picked some up in the palm of her hands and blew them at him while laughing.

"You love me huh?" she asked playfully.

"Pretty much," he replied, only half joking.

"Well we still have a few days here. So you don't have to worry about me going anywhere anytime soon. You have me all to yourself. I'm loving France, even though I haven't seen that much of it," she said with a chuckle.

"So we need to change that then. How about we go out on the town today. Do some sightseeing and shopping," Nahvid offered.

"I'd like that," she answered. "I want to be able remember something about this place besides the hotel room. Although last night will probably be my fondest memory."

Thinking back on the way her pussy had hugged his dick as he entered her from behind he licked his lips and replied, "Yeah, ain't nothing topping that. How about a round two?"

Raegan stood up out of the water and hopped out of the tub, quickly wrapping herself in a plush towel. "Agh, agh, agh. If we start that we won't get to see anything today," she said. "And I want to see the Eiffel Tower!"

Nahvid and Raegan left the hotel arm in arm, eager to explore the city. Nahvid felt like an entirely new person in the foreign land. He couldn't remember the last time he had stepped foot outside without a burner on his waistline. His guard was forever up, cemented around him like a personal fortress, but here with Raegan, he was free to live. Fully prepared for the damage that Raegan was about to put on his black card, he entertained every outfit that she tried on. He had never seen shopping until he saw her in action. She was a fan of fashion and with no spending limit she was like a hurricane as she ripped through the stores. She was hesitant to spend until he reassured her that it was okay and once he gave her the green light there was no stopping her. Paris was like Candy Land to a material girl like her and the smile on her face was enough reward for Nahvid. Nahvid didn't mind lacing Raegan and treating her to a lifestyle that she had never experienced. He enjoyed her presence and the feeling that she gave him in the pit of his stomach. His attraction to her was pure, like a teenage love affair and growing up in the streets it was the simple things like a first crush that he had missed out on. That was it. He had a crush on Raegan and although she didn't know it, she had him wrapped around her finger. Not on no sucker shit, but he was attracted to her in the worst way. Nahvid was grateful that she had decided to come.

Paris was the perfect atmosphere to get to know someone. Being so far away from home, they were in their own little world. Neither of them spoke French so they only conversed with one another. They were each other's friend, ally, and mate all at once. One week felt like one year to them and even they were surprised at how connected to one another they became. She told him everything about her, except for how she made her money. That was the one secret she kept because she knew it would change his perspective of her. Uninterrupted, they were able to get to know each other. It had been a long time since Nahvid had given a woman so much attention, but with Raegan it felt right. It felt natural. It was inevitable that those three little words slipped out while they were there. Paris was the city of love and they had gotten drunk on it, night after night. The time flew by so quickly that they didn't want to leave, but as they sat on the international flight they both knew that they had to go back.

"I don't want things to change when we get back," she whispered in his ear as she kissed him repeatedly, gently.

"They won't. You're mine, ma. Nothing in the world can change that. Not after everything we've done this week. I'm selfish and I want you to myself."

As soon as Raegan stepped foot inside her home her cell phone rang back to back, first with Gucci blowing her up then with Chanel calling.

"Hey?" she answered. "What's up? I just got home," she said.

"Look outside, bitch," Chanel yelled excitedly.

Raegan went to her window and dropped the phone when she saw her girls lined up outside in a parade of foreign whips.

"No, they didn't!" she yelled excitedly as she slipped into her UGGs and threw on a peacoat before rushing outside.

"Bitch!" she shouted.

"You like 'em?" Gucci asked.

"Of course. I'm about to cop me one today!" Raegan said. Lisa came up and shook her head. She tossed her the key to the car that she had driven over there.

"No need to," Lisa said. "You know I can't afford a Benz. It's yours." She laughed as Raegan jumped up and down like a kid on Christmas.

They all hopped into their cars, Lisa riding shotgun with Raegan as they skirted out with no destination, stunting around the city.

When Nahvid returned home he called Nita repeatedly but she wouldn't answer his calls. He looked at the roomful of new furniture and clothes that he had purchased for her, shaking his head. He should have known that she would disappoint him . . . this had become a routine. She would get his hopes up only to shatter them when she chose to hug a crack pipe instead of her baby boy. Nahvid was a ruler and everything in him wanted to control his mother. He wanted to lock her away and hide the key until her body was clean, but of all the things he had a hold over, Nita had never been one of them. He was disappointed that Nita had stood him up. She had a monkey on her back that trumped any and everything. Today she hadn't been ready to come home, but one day, when she was ready . . . he knew she would come and that room would be waiting for her.

Chapter Twelve

The girls popped bottles in the club. Cristal and Louis XIII flowed freely at their table as Raegan, Gucci, and Chanel partied like socialites. Everything about them rang new money. Lisa couldn't believe the way that her friends had grinded to the top. As she sat partying at their expense she silently wished that she had gotten down from the beginning. They had come up in a major way. Well into their sixth heist, the girls were getting paid. Raegan had $250,000 put up on her own and she barely touched it thanks to Nahvid's generosity.

Easy money.

Dirty money.

More money.

Was their thought process . . . now that they had taken their first hit of the fast life they had become indulged by it. Mega shopping sprees filled their days and they spent frivolously because they knew that it could be easily replenished. The girls were in a circle on the dance floor, dancing their asses off, feeling like rock stars for the night. As Nahvid and his crew sat back, he admired his lady from afar. She was definitely the bell of the ball and he loved how she stole the show. Raegan blew him a kiss and smiled sexily as she wound her body while staring him in the eyes. He was completely satisfied with Raegan.

Reason leaned into his man's ear and whispered, "Yo, I'm not feeling your girl, Nah. Her and her girls are flossing a whole lot of paper. You know them bitches that been going around robbing stash spots . . . From the looks of it, that's them and your girl is shining like the ring leader."

Nahvid shot Reason a look that would have bodied him where he stood if looks could kill. "She don't got to rob nobody, fam. I'm taking care of that. Don't come out your mouth reckless about her," Nahvid said in a low, controlled tone. The last thing he wanted to do was beef out with his man over Raegan, but he had to make it known that she belonged to him now.

Reason's temple throbbed in anger. *This ol' pussy whipped-ass nigga. I'ma have to watch that bitch. Closely,* Reason thought. He didn't think Nahvid could see through the trance of a beautiful woman, but nothing was more attractive than his paper and Reason wasn't about to let Raegan or anyone else eat off his plate.

"No disrespect, Nah. You my man a hundred grand. I just don't want some broad to interrupt the paper flow, nah mean?" Reason asked.

"Has anything ever stopped me from getting money? Nigga, have I ever stopped you from eating? Everybody eats, but let me tell you something, fam . . . it's nothing if you don't have somebody to share it with. All them square feet I'm living in is pointless if I'm in it by myself. I want a wife and some kids, fam. It's time and she's it," Nahvid said seriously.

Reason nodded and tapped his Remy glass against his man's to show support, but in the back of his head his skepticism ate away at him. He didn't trust Raegan . . . point blank and would keep an eye on her. It took more than a happy face and a magnificent ass to catch him slipping.

The girls finally made their way off the dance floor and returned to their table. Raegan and Nahvid had been on each other all night. Their eyes never left one another as they flirted across the room. Raegan didn't crowd him in the club and he loved that. Even when other chicks approached Nahvid, Raegan never flipped. She just sat in the cut with amusement in her eyes as she watched Nahvid turn hoes down. The night was full of good-hearted fun but she was ready to put in personal time with her man. Nahvid nodded to her, summoning her to him and as she arose from her seat, Chanel leaned into her ear to whisper over the music.

"Gucci and I need to talk to you," she said to Raegan as she grabbed her hand, pulling her through the crowd.

"Guch!" Raegan shouted and nodded her head toward the bathroom to tell her to follow. The three girls left Lisa at their table to watch their handbags as they made their way to the back of the club. Lisa knew how they got down, but they never cut her in on any of the details. She didn't need to know the when's and where's. It was better for all of them that she remained untainted.

Nahvid stopped her just before she entered the restroom.

"You coming home with me tonight, ma?" he asked as he pinned her body against the wall.

"I've barely slept one night in my place since we got back," she whispered. She wanted to tell him no, but they both knew whose bed she would end up in tonight. He trapped her words in a kiss and grabbed her aggressively behind the neck to devour her tongue, teasing her and making her love button pulse.

"I've got a surprise for you, ma. Let's bounce," he said.

She grabbed the hand that caressed her face and kissed his wrist. "Okay. Meet me at the car in fifteen minutes. I need to talk to my girls real fast and settle our bar bill," she said.

He gave her a knowing look and said, "You know I already took care of you. Just holler at your people and meet me outside."

As soon as she walked inside Raegan could see that Chanel and Gucci had a lot on their minds. They stopped talking as soon as she stepped foot inside the restroom. "What's up?" Raegan asked.

"Gucci and I think it's time to hit another lick," Chanel said.

"You and Gucci? Or just you, Chanel?" Raegan asked.

"B . . . both of us think it's time," Gucci spoke up, stammering nervously.

Raegan shook her head in disbelief. They were lucky to have kept a low profile this long. Hustlers all over the city were talking about the group of chicks who were sticking up dope houses. They had a schedule and Raegan was sticking to it.

"I'm not for it. We need to lay low and take a month off," Raegan advised. "Niggas are on edge all over the city. It's best if we just fall back and then start up again in thirty days," Raegan said.

"I don't know about you but I can't wait thirty days, Raegan," Chanel said.

"Me neither," Gucci added.

"Fuck is you bitches playing broke for? I know how much y'all getting cuz I'm getting it the same way . . . the same amount. We're falling back. That's the smartest thing to do right now," Raegan said.

"Smart for who, Raegan?" Chanel countered. "Everybody ain't fucking with a rich nigga like you. These diamonds, the clothes, the shoes, the cars . . . it all costs and it's coming out of *my* pocket. Homeboy out there got your head in the clouds. We need to hit a lick . . . like tomorrow."

"I'm strapped right now too, Raegan. It is time. Putting my mama in that home is a big expense. I can't miss no money. Thirty days is too long," Gucci admitted.

"I'm out of here. Y'all tripping and you're getting risky," Raegan said as she headed for the door. Chanel rushed and pushed the door closed, then grabbed Raegan's hand to make her face them.

"We're doing it. Tomorrow," Chanel said sternly.

"Don't get fucking greedy, bitch, just stick to the plan. We hit one spot every month. That's how we been doing it. That's how we should keep doing it," Raegan whispered harshly as she snapped at her friends as they stood inside of the marble-tiled bathroom in the plush, upscale nightclub. The three ladies were dressed to kill as they discussed business in an unconventional setting. They heard the toilet flush behind one of the stall doors and Raegan's eyes bugged out in disbelief. "You bitches didn't clear this mu'fucka out?" she asked incredulously. "You must want to get caught the fuck up?" She stormed over to the stall and banged on the door with a flat hand. "Hurry the hell up, bitch. Time's up."

The stall door opened and a girl frowned as she stared Raegan down. "Excuse me?" she asked.

"You deaf or something? Get out!" she shouted harshly as she pushed the girl toward the door. There wasn't a scary bone in Raegan's body and it was nothing for her to strong-arm the girl out of the restroom. Once they were alone Raegan pushed open the other stall doors to make sure there was no one else inside. The last thing she needed was some ear-hustling-ass bitch blowing up her spot.

"Why are you so paranoid? I know Sunny Rae ain't scared?" Chanel asked with an accusing stare.

"Ain't a damn thing about me scared, bitch. I'm smart and I'm not down for hitting another spot a few days after we just wrapped up the last job. That's what we agreed to. Hit one stash house a month. If we do it right we don't need to go back in every other week looking for more. That's just greedy. Our luck is sure to run out if we play this thing the wrong way. Shit has been lovely. I don't know about y'all but I'm sitting on more cash than I can spend. Why press our luck?" Raegan argued.

"Look, Raegan, you're lucky. You get to stack your paper because you have a good man who takes care of business. We gotta live the best way we know how and this is how we eat. You're going soft, Raegan," Gucci shot at her. She pulled a small compact mirror out of her Hermes bag and removed a small bag filled with white powder. The substance was so pure that it sparkled slightly under the dim bathroom light. She quickly set herself up and hit two fat lines of cocaine. It was a habit she picked up by being around so much coke. The girls hadn't found any buyers for the product they stole so Gucci sampled it from time to time . . . a recreational high.

"I'm not going *soft*, Gucci. I just don't want to change things up. If it ain't broke why fix it?" Raegan argued. "And since when you hitting blow? Fuck are you doing?"

"I'm a big girl, Raegan," Gucci said as she sniffed and cleared the extra powder from her nose.

"Look, Raegan, I'm broke and my pocketbook needs fixing," Chanel said as she stared challengingly at Raegan.

Their friendship was new, but they were extremely loyal to each other. They had become thick as thieves. They each had been groomed for the game. Treachery was bred within them . . . larceny their religion . . . money their motivation.

"I'm out. This is not a negotiation. We are not doing this," Raegan concluded.

"We are doing it. I've already scoped the spot and everything. It's out in Trinidad. You're acting real brand new but it's fine . . . we'll do it without you," Chanel spat as she walked past Raegan, her Louboutin stiletto boots stabbing the floor as she walked out.

Raegan looked at Gucci desperately for support, but Gucci just shook her head in disappointment. "We would never leave you hanging like that, Raegan. You know we need you out there," she said before following after Chanel. Raegan went back to the table and air kissed Lisa good-bye before grabbing her handbag and leaving the club.

Chapter Thirteen

Lying underneath the crumpled satin sheets Raegan's head spun out of guilt. She tossed and turned, feeling guilty for not riding with her girls. Restless, she crawled out of bed and wrapped Nahvid's robe around her shoulders. The moon was full and although it was freezing outside, she needed to clear her head. She stepped out onto his balcony and stared up at the night sky. The crisp air hit her instantly, refreshing her as she stared out on to the sparkling snow.

She heard the sliding door open behind her and she closed her eyes as she felt Nahvid's lips grace her neck.

"It's freezing out here, ma," he whispered. "Come back to bed."

"It's beautiful though. It's so still at night," she said.

"You wanna talk about it?" he asked, thinking that she missed her son. He hated to see her sad. He could tell by her tense shoulder and the heaviness in her tone that her heart was burdened.

She shook her head and turned around to kiss his lips. "No, not really. I just want to be with you. When I'm with you everything in my world seems right. I forget all of the bad," she whispered.

"Me too, ma. Me too," he whispered. "You're my get right."

He led her back inside and lay down in his bed, wrapping his arms around her. "I feel like I want to take things to the next level with you. You're my Sunny Rae. I'd like you to meet somebody," he said.

"Who?" she asked.

"My mother," Nahvid answered. "You're the only woman who I have ever cared for besides my moms. I would like for the two of you to meet. I called her when you fell asleep to see if she was available." Nahvid waited for her to respond. "I've arranged a dinner at the restaurant tomorrow night. Is that okay?" he asked. He wanted Raegan to know where he came from and to meet the woman who had birthed him and the one who he had let break his heart repeatedly.

"Of course," she answered. "I'd love to meet her, baby." As she thought about her girls she feared that they may be right. She didn't want to let them down just because Nahvid had chosen to upgrade her life-style. *I have to be there for them. I have to do this,* she thought. She turned to Nahvid and added, "I just have to go get pampered in the morning. I'll have to meet you there. I want to make a good impression on her."

Raegan had the best Brazilian blowout in town and she was always well maintained. Pampering herself was the last thing on her mind, but using it as an excuse was the perfect lie to give herself enough time to hit the lick with her girls before the dinner. She cared about Nahvid and she gave herself to him like no other man before, but she owed this to her girls. *When he wasn't in the picture they were all that I had. I can't let them down.*

Raegan hesitantly came out of her sleep, wishing that she could live in her dreams forever. Her son was always available to her in her dreams and as she opened her eyes she could still hear his coos in her head. She crawled out of bed and did her morning beauty regi-men before making her way downstairs.

"Nahvid!" she called as she descended the stairs. He met her at the bottom and lifted her off of her feet as he kissed her lips.

"Good morning, beautiful," he complimented. "I need you to be quiet though. My homeboy is asleep in there on the couch."

"What?" she questioned in confusion.

"Go take a look. I'm about to make breakfast. Wake him and see if he's hungry for me?" Nahvid asked.

Raegan frowned in confusion as she made her way into the living area. She stopped mid-step and her hand shot over her mouth as tears came to her eyes. Her son lay comfortably on the couch with his thumb in his mouth. It had been so long since she had seen him. He was seven months old. "How did you? When did? Oh my God," she whispered in disbelief. "How long do I have with him?"

"A lifetime, ma. Your baby's father and I had a talk. He sees things much clearer now and he sends his sincere apologies," Nahvid said seriously as he wiped the tears from her face. "He's all yours."

Raegan ran to her baby and woke him up with hugs and kisses. Her heart swelled so much that it hurt. It was the greatest gift that Nahvid could have ever given her . . . It was one that she would never forget.

She played with her son for hours, wearing him out with laughter and love. She was relieved that he seemed to recognize her and she did all that she could to make sure that she showed him how much she had missed him. As time slowly ticked by she wished that she didn't have to leave him, but she had to take care of one thing . . . one lick with her girls. Nahvid came over and took her son, cradling him as if it were his own child. "Let's put your mommy out so she can get ready for tonight, li'l homie," Nahvid said. Baby Micah seemed to take to Nahvid and as Raegan looked up at the two of them she realized that she loved Nahvid. He was her man . . . they were built for one another. *After today I'm done with this. I have enough money put up to last at least a couple years if I live modestly,* she thought. As she stood, sadness filled her eyes.

"He'll be here when you get back. Go ahead. Take whatever you need out of the knot on the kitchen counter. Enjoy yourself and li'l man and I will meet you here at eight P.M."

Raegan nodded and then kissed her son before heading out to meet Gucci and Chanel. Whether they liked it or not, this would be the last time she put her life on the line.

Chapter Fourteen

"Hurry up before I put your brains on the floor," Gucci shouted as she pointed her gun at the guy. Her nerves were all over the place. She was scared to do the job without Raegan and had hit a few lines of coke to give her the courage she needed to carry this lick through. She was quickly regretting it, however, because it felt like her body was on overload and she couldn't quite focus on the task at hand.

"He thinks we're playing with his ass," Chanel yelled harshly. The guy was moving extremely slow. They had already been in the stash house too long. She hated to admit it, but things were much harder without Raegan. There were just too many niggas in the room to watch. She felt out of control and frantic without the extra security that Raegan contributed. Uneasy and a bit fearful Chanel was ready to shake, but she wasn't leaving there without the money she had come for.

Chanel felt completely unprepared. In her rush to come up on some new paper, she hadn't done her homework well enough. She had scoped the spot briefly, but had been far from thorough. If she had done her job she would have known that the five hustlers in the room were one man short. So as the dude stuffed the money in the duffel bag, he moved molasses slow, purposely trying to give his man time to return to the spot.

The situation was out of control. A smoker who had come to cop lay quivering in the corner of the room and as she tried to stand Chanel almost lost her cool.

"Sit the fuck back down!" she shouted as she applied pressure to her trigger. "All of you sit! On your hands!" The various fiends in the room sat down on top of their hands wishing that they had kept their promises to God to kick crack. Maybe this was their punishment for living life addicted to the devil's smoke. Chanel was overwhelmed. There were simply too many people in the room and not enough firepower to keep things looking favorable for the girls. Feeling as though they had gotten in over their heads, Chanel decided to get what they could and retreat. "Get the bag," she told Gucci.

As she hit the back door she was met with a Beretta to the face. "Bitch, get your ass back inside," the guy said as he snatched the gun from her hand, catching her off guard.

"Put your gun down!" Gucci demanded as she immediately placed her pistol to the head of the man who had been bagging the money.

"Bitch, you put your gun down," the dude shot back.

BOOM!

Without warning a shot let off and the dude was met with a slug to the back of the head as Raegan stepped into the room.

"You already know what time it is. Move faster or don't move at all," Raegan threatened.

Distracted by Raegan's presence Gucci never saw the guy reach for the pistol he had taped beneath the table. He popped off, his bullshit aim causing him to miss, but inciting a shootout. Gucci grabbed the money and shot out the front door as Raegan and Chanel held it down inside. Bullets flew and when Chanel's clip ejected itself, empty . . . Raegan kept firing, relentlessly. She had toe tagged that nigga before he left her son without a mom. Raegan dumped on him until she heard him stop firing and when Chanel went to check the body her eyes bugged as she announced, "He's dead."

The men on the floor trembled. Their hands and feet were bound and they anticipated being executed one by one, but Raegan wasn't cold-blooded. When she saw the woman dead in the corner, blood trailing from a dot in her forehead, her stomach turned. Things had gone bad . . . fast and there was no turning back. "Get the rest of that money and let's go," she said harshly as she walked out of the house dazed from all of the carnage she left behind inside.

Chapter Fifteen

"You came," Gucci mumbled as she drove away from what was now a crime scene.

"I wish I hadn't," Raegan shot back. "I told you bitches . . . I told you! We were supposed to play it smart, not reckless. Now three people are dead . . . *dead!* You couldn't see that the stupid nigga was stalling?"

Chanel and Gucci thought it wise not to argue back. Raegan was livid and they knew she was right. They had overestimated their game and now it had back-fired. Chanel drove back to her house and they quickly went inside. Blood covered Raegan and she trembled as she rushed upstairs.

"Count the money and put it in Lisa's room. Nobody touch it. Nobody. I have to get cleaned up and get out of here. I have to meet Nahvid somewhere. Just don't get to spending this money right away. Lay low for a couple weeks until things die down," Raegan suggested.

Chanel and Gucci nodded while looking guiltily at each other. When Raegan stepped into the shower she broke down. She cried good and long. Her soul hurt. Her conscience was heavy. They had been greedy. After the first hit they should have stopped, but their insa-tiable love of material things had led them straight to the breaking point.

***

Raegan walked into the room looking as beautiful as ever. A borrowed Badgley Mischka dress out of Chanel's closet helped cover up the sins she had committed just moments before. As she walked over to Nahvid, she hoped her eyes weren't red. He held her little man in his strong arms and embraced her gently.

"We missed you, ma," he whispered into her ear.

She blushed and took her seat. Her heart melted when he passed her baby Micah. He was her joy. He instantly distracted her from the events that had just taken place.

"Where's your mom?" she asked.

Disappointment filled his face as he replied, "I don't know." Raegan's heart went out to Nahvid. He was normally so poised and strong, but the devastation that took over his features made him look like a lost little boy. "I shouldn't even be surprised. This is typical," he said. He picked up his menu. "Let's just eat."

Raegan reached over the table and grabbed Nahvid's hand, squeezing it reassuringly. "No, Nah, we can wait."

Baby Micah distracted them both as they sat with him like doting parents as they waited for their guest of honor to show up. With every minute that passed Nahvid's face revealed more of his hurt. "How can a mother do this to her son? She's never been there. Tonight I wanted her to meet you because I've grown to care for you . . . I wanted her to be normal . . . to scrutinize you like any normal mother would. For once I just wanted her to be the parent, nah mean? I wanted that fairy tale shit," he admitted. Raegan's eyes watered and as soon as she went to hug Nahvid, baby Micah cried out.

"I'm sorry . . . He has the worst timing," she said as she picked up her son and cuddled him close to her chest.

Nahvid smiled and shook his head. "Never apologize for being a good mother, ma. What you have with him is what I wish I could have with my own mother. I admire the love you have for your son," he said.

Raegan walked over to Nahvid and sat on his lap with her baby still in her arms. She looked at him as he welcomed the two of them into his lap. His embrace was warm, but his eyes were cold from the abandonment he felt. "She is crazy for not loving you, right," Raegan said. "She's the one losing out, Nah . . . not you. You are an extraordinary person. The best man I've ever met."

"You're the first person I've ever talked to about her . . . about missing her. I'm not gonna lie, Rae. It hurts," Nahvid admitted as he inhaled her scent, burying his head in her neck. "You being in my presence makes life a little less lonely."

"I'll be here as long as you want me too, Nahvid," Raegan replied with a kiss on the lips. They waited for an hour before deciding to order.

"I love you, Nah. Don't be too mad at your mother," Raegan said. "I'm sure that she loves you, baby. She'll come around. I'm not going anywhere so I will be here whenever she's ready to meet me. I wouldn't want to share you with another woman either. You are her baby boy. I know when Micah brings home some little floozy I'm going to be reluctant to accept her too."

Her smile lit up the room and caused Nahvid's night to turn around. Even though he knew that his mother's issues were much more complex than Raegan could ever know, she had a way of making even his most miserable moments seem worthwhile.

"You're an amazing woman and mother, ma," he complimented. "The more I'm around you the more I can't stand the thought of losing you."

"You won't. I am here, Nahvid. I am the one person who will always come back to you," she said as she held his hand up to her mouth and kissed it softly.

Nahvid put his napkin over his plate and looked at her seriously.

"What?" Raegan asked, feeling as though she were transparent.

"I want to share something with you. There's a place that I need to show you," he said as he stood and held out his arm. "Take a ride with me."

Nahvid loaded baby Micah into his back seat, opened the door for Raegan, and then climbed inside his car. Raegan had him feeling a certain type of way about her. He was experiencing love like never before. Usually he lost interest in women quickly, but Raegan stimulated his mind, body, and soul. She was imperfectly perfect and he felt that he needed to open his entire world to her. They rode in silence, but Nahvid gripped her hand tenderly, protectively as he whipped through the city's streets . . . his streets . . . the ones that he had put in years of work to own. Raegan could feel that his mind was racing and she gave him time to think. She sat back and just enjoyed the feeling of being his queen. There were a million and one bitches who would love to be sitting next to him, but he had chosen her and it felt good. They arrived at a closed storage facility and Nahvid turned off the car.

"Come on, I need to show you something," he said.

She grabbed her son out of the car and followed him inside. "What is this place?" she asked as she entered and discovered the contents that lay inside. There were luxury cars, furniture, and boxes everywhere.

"This is my stash spot, Raegan. I'm showing you this because I trust you. I'm trying to be with you, ma, and I want you to know where my worth lies in case anything ever happens to me. No one knows where this is. If I'm ever at a point where I can't handle my own business I want you to be able to provide for you and your son. You tell no one where this is, Raegan. Not even your best friends. This is for your knowledge only, just in case," he said.

"Just in case what?" she asked, feeling as though he was foreshadowing an inevitable death.

"Just in case," he repeated with a knowing nod. "Can I trust you with this?"

Raegan went to him and rubbed his face reassuringly. "You can trust me with anything."

Their bond was so strong in that moment and Raegan was honored that he was positive in her loyalty. She knew that Nahvid was very protective over his empire and the fact that he would let her in on such a sensitive matter made her feel exclusively loved. In a short period of time they had come to cherish one another and now more than ever before, she was confident that they would be long-lasting. Nahvid's phone rang and he kissed the top of her head as he answered the call.

"Yo," he answered. Raegan felt his body stiffen as he received the news on the other end and she looked up at him curiously. His mood went from calm to enraged in the blink of an eye as he ended the call. He looked at her and kissed her cheek. "We have to go. I have something important I need to handle."

They drove in silence but Raegan knew that whatever news he had received had changed Nahvid's entire mood. The tension in Nahvid's brow caused him to frown and his jawbone clenched as he gritted his teeth. Raegan wanted to speak, but for lack of words remained quiet, until they pulled up in front of the very house that Raegan had just robbed. Her chest became tight as she fidgeted nervously. It felt as though her heart fell into the pit of her stomach. "Why are we here?" she asked.

"Just stay in the car, ma. This is one of my spots. Somebody robbed me," he stated. "Lock the doors and don't open then for anybody." He got out of the car and walked up to the door where Reason was waiting for him.

Raegan watched in horror. She didn't know if she should get in the driver's seat and peel out or if she should stay put. Uncertainty took over her mind as the threat of being caught up made her feel as though she would vomit. *There is no way he knows it's me,* she thought as her breathing became deep . . . panicked.

She saw him emerge from the house grief-stricken as blood covered his shirt. She got out of the car, running to him as worry filled her. The look on his face was one of pure heartbreak. "What's wrong? Nah, talk to me," she begged as she cupped his face in her hands. She could see the pain seeping from within him, but he refused to cry. *It's just money. He can't be this broken up about money,* she thought.

"My mother was in the house when it was robbed. They killed her," he said. "It's been a long time since I've put my murder game down . . . but the bitches that did this is gonna see me."

"Bitches?" she said feigning shock as if she weren't a part of the very crew who had orchestrated the heist.

"One of my li'l niggas . . . they left him alive. He said it was three bitches . . . red-bottom heels, trench coats, and winter scarves wrapped around their faces," he described.

As he spoke she dug her heels into the plush grass. She was wearing the exact pumps she had worn during the robbery and she discreetly hid them, not wanting him to put two and two together. He knew that she owned many pair. Hell he had purchased most of them, but suspecting her was the last thing on his mind. She felt like a snake. She truly cared for Nahvid and knew that they could be so great together, but their courtship was built upon a foundation of lies . . . deceit that she had started . . . lies that she had told and would have to keep up to save her own neck.

"Let's go home, baby," she said. "I'm so sorry."

He had no idea that there was more to her apology than sympathy. Her mind spun as she got into the driver's seat and made her way back to his house.

He didn't speak and the spark that usually lit up his eyes when he looked at her was now so dim she almost couldn't find it. Her guilt and insecurity made it feel as though he already knew the truth. She wanted to probe into his head . . . to hear the emotions so that she could make sure he was clueless of her involvement but she said nothing. Raegan put baby Micah to sleep, in the crib that Nahvid had purchased. As she looked around the room she was overwhelmed in regret. *How could I do this to him? How could I contribute to this pain? He'll never forgive me for this.* Raegan kissed her son and packed a bagful of his things, quietly tiptoeing around his room until she had gathered baby Micah's most important things. She knew that she would have to leave Nahvid. Too much had gone down. There was no taking back this mistake and as soon as she got the opportunity she would blow like the wind, no matter how much she wanted to plant roots. She hid the bag in his closet and then returned to find Nahvid. Tears gathered in her eyes when she saw him standing at the window. His back was turned to her so she couldn't see his face, but the way his shoulders slumped in defeat revealed his broken spirit. Raegan knew that she had squandered a good thing, thrown away what could have been a storybook love, all in the sake of chasing dead presidents. She had never meant to hurt him, but as she walked up behind him and wrapped her arms around his body she knew that he had.

"I love you, Nahvid. I am sorry, baby," she whispered.

He stayed up half the night drinking his guilt away as Raegan sat on the couch rubbing his back to ease his tension.

"I should have pulled her out of the streets a long time ago," he said regretfully.

"You didn't know this would happen, Nah," she soothed, all the while fighting her inner turmoil. Everything in her wanted to tell the truth but she feared the repercussions. She knew of his power in the streets and had heard of the things that he had done to those who crossed him. She hadn't known him long enough to be the exception to the rule. She was sure that she was beginning to fall hard for him. She would even go so far as to say that she loved Nahvid, but she wouldn't bet her life on it that he felt the same. Nahvid wouldn't hesitate to end her life. The doorbell rang loudly throughout the house and she stood to answer it.

"It's four o'clock in the morning," Raegan noticed, wondering who it could be.

"It's Reason," Nahvid announced as he stood too. He went to answer the door and Reason walked in with a badly beaten young boy at his side.

"Take him to the garage," Nahvid ordered. Raegan watched timidly as Reason pushed the boy toward the garage door.

"I didn't have shit to do with it, fam. Nah! Please, man. I was at home with my sister, fam! I swear on everything!"

Reason dragged him kicking and screaming all the way out of the house. Nahvid walked over to Raegan and noticed that she was shaking.

"Nah, please don't hurt that boy," she pleaded. She gripped his hands tightly and stared him in the eyes, begging him not to do this. She knew that whatever happened to that young man was on her, yet she still couldn't open her mouth to stop what was about to go down. She couldn't implicate herself. Raegan wasn't ready to confess . . . to show her true self to Nahvid. "Nah?"

"Don't worry about that, ma," he said. He kissed her forehead. "Go upstairs and get some rest. I'll be up after a while."

The soundproof garage masked the torture that was going on inside but Raegan wasn't naïve. When Reason left dragging a heavy-duty bag behind him, she knew what lay inside. She closed her eyes knowing that she was responsible for all of this. She had to go talk to Gucci and Chanel. They had no idea what was going on and she needed help figuring out what to do next. She loved Nahvid and was positive that he adored her . . . but that line between love and hate was so thin that she knew if he ever found out what she did, things would never be the same.

First thing in the morning I have to think of an excuse to get out of here. I'm not going to stick around until he finds out what I did. By the time everything comes to light I'll be long gone, she thought.

Raegan awoke first to find that Nahvid hadn't been to sleep. The stress in his brow was evident and she stood on her tiptoes to kiss his ails away.

"Li'l man is still sleeping. I just checked in on him," Nahvid said.

"Thank you. Why are you so good to me? I don't even deserve you," she whispered.

"You and baby Micah are all I have right now. I see you in my future. I want you and your son to be a part of my life for a long time," he said.

"Me too," she said. "But if something ever happens to make you feel otherwise . . . know that I always loved you and that I would never do anything intentionally to hurt you."

He pulled her close and inhaled her scent.

"Are you hungry? You have to take care of yourself," she said, sincerely concerned. Raegan had never seen him so bothered. He always seemed to carry the weight of the world on his shoulders without falter, but the death of his mother had him thrown.

He nodded and placed his forehead against hers.

"I'm going to go grab a few things from the grocer. It'll give you some space to think. We'll be back," she said as she went to get her son dressed.

"Leave li'l man here. I don't want him to get sick," Nahvid stated.

Raegan nodded reluctantly knowing that if she had taken her son she would have never returned. Raegan dressed slowly as she tried to think of a way to get her son out of the house with her.

"Go ahead, baby girl. Micah is straight here with me. Take your time," Nahvid said as he walked into the bedroom. He could sense her hesitance. "Is everything okay?"

She continued to slip into her things and nodded distractedly. "Yeah, it was just a long night. Everything is fine. I just want to make sure you are okay . . . we're okay . . . right?" she asked.

Nahvid kissed the tip of her nose and said, "You're the only thing in my life that's okay right now. Now hurry back to us. You're only going to the store . . . you don't got to get all fancy, ma, just slip into something and come back home to me."

Raegan left, but as she walked out of the house an eerie feeling overcame her. She looked over her shoulder, feeling as if she would never come home again. Shaking off the bad vibes she got into her car and sped to see Chanel and Gucci.

When she arrived the front door was wide open and the house was in shambles.

"Guch! Lisa! Chanel!" she called out. She made her way upstairs and ran from room to room looking for her girls. When she saw Lisa bound to her bed, tongue lying on the pillow beside her, eyes gouged out of their sockets she hurled on sight. She rushed to the closet to retrieve the cash and when she saw the empty safe open on the ground her entire body went numb. She rushed out of the house, so frantic that she could barely dial the numbers on her phone.

"Hello?" Gucci finally answered.

"Where are you? Where's Chanel?"

"We went to breakfast. What's wrong? Where are you?" Gucci asked.

"I'm at your house staring at Lisa's dead body. The stash house we took was Nahvid's!"

"What?" Gucci slipped. Raegan got their location and raced to meet them. She was pissed. She could tell by the way that Gucci had reacted that she hadn't known they were hitting Nahvid's spot, but it was a little too coincidental for Raegan. Her girls were waiting in the parking lot of the restaurant and when Raegan pulled up, she got out of her car and ran up on Chanel. Her fist connected with Chanel's lip, bursting it on impact.

"You bitch! You knew that was his spot. Why would you target him?" she asked.

Chanel knew that Raegan would be in her feelings when she finally found out so she held her composure as she wiped her mouth with the back of her hand. She spit blood onto the pavement and replied, "Because the nigga is loaded and I knew you would never agree to it if you knew. Robbing him was the only way we would hit it big! Ain't nobody getting money in this city but Nahvid and you know it! Nobody was supposed to get hurt."

"Yeah, well somebody did. His mama! She was in the house, Chanel! She died and now Lisa's dead too. The money's gone!"

"What?" she asked. "We just saw Lisa two hours ago. Fuck you mean the money's gone?"

"Yeah, well she's dead and Reason killed her. There is no telling what she told him before she died. They tortured her. Cut out her tongue. I know she talked," Raegan said. "He knows it was me . . . He knows." She frantically paced back and forth.

"We have to skip town," Gucci said. "We have to get out of here."

"And go where? Huh? We don't have any money. Besides Nahvid has my son! Micah is there with him. I left him there!" she shouted as tears welled in her eyes. Raegan remembered the feeling that had passed over her before she had left Nahvid's house and she shook her head, wishing that she had made a different decision. "He has my baby."

"He's not going to hurt Micah. You know that," Chanel said.

"I'm going back," Raegan stated.

"You can't, Raegan. You have to leave him there, at least for now," Chanel said. "Whoever murdered Lisa the jokes on them. The security system tapes the property around the clock. I can upload the tape online and we can use that as leverage to get Micah back. But right now we need to let things cool down. We have to skip town."

"And go where?" Gucci asked.

"I know someone who can help us. A friend of mine owns a boat in Florida. If we can make it there, he'll take us wherever we want to go. He's powerful and prestigious. He can get us passports . . . whatever we need. I know that he will help," Chanel said. "I stopped talking to him awhile back, but I know he won't turn me away. If we can make it down there, we'll be okay."

"I can't believe this," Raegan cried. "I don't even have any money on me right now. We can't make it too far on broke and this fucking credit card is going to give Nahvid a damn GPS to come find my ass."

"We've got to take a bank," Chanel whispered.

"What?" both Gucci and Raegan exclaimed, looking at her as if she had lost it.

"Stop talking stupid," Raegan shouted. "I should slap the shit out of you for even saying some airhead shit like that."

"What! You got a better idea? What's the other option, Raegan?" Chanel countered. "Go back to Nahvid and hope he doesn't dead you on sight? We need money and this is the only way."

"A stash house," Gucci spoke up and said. "We could hit another one."

"Every hood nigga in the city is on to us now. A bank is our only other option . . . We have to hit a bank . . ."

Chapter Sixteen

"I don't know a damn thing about banks. There is too much that can go wrong," Raegan said skeptically as she sat on the bed of the seedy motel room.

"You didn't know anything about robbing stash houses either but we pulled that off. At this point, Rae, we really don't have a choice," Chanel replied.

"And you're comfortable with this?" Raegan snapped, looking for Gucci to back her up.

"If this is what I have to do to stay alive then yeah . . . I'm in," Gucci replied.

Raegan had a feeling in her gut . . . a warning sign that was trying to stop her from escalating matters. Everything in her wanted to call Nahvid and run back to him. Common sense was screaming at her.

"No! Stop! Don't do it! Nahvid will understand once you explain! Put on your grown-woman panties, bitch, and go back for your child!"

But she didn't listen. Her cowardice wouldn't let her do the right thing. She wished that she could turn back time and take back the role she played in robbing Nahvid. She cared deeply for him and in his world she felt safe, secure, and kept. With him all she had to be was a girl in love . . . she didn't need to struggle for survival because he took care of her effortlessly. *How did I fuck that up?* she wondered as she shook her head in utter shame. Now here she was separated from her son once again and on the run for her life. Shit was real, nothing about her life was a fairy tale . . . even her love story with Nahvid had a tragic ending. She didn't know what Lisa had told Reason but she knew that no human being could handle the torture that she had endured. Raegan was sure that Lisa had talked and she could only imagine what was said. Lisa's words would forever be secrets of a ghost . . . Reason had made sure of it. Raegan could not fathom the betrayal that Nahvid felt and the measures he would take to get revenge. There was nothing about Raegan that was naïve. She had only known Nahvid for a short time. His feelings for her would not get in the way of his business and they especially didn't trump the love he had for his mother. When Nahvid found her he would kill her and it broke Raegan's heart that her son was still in his possession.

"We'll take Security One Credit Union first. It's a small company so their security won't be as advanced as a national chain bank. They will never see us coming," Chanel schooled.

"And if we get caught?" Raegan countered.

Chanel sighed and looked back and forth between her friends. She was scared shitless just like them. There was nothing brave about her, but she had never been one to roll over and die without a fight. The way she saw it, they had no other options. It was either go up against the streets or hit a bank and blow town . . . In her mind the bank was where the odds lay in her favor.

"Look. I fucked up. I never thought that Nahvid would ever find out that we hit his spot and I certainly didn't think that we would walk out with blood on our hands. I'm scared. I know what type of reach that man has and I'm not trying to end up like Lisa. I just want to get as far away from D.C. as possible," Chanel said sincerely. "We have to stick together . . . no matter what."

Raegan wanted to slap the shit out of Chanel for messing everything up. *If she hadn't gotten out of pocket none of this would have even happened,* Raegan thought. At this point shifting the blame was redundant. It was too late for finger pointing. She simply had to play the hand that she had been dealt.

"Let's just get some sleep," Gucci spoke up, trying to be the buffer between the two natural elements that were threatening to erupt. Among the three young women she was the most timid of the group. She thought that it was sometimes best to listen rather than shout to be heard. "We're going to need to be alert to pull this off. There's no point in continuing to debate it. We all know what we have to do."

Raegan and Chanel both nodded in agreement. Chanel and Gucci took the double beds and Raegan pulled out the sofa as they prepared for a restless night's sleep. Raegan wanted to desert her friends and go begging for Nahvid's forgiveness, but she could never be that selfish. Chanel had been there for her when her bum-ass baby's father had repeatedly dogged her. She was a good friend and Raegan knew that no matter what they were in it together until the end. Loyalty was all they had.

Raegan thought of baby Micah and a lone tear crept from her eyes and rolled down her face. She wiped it away as she turned her back to her friends, but both Chanel and Gucci noticed her distress. Raegan had the least to gain and the most to lose in the situation. Not only was she thinking of herself, but she was accountable for her child and neither Gucci or Chanel could understand that.

"Raegan," Gucci called out.

Raegan didn't respond. She was too choked up and overwhelmed to even speak.

Gucci and Chanel gave each other a knowing glance, both feeling regret that their overzealous antics had led them down this path. They walked over to Raegan and sat down beside her.

Wrapping their arms around their friend they formed a cocoon of support. "I'm sorry, Rae. Micah is going to be fine," Chanel said.

"And so are we," Gucci added.

"Why the hell do I have to sit in the car?" Chanel asked. "This was my setup and now I'm stuck being the getaway driver?"

"Because you're reckless and we are doing this my way or no way," Raegan said as she handed Gucci a gun.

Gucci cocked it back. Adrenaline mixed with fear caused her heart to beat irregularly. "In and out," Gucci whispered.

Chanel smacked her lips and rolled her eyes. "So you're going to have Gucci scary behind watching your back? If something goes wrong we all know that she's not popping off."

"Nothing is going to go wrong if we keep a cool head and you clearly cannot do that. I'm not beat for the bullshit today. Gucci and I got this part . . . you just be ready to get us the fuck out of here," Raegan replied bossily.

The girls didn't have many options for disguises. All of their pockets were on E and the only thing they had to conceal their identities were the very same getups that they had worn when hitting the stash houses. Louboutin red-bottom heels and trench coats. Gucci had shoplifted three wigs and sunglasses to hide their faces so it was what it was. That was as good as it got.

There was no point in prolonging it. They were either in or out and if they chose the latter, they would be sitting ducks.

"Let's just get it over with," Gucci said as she inhaled anxiously. Raegan nodded her head and Gucci walked into the bank first, her long red wig flowing behind her as she went inside. Her nerves were so bad that she tapped her foot against the tile floor, causing her heel to echo with every *click clack* as she stood in line. Her bowels flip-flopped uncontrollably as the possibility of getting caught sent her stomach into a frenzy. It felt as if she would throw up at any second. She looked nervous and it felt as if everyone in the bank knew her intentions before she ever made a move.

She looked around and noticed that the bank was crowded. It was Friday . . . payday, which meant that the bank had a large amount of cash on site. In her mind, she already had her cut spent. She would send her mother's adult care home enough so that her mother would be straight for a while and then Gucci would give D.C. her ass to kiss. As she turned her head she saw Raegan walk into the bank. From appearances alone, Gucci would have never thought that Raegan was out of her element. She was calm, collected, coordinated. She didn't stumble or falter . . . she simply walked into the place as if she owned it and stood in the next line over. There were only two tellers on duty in the small credit union and Raegan and Gucci would both handle a teller to make sure that no silent alarms were tripped. Gucci felt as if she had a thoroughbred racing in her chest from the rapid beating of her heart. She took deep breaths to calm herself. She didn't want to be the one to fuck this up. She knew what was on the line. Her eyes scanned the entire room. She had only been in the building for forty-five seconds but it felt as if she had been standing there for hours. Sweat shone lightly on her brow and her stomach turned. It was one thing going up against a bunch of hood niggas but to be putting her freedom on the line was intimidating. Gucci was confident in her girls' abilities to outthink a dope boy, but to outwit an entire institution was a completely different ball game. The stakes had been raised the moment they had decided to take a bank. She looked at the clock . . .

Fifty-five seconds.

At the one-minute mark it would be time to put in work.

Each tick of the long hand taunted her . . . dared her to put the plan in motion.

Fifty-six seconds.

The lady in front of her stepped out of the way and Gucci stepped up to the counter.

Fifty-seven seconds.

"Hello, what can I do for you today?" the teller asked with a genuine smile. Gucci hated to be the one to fuck up the woman's day.

Fifty-nine seconds.

But that's exactly what she was about to do.

As the hand hit the number twelve Gucci's eyes went from the clock to the teller. Time seemed to slow dramatically as Gucci leaned over the granite slightly and whispered, "I've got sixteen bullets in my pistol and if you don't want one of them to land in your head I suggest you open the drawer and empty it now."

Gucci smiled the entire time she was speaking to make the transaction appear to be as normal as possible, but the look of alarm was clearly transparent in the teller's eyes.

Her mouth fell open and Gucci shook her head slightly. "Unh uhh. I wouldn't do that. Just calm down and you will walk out of here with your life," Gucci said. The woman's nodded frantically as tears filled her eyes, but at Gucci's orders the woman held them at bay . . . not allowing one single drop to fall onto her face. Her hands trembled so badly that she could barely get the money out of her drawer. Gucci quickly gazed to her left and saw that Raegan was handling her own and that no one else in the bank noticed that anything was out of the ordinary.

Gucci found her rhythm and her nervousness gave way to pure adrenaline as she gripped her gun that was concealed in her oversized handbag. Safety off, bullet locked and loaded, she was ready for anything but so far she didn't even see a reason to use it. She held the steel so tightly that her hand tingled and her fingertips turned white.

"That's it . . . That's everything," the teller whispered as she slid the stacks of banded denominations over to Gucci. Gucci quickly put the money in her bag and while she was distracted she noticed the teller's hand inching to the right.

Gucci reached over and grabbed her wrist tightly. The woman withdrew quickly.

"Please, please, please don't kill me. . . ." she whispered pleadingly. "I'm just—"

"Go to the bathroom and count to sixty before coming out. If you alert anyone on your way I will make sure that I kill you before the police ever arrive," Gucci threatened.

The woman nodded and stepped back from her station as Gucci took her handbag and backpedaled for the door. Raegan wasn't far behind her. She could hear her heels on the tile floor. When they finally exited, they took off for the car, sprinting full speed.

"Pull off, pull off, pull off!" Raegan shouted as soon as they hopped in.

Chanel put her foot to the gas and sped out of the parking lot.

"We did it!" Gucci exclaimed in disbelief.

"We did it?" Chanel asked as she kept looking back at Gucci as she stared inside of her handbag.

"We did it!" Gucci said again, this time in excitement.

"We did it?" Chanel asked again as she searched for answers while looking over at Raegan who rode shotgun.

"We did it," Raegan confirmed with a head nod. She rested her head back on the headrest and sighed as she let go of the anxiety that had filled her. She couldn't help but to crack a smile, however. She turned to Chanel and screamed, "We did it, bitch!"

Chapter Seventeen

"How much is it?" Gucci asked anxiously as she paced back and forth, awaiting the final total.

Raegan peeked out of the blinds of the dusty motel. Both she and Gucci had been on pins and needles.

"Y'all did it wrong. You hit the teller's drawer instead of hitting the bank's safe. This is only fifty racks," Chanel said with a slight attitude as she shook her head in frustration. The thrill of accomplishing the impossible faded once they realized they had come up short.

"Fifty thousand dollars?" Gucci exclaimed. "What the fuck are we supposed to do with that?" she asked.

"We're supposed to hit another bank," Chanel responded. "Y'all fucked up. You got away with it but you didn't take shit. I told you I should have gone inside. I would have hit the safe. They won't even miss this little bit of money."

Raegan turned around and looked at Chanel incredulously. "What? I'm not hitting another bank. Are you crazy? We were lucky that everything went smoothly this time. It was a one-time thing. We'll just have to make the best with what we got."

"Fine, Raegan," Chanel said as she grabbed a small stack of money and stood to her feet. She walked over to Raegan and reached for her wrist then placed the bills into Raegan's hand. "$16,500 is your cut."

"It's not enough," Gucci whispered as she brought her hands to her face. "I can't tie up my loose ends with that!"

"Then we hit another bank and this time we'll do it right," Chanel said.

"I have to get out of here . . . this is too much. I should have never come through for y'all. If I wouldn't have been there I wouldn't even be in this shit."

"So you saying you wished you had left us hanging? You saw how stuff went down that day. If you hadn't shown up we might have died," Chanel countered.

"We're a team, Raegan . . . Whether you like it or not, you're in it. We all are," Gucci said.

"I need to clear my head," Raegan stated. She grabbed her handbag and stormed out of the room.

As soon as she looked at her phone she noticed that she had a missed call from Nahvid. A grocery store run had turn into her being MIA for two days. What could she say to him? What would he do to her child? Terror gripped her like never before as she dialed Nahvid's number.

He sat behind his desk, his pulse racing from a mixture of rage and hurt as he listened to Reason tell him of Raegan's deceit. She had been the first woman he had ever put his trust in and she had let him down.

"I never trusted the bitch, Nah," Reason said, hyping the situation. "Honestly I was just holding my tongue cuz I knew you were feeling shorty . . . but she had snake written all over her."

Nahvid wanted to defend the allegations against Raegan, but the more time that went by without him hearing from her the guiltier she looked.

"I can't believe that she and her girls were behind the robberies all along. They were straight jacking niggas for they shit. Shit would be sexy as hell if they hadn't tried to eat off my plate," Reason said. Reason was talking a little too much for Nahvid. He just wanted to hear from Raegan so that he could confront her about the situation. He had to hear her admit it from her own mouth. Although all fingers were pointed at her he was still holding out hope that there could be a reasonable explanation. In his eyes she was innocent until she admitted guilt, despite the proof in his face.

"She didn't do this . . . not Raegan. I don't see her doing this, fam. Her son is here. She wouldn't leave him here. This ain't her. Can't be," he mumbled to himself.

Reason frowned in disapproval. "Look, fam. I don't know what the bitch did to you but you're going soft. I cut her homegirl tongue out her mouth, baby . . . and the name she was screaming was Raegan's. Raegan, Gucci, and Chanel. Them same bitches you be sending bottles to in the club. Your girl hit our spot and your mom got murked behind that shit. You really telling me you gonna let that shit ride?"

Before Nahvid could respond, the phone rang loudly interrupting the conversation.

Sunny Rae came up on his screen. He looked up at Reason who nosily inquired, "That her, fam?"

Nahvid shook his head and replied, "Nah, but I do need to take this. Give me a minute, bro, to handle this business." Before Reason headed out the door Nahvid added, "And make sure that mess you made is cleaned up . . . You know the motto . . . no body, no murder. Send the cleanup crew through there."

Nahvid watched as Reason stood and excused himself from the room. He didn't need Reason hearing the conversation that was about to take place. Nahvid didn't like to show his cards to anyone. Raegan was a weakness and she had penetrated his fortress. He needed to speak to her about her possible betrayal without prying ears. He exhaled to release some of his stress before answering the call.

"Nahvid . . ." she said, her voice calling to him desperately, breaking out of emotion and tearing his heart out of his chest all at the same time.

"Where you at, ma? I'm hearing some real foul shit about you right now," he said, heated.

"Nah, listen to me. There are some things that you don't know about me . . . stuff that I'm ashamed of . . ."

"Did you do it, Raegan? Yes or no? Don't hit me with the bullshit sob stories. You the bitch that's been taking niggas for they stash spots?" His voice was serious, stern, harsh almost and it frightened her into shame and silence.

"Baby, listen to me . . . please just hear me out . . . I'm not trying to tell you sob story, but you have to give me a chance to explain. . . ." she cried. There was no shame in her breakdown. Raegan sat outside on a concrete stoop, snot running down her face, and pure emotion leaking from her eyes. She was usually so composed. Raegan took pride in her ability to always appear in control. That's what bad bitches do, but in this situation she was a woman . . . a vulnerable woman who had made the biggest mistake of her life . . . a woman who was terrified of losing the love of her life.

Nahvid could hear her fear; sense that her back was against a wall. His girl needed him to save her . . . to rescue her . . . to tell her that everything would be okay. If it was only about the money he could have, but his mother was dead and on behalf of her this was a score he was obliged to settle.

"Yes or no?" he repeated. "Was it you and your girls that robbed my spot?"

Reason sat back silently and listened to the one side of the conversation he could hear. *What more do this nigga need? Find out where the bitch at so I can go see her,* he thought as his trigger finger itched at the thought of serving revenge to Raegan. Reason was cold-blooded to the core. He would put a hollow through her dome and then be the pallbearer at her funeral if need be. All Nahvid had to do was call the play and let his team do the work.

"You're going to hurt my son! Please, Nah, please don't hurt my baby. Just take him to his father. Please. I'm sorry. I didn't know. I was in over my head . . ." She was rambling and incoherent she was crying so loudly.

"Where you at, Raegan? Let me come get you. We'll talk about it. I won't hurt your son. You know me better than that. I'm the one who didn't know the real you. How could you step on my toes like this? Didn't I take care of you? Huh? Didn't I feed you? Clothe you? Throne you, ma? Huh? You were in the place that every bitch in the hood wanted to be and look how you do? Look how you disrespect me. You shot my mother, Raegan. My Sunny Rae. You got niggas laughing at me out here, baby girl," Nahvid stated sincerely. His head was lowered as he gripped his cell tightly in one hand and pinched the bridge of his nose with the other. Torn up over her deceit he wanted to ring her neck. Nahvid was used to punishing . . . to sentencing death to those who had crossed him. He was judge, jury, and executioner and he never varied from these roles when it came to business. He couldn't understand why things with Raegan were proving so unique. New to the whole love thing, Nahvid failed to realize that what he and Raegan shared was far from business. Women before her were there for a specific reason. They served him sexually and in return he gave them material things. Fair exchange wasn't robbery and with other women everyone always walked away unscathed and overly compensated. Raegan, however, was getting him. She had upped the ante and was playing for keeps. What they shared was far from an arrangement . . . he was ready to make a commitment to her and she was proving to be like the women he had sworn to avoid. She was running away with his heart and leaving his chest full of spoiled disappointment. The sick feeling that she had left him with was unbearable. She had ailed him and ironically she was the only one who could heal him.

"Nah, it wasn't like that. I swear to you! I know you can never forgive me after all that has happened, but just please. I'm begging you. Just don't hurt Micah."

Nahvid had never felt anyone tug at his heartstrings the way that Raegan was. It was then that he realized exactly how deeply he loved her. He would never harm baby Micah because he was a part of her.

"I won't. Where are you?" he asked.

"I can't tell you," she answered.

"Fuck all that, Raegan. Where are you, ma?"

"I'm scared, Nahvid. I can't tell you. I saw how you did that boy. I saw the bag that Reason carried out of the garage. You'll kill me. You'll send Reason for me," she whispered.

"Reason?" Nahvid exclaimed. "Reason works for me . . . If I say you'll be okay then you'll be okay. You don't have to worry about Reason, Raegan."

Reason stood outside the door shaking his head in disgust. *This bitch got this nigga on some real sweet shit. I'm deading that bitch on sight,* he thought. He couldn't believe that Nahvid was slipping the way that he was. This wasn't the same best friend who had been his partner in crime since they came out of the sandbox. The Nah he knew would have had his entire team scouring the city looking for Raegan. An easy twenty stacks could have had the mess cleaned up in no time, but Reason had never been in love. He didn't understand the inner battle that Nahvid was fighting.

Was Nah supposed to love Raegan through it all or was he supposed to push the end button? He knew once he sent his wolves out into the field they were coming back with her carcass. He at least needed to hear both sides of the story first because deep inside he knew that once Raegan was gone, there would never be another woman to take her place. Every plaything after that would be just a fling . . . a random fuck dummy to pass time with. No one would be able to fill the void she would leave in his life. He had the power to make her extinct, but he had to be ready to deal with the pain he would be causing himself by doing so.

"Just let me see you, Raegan. We need to talk. I can't guarantee that I can help you or forgive you, but I can at least hear you out. I swear that nothing will happen to you tonight. That's my word. Just meet me. Trust me," Nahvid demanded. He had mixed emotions regarding her. Something in him just wanted to lay eyes on her, just to see how he felt about her now that he knew everything. Now that her secrets were laid out in front of him, would he still want her? It was a question that they both needed to answer.

"Okay. I'll meet you on one condition. You bring my son with you," Raegan negotiated.

"Done," Nahvid replied. "Just make sure you show up."

Raegan called a cab and arrived at the restaurant first so that she could watch her surroundings. She didn't know how Nahvid would react to her. He could be setting her up for all she knew and she wanted to be on point.

"Hey, lady, you gonna get out or what?" the cab driver asked as he watched her curiously in the rear-view mirror.

She handed him a hundred-dollar bill. "Just keep the meter running. I need a minute. I'm waiting for someone." Her nerves were so rattled that the hairs on the back of her neck stood up. She held her breath when she saw Nahvid's car pull up and her eyes nervously scanned the entire block as she looked for any sign of his goon squad.

"If you're not out in fifteen minutes I leave," the Middle Eastern cabbie said impatiently, despite the generous tip she had blessed him with.

"Just wait damn it," she shot back, her eyes never leaving Nahvid. The darkened block was deserted. He had come alone and she let out a small sigh of relief, but when she saw him get out of the car without her son she was livid. Raegan waited until he had stepped inside of the restaurant before she got out of the cab. He didn't even have time to turn on the restaurant lights before she snuck in and put her gun to the back of his head.

"Where's my baby?" she asked.

"Whoa . . . whoa, Raegan, chill out. Put the gun down," he said in a strong, calm, reassuring tone as he held his hands up.

"We had a deal . . . I meet you, you bring my son to me," she said, her voice quivering. "Did you come here to kill me? Is that why he's not with you? Is he still alive?"

"Raegan—"

"Answer the question!" she shouted as tears began to come. "Is my son still alive?"

"Of course he is . . . I dropped him off at one of my worker's spots. My homeboy wife is taking care of him. He's in good hands. I came to bring you home, ma. Now put the gun down, Raegan . . . let me turn around. I need to see your face when I talk to you." Despite having a gun to his head his voice showed no sign of distress. He had the upper hand in the situation and they both knew it.

Raegan put her hand on his back and led him through the dark restaurant to his office. She turned on the light, gun still aimed, eyes still searching for the setup. She was terrified and playing out of her league. She wasn't built for this . . . not when her adversary was the man she loved. Raegan never claimed to be a gangster; she was simply a woman who had been put between a rock and a hard place. She was stuck.

"Sit down," she said, trying to appear assertive, but Nahvid was a predator in any situation. He could smell her fear. Her aim was timid. There was no bite behind her bark, but most of all she was his bitch. He could hear her cries for help without her ever having to open her mouth.

Nahvid walked up on her.

"Don't come near me," she said.

"Come on, Raegan. This ain't you . . . or is it? Is this you, ma? Cuz right now I'm feeling like I've been sleeping with the enemy. Like I don't know you. Like I've been a mark to you all this time," he said as he continued to step toward her.

He was within arm's reach and he wrapped his hand around the gun. He clasped her hand between both of his, applying pressure until she let go of the pistol.

"I'm so sorry," she sobbed as she fell into his arms. He resisted at first, feeling mixed emotions. A part of him wanted to murder her, but a huge part of him wanted to hold her. His arms closed around Raegan's svelte figure and held her tightly. Nahvid could feel the frightful rhythm of her heart as it beat frantically . . . desperately . . . unsurely. He could tell that she was putting on a brave front but the tremble in her back gave away her apprehension.

As much as he hated her for taking his mother away, he adored her for giving him what his mother never could. Raegan had showed him what it was like to feel true love.

"How did we get here?" he asked.

Raegan stepped away from him and looked directly into his face. "I didn't know that we were robbing your spot. I swear to God on my son's life. I didn't find out until you drove me there later that night. It was only supposed to be one time. I needed money to pay Micah back so that he would return my son. I didn't have time to do it legit, so me and my girls started pulling capers on hustlers around the city," she said.

"What am I to you? Was this planned?" he asked angrily.

"No! No! Nah . . . I am crazy about you. I just felt so disloyal to my friends. I was taken care of with you. You kept me the way I deserve to be kept, but they were still hustling . . . still struggling. They needed more money and they wanted to hit more stash houses. I told them no. I said I was out, but then I started feeling guilty like I was turning my back on them. Before you came into my life they were the only support system that my baby and I had. They were my family, Nahvid, and I just couldn't turn my back on them. The morning I told you I was getting ready for the dinner with your mother . . . I was really out hitting a stash house with them. Things just went bad and bullets started flying and your mom . . ."

Nahvid felt nothing but love for Raegan in that moment. She had been forced into the situation all because of her son and when she was ready to leave, she felt obligated to her friends. She was loyal and if she truly didn't know that she was taking his operation, he couldn't blame her. She was a diamond in the rough with evident flaws, but even a blind man could see her worth. She just needed him to clean her up a bit, smooth out her imperfections, and give her value.

"Now we're on the run from you . . . robbing banks just to make it out of town . . ."

"What?" he exclaimed, realizing that the situation was completely out of hand. Raegan was federal and if he didn't pull her back off the ledge she would be at the point of no return. He could squash her beef in the streets without a problem, but she was moving reckless and if the heat came down on her . . . she would be connected to him. He couldn't protect her from a federal indictment. Shocked that he had allowed someone so treacherous into his life he wiped his face in frustration. "Where is your head, ma? Huh? You reckless out here . . . You moving so stupid. You're so beautiful but right now you're looking real ugly. Can I trust you around me, Raegan? I'm a man of great stature. I have a lot to lose by fucking with you, ma. I don't need no Eve to my Adam, Raegan . . . You're poisonous, ma, and I'm second-guessing everything about you."

His words silenced her and she dropped her head as her mind searched for the words that could fix this. What could she say? What could she do? Was she just a slow death for him? Raegan didn't want to be the one to bring Nahvid to his demise, and she honestly had no intentions of doing him dirty. Her world was chaotic. She and her friends had made it this way. She wanted to be hurt but she couldn't blame his skepticism. She deserved to be doubted. Raegan had done nothing to prove the love she professed.

"Don't say that. Please, Nahvid, just believe me when I say I would never intentionally hurt anyone! Especially anyone connected to you!" she claimed. "Shit is just out of control. I can't get time back. I did what I did and I'm standing here in front of you taking responsibility for that. I'm so sorry for what I did. You are the last person who I would betray. I need help. I just want all of this to go away," she whispered. She hoped that her transparency was enough to make him see that she was being authentic. Her eyes burned with sincerity and she breathed heavily from the turmoil of it all. This was hell; they both were burning in a love affair that was highly unlikely . . . yet one that they each yearned for.

Nahvid turned his back to her and placed his balled fist to his forehead as he leaned against the wall, eyes shut, mind racing, heart banging. Raegan's offense against his camp was huge and her offense against his life was even greater. Nahvid had murdered men for much less but he couldn't deny that through all the bullshit he cared for her. He knew that at their greatest, their love was one unrivaled by any the history books had ever seen. More attractive than Zya and Snow, more notorious than Young Carter and Miamor, more dedicated than Anari and Von, and more unpredictable than YaYa and Indie's . . . their story hadn't been written yet. It was too new and the invisible forces of the universe were too strong. She was like a magnet: her pull on him was insane. Nita's face flashed through his mind and he felt a lump form in his throat. His mother had been living wrong for so long so could Nahvid truly place all of the blame on Raegan?

Raegan stood back silently as she watched the inner battle he was fighting and she was sick because she was the cause of it. She shuffled in her stance nervously, her face twisted in uncertainty and agony. Love had a way of hurting the most when it wasn't on track and they both were suffering for different reasons. She walked over to him reluctantly and wrapped her arms around him as she rested her cheek on his strong back. He didn't turn to face her, but the sensation of her arms around him seemed to fill him up. His entire life he had been walking through the world half loved, half appreciated. Nita hadn't been able to love him fully because she was too in love with herself. Her crack addiction had taken all of her to the point where she had nothing left to give to her son and when Raegan stepped in she seemed to fill the void. He had not allowed himself to love but she had melted his frozen emotions. He had had badder, richer, slimmer, nicer, women than she . . . but none had been she. No other woman had been able to position herself next to him and carve out a spot in his life that was only fit for one. It wasn't her perfections that he adored . . . it was her imperfections.

"Please, Nahvid. You have to know that I love you. I need help. I just need you to help me, Nah. Forgive me and just take all of this away," she whispered as her tears wet the fabric of his shirt.

"I'll make it go away, ma," he whispered. The words tasted like vinegar falling off of his lips, but he said them anyway. He couldn't let his pride stop him from being there for her. Seeking revenge against her would be like biting off his nose to spite his face. He turned toward her and gripped her face between his strong hands as he stared at her intensely. "Just be loyal to me. You should have come to me from the beginning. Your girls wanted to make their paper, I could have put 'em to work, ma. Nobody around me is starving, but loyalty is what I require to be in my circle. You understand?" he asked as he held her chin firmly, scolding her and loving her all in one speech.

"I understand," she answered. "I'm afraid of you now. I feel like you're going to punish me for what happened to your mom. I'm terrified that you'll hurt Micah or hurt me."

Nahvid swallowed her words as he bent down to kiss her lips. It was crazy how in an instant he could make her world better. He slid her dress up and found that she wore no panties. It took no time for him to fill the space between her legs. Dripping wet she soaked him as he bounced her up and down on his thickness, hitting every spot so right that he made her sore.

"I love you, Nah," she whispered in rapture as her head bobbled back on her neck in ecstasy.

"I love you too. You're my Sunny Rae. I need you to keep me sane."

He grieved his mother, but she had always chosen her drug of choice over her son. Well Raegan was his drug of choice and now he understood his mother's strife. She loved her son, but she was addicted . . . as was he, to Raegan.

He drilled into her as he laid her across his desk, cupping her breasts as he admired her beautiful physique. She was thick, voluptuous, and still carried the weight from having a baby . . . but it was all in the right places. She was a real woman and Nahvid knew that if they could get through this obstacle intact, she would be his for life. He felt the grime of the situation stick to his heart. His mother wasn't even in the dirt yet and he was bedding someone who had contributed to her death. It was a choice that he would have to live with for the rest of his life, but one that he felt was worth it. He had never felt more whole; as a matter of fact he had been half fulfilled until he met Raegan.

As Raegan enjoyed the sheer bliss of his stroke she cried the entire time. She didn't know that someone could love her so perfectly. His love was loyal . . . flawless . . . unconditional. She found everything that she had been looking for in dudes over the years within him. He hit the back of her pussy like no one had ever done before. Her legs shook violently as she creamed all over him. Nahvid was still hard and his stamina was incredible as he pulled himself out of her. His dick was thick and deliciously chocolate. The veins on his length throbbed and begged for her to lick them. Without hesitation she got on her knees and took him into her mouth. Womanhood dripping onto her thigh as she swallowed him, deep-throating him as she bobbed down and planting loving kisses on the tip each time she pulled back.

"Come here," he ordered. "Get on this dick, ma."

She straddled him and gasped as he split her walls.

"You forgive me?" she whispered in his ear.

He touched her face and looked her in the eyes. He could see the remorse as he stared into her soul, but the motherless child inside of him would not allow him to fully forgive her sins against him. The overwhelming urge to hurt her surged through Nahvid as he lifted her off of him and turned her around. He entered her from behind, unyielding as lust mixed with anger caused him to be a bit rough. She winced and moaned all at once as Nahvid danced along the line of pain and pleasure. "Don't run from me, ma," he whispered as he gripped her hips and pounded into her middle. He spread her ass cheeks. She bit her lip to stifle the animalistic sounds that escaped her lips. Nahvid was punishing her and Raegan was taking it like a champ. She threw the pussy back at him like she was an all-star pitcher. Raegan knew her man and she could feel his frustration in the way that he stroked her. He was usually gentle and caring, but this session contained no sensitivity. It was raw and passion filled, but it was fueled by pain and Raegan recognized the difference. This wasn't lovemaking . . . it wasn't what she had become accustomed to with him. Not with Nah, not from her man . . . or was he even still hers?

Raegan's heart hurt because of the pain that she had caused Nahvid. He had been good to her and she had repaid him with disloyalty. Knowing that she couldn't take his strife away killed her, but she gave him her all sexually as her nails left markings in the wooden desk that she was sprawled across. She laid all her cards out on the table and tried to seduce him into forgiveness. Atonement. That's all Raegan needed from him, but she was unsure if he was really capable of letting something so big go unchecked.

She had crossed him and she was well aware of his ruthless reputation in the streets. Her eyes would always be open for the double cross she expected to come her way. She would be paranoid with him and the two would never fully trust one another. Their relationship could never be exactly as it was. Nothing was the same as it had been and everything had changed for the worse.

Nahvid's mind spun as he pressed her head down into the desk while he rocked in and out of her. It was too soon for him to even be in her presence, but like a moth to a flame he was drawn to her. Being with her was like self-destruction, yet still here he was dick deep inside of her womb, making promises of forgiveness that he wasn't sure if he could keep. He wanted to be the noble man she had come to know, but the hood nigga in him wanted retribution. No one had ever disrespected him in the way that Raegan and her girls had. Love, he concluded, had softened him. The devotion that a man usually felt for his mother he felt for Raegan, and guilt plagued him because he held the woman of his dreams at higher regard than the woman who birthed him. Consumed with rage, lust, hate, love, and every emotion in between he took it out on Raegan's body until he had nothing left. He came hard, causing her body to shudder as she shared in his satisfaction.

In the aftermath of their rapture neither knew exactly what to say. Eerie and doubtful of his affections for her, Raegan instantly doubted that they could ever go back to what they were. She wished that she could just hit reset and do things over again, but life wasn't a game.

"What now?" she asked, as they adjusted their clothes. Her head hung low, unable to keep eye contact with him out of shame and remorse.

"Now we go home," he whispered.

She looked up at him in disbelief. Pools of fresh tears sparkled in her eyes and fell gracefully down her cheeks. "Really?"

"I'm not saying we can fix this today, tomorrow, or the next day . . . but one day things will be right again. I just know that I don't want to lose you, ma." As he said the words he felt like a sucker. He was going against everything that he stood for and all that he knew for her. If he had been watching from the outside he would have called himself a tender-dick nigga. He was moving like a chump and he was aware of that fact. This time he was putting logic to the side as he allowed his emotion to lead. He only hoped that he was making the best choice. Nahvid pray that Raegan was worth it.

"I can't just desert my girls," she said. "I just need to tell them—"

Nahvid shook his head and interrupted her. "That's your business, but I can tell you that I don't want them snake bitches around me. They're on some federal shit so I can't have my woman associated with that. Cut them off, Raegan, and when you're done come home to your man."

Chapter Eighteen

Reason watched as Nahvid left the restaurant. They had come up in the game together and had reigned supreme in D.C. with their iron-fist tactics. The way that Nahvid was handling this situation with Raegan was completely out of character. Reason had never jumped stupid or tried to overthrow the empire in the sake of greed, but the way things were looking it seemed as though it was time to dethrone the king. There was a crack in Nahvid's armor and Reason was the only nigga close enough to see it. Reason wasn't a grimy man, but he was loyal to the money above all else. Nahvid was jeopardizing everything they had built to chase pussy and Reason wasn't having it. The D.C. nigga in him wanted to pop his melon on sight. He gripped the .45 that lay in his lap. If Nah had been any other nigga he would already be leaking on the sidewalk and before his body was cold in the ground Reason would have been courting the connect to a $500/plate dinner, but the years of friendship that they had established kept Nahvid breathing . . . for now. Nahvid wasn't the true problem. *Everything was butter until that bitch stretched the nigga nose wide open,* he thought.

Many women had divided many men, but Reason refused to allow Raegan to become a modern-day Helen of Troy. If Nahvid didn't have the moxie to eliminate the issue, then Reason would gladly step in. There wasn't a day that he woke up that Reason wasn't prepared to put his murder game down. While Nahvid was the one calling in the death warrants, Reason was the actual one pulling the triggers. There was no hesitation when he was involved. He lived, ate, breathed, and shitted on these streets.

Raegan emerged from the restaurant and walked down the darkened streets swiftly. Her heart was heavy because she was about to step out on a limb with Nahvid, but it wasn't strong enough to carry any extra weight. She had to cut her friends off.

She finally hailed a cab and made her way back to the hotel. Raegan was so distracted and torn over what she was about to do that she never noticed the vehicle tailing her. If she had been on point she might have seen the headlights reflecting through the rearview mirror. Instead she sat, unknowingly, as Reason preyed upon her.

"Wake up!" Raegan said as she turned on the light, illuminating the room.

"Hmm! What are you doing, Rae? Turn that shit back off. Whatever it is it can wait until morning," Chanel groaned as she turned over and pulled the covers over her head.

"It's important. Get up," she said, antsy as her voice quivered.

"Are you okay?" Gucci asked, hearing the angst in Raegan's tone. She sat up in her bed and instantly knew that something was awry. "What's wrong?"

"I'm going back to Nahvid." Raegan let the words fly from her mouth and she braced herself for their response, but silence filled the room as Chanel sat up also.

The stare down between the three girls was intense as animosity built in each of their hearts.

"So I guess that leaves us on our own? That's how you playing it, Raegan? We're supposed to be in this together! That's where you ran off to tonight?" Gucci whispered harshly, clearly upset.

"He has my son!" she shouted back.

"Raegan, stop! Stop acting like this is about Micah. That nigga got your head that's what he got. If your kid was lying right here in this room your ass still would have gone back to that nigga. So now what? Of course you can go back cuz you're fucking him, but what about us?"

Raegan didn't respond, she opened her mouth to defend herself, but no words would come to her.

"Let me guess. We're the grimy friends that corrupted his precious Sunny Rae? Right? That's the way the story's spinning? Well let me ask you something, Raegan. Did you tell him that this entire scheme started with you? If I recall the shit correctly robbing stash houses was your bright idea!"

Raegan knew that Chanel was speaking truth. She wished that she had never proposed the thought to start pulling capers.

"If she want to go then let her go," Gucci said with a wave of her hand. "We're all grown. I don't know what makes you think he's going to just forget that you played a role in killing his mama. She's dead behind what *we* did. What makes you think he just gonna let you breathe when she's no longer able to?"

A knock at the door interrupted the heated conversation and sent each girl into a panic.

"Who the fuck is that?" Chanel asked.

"Did Nahvid follow you here?" Gucci asked.

"No," Raegan said.

"You sure?"

"Yes!" Raegan whispered.

Chanel reached under her pillow and removed her pistol, clicking the safety off like a pro as Gucci followed suit.

"You strapped?" she asked.

"You know it," Raegan replied.

KNOCK! KNOCK! KNOCK!

"Housekeeping!" a woman's voice rang out. The girls looked at one another knowing that they were being set up.

"He promised me," Raegan whispered.

"He lied," Gucci replied.

There was no way that housekeeping was coming through their room in the wee hours of the morning in a fleabag motel. They already knew who was on the other side of the door and there was only one way out.

Raegan cocked her pistol, her heart silently breaking as she walked over to the door. "Fuck it," she said as she unloaded her clip into the wood.

BANG! BANG! BANG! BANG! BANG!

She kicked the door open and saw a bleeding woman fall backward into a man's arms. Their eyes met for only a brief second before he raised his gun. The color drained completely from her face when she saw Reason.

He sent Reason after me, she thought.

Raegan had caught him off guard. He had never expected her to shoot first and ask questions later. Reason had underestimated her ruthlessness. He certainly wasn't prepared for all three of the girls to be strapped. They let their cannons bark, making it rain lead all around him. Reason shuffled backward, firing reckless cover shots and holding the woman he had paid to knock on the door as a human shield.

He was outgunned and he wasn't one to defy the odds. He backed all the way up to his car, dropping the dead woman at his feet, before hopping in and speeding out of the parking lot.

The girls fired on him until they saw his taillights disappear from sight and their clips ran dry. "Fuck!" Chanel shouted.

Raegan's stomach felt as if it were suddenly hollow as she gripped it in agony. "He lied to me . . . he lied. My son . . ."

"You fucked us!" Chanel shouted. "Your love-struck ass led Nahvid straight to us!"

Chanel and Raegan ran toward the room while Gucci headed toward the office. "The tape! I'm getting the tape!"

The bell above the office door rang as she stepped inside. She looked around, seeing no one, but she could hear a young girl whimpering. Gucci rushed behind the counter to find a white girl trembling beneath it.

"Get up. I'm not going to hurt you. You're good. I just need the tapes of the property," Gucci said.

The girl's black mascara ran down her face and her hand trembled as she pointed to an old television set and VCR in the corner.

"Get it," Gucci demanded as she pulled the girl to her feet. Sirens rang in the background drawing louder the closer they got. Gucci saw Raegan and Chanel running for the car. She silently wondered why she had ever gotten involved in something so dangerous. Maybe it was because for most of her life she felt as if she didn't belong. She felt different and as though people didn't respect her. Chanel and Raegan were the only friends she had ever really connected with. They accepted her without judgment and because of that she knew that she would ride this thing out with them until the very end. Gucci threw her head toward the TV set and said, "Get the tape and hurry," Gucci ordered the girl. "We've got to get out of here," she said to herself as the fear of being caught invaded her brain.

Nahvid sat in the plush rocking chair staring through the bars of the crib, watching baby Micah's chest slowly rise then fall. His heart was in distress as he watched the golden rays of the sun slowly peek through the horizontal blinds that covered the windows, inevitably turning dark to light. The long sigh that escaped his lips gave him no relief. He had been waiting for hours . . . hoping . . . wishing . . . wondering when Raegan would come home. It was at that moment that he remembered why he had never allowed himself to love a woman. He hadn't known Raegan for that long and already she was turning his world upside down. There were no feelings of bliss or fulfillment as far as he was concerned. Love had always been like a thorn in his side . . . it hurt. Now he was left with so many split ends, ends that he needed to clip.

The small cry of an infant interrupted his reverie and he arose to comfort baby Micah. There was a monster inside of him that lay dormant when it came to Raegan. From the trespasses she had committed against him she should be lying face down in a ditch with her dead baby by her side, but he couldn't bring himself to make that call. He felt a unique connection to this woman and as he thought of her he brought her child to his shoulder. Nahvid sat down in the rocking chair and slowly glided back and forth.

"Shhh . . . it's okay. Everything is going to be okay, li'l homie. I'm going to find her and I'm going to bring her home."

Nahvid had no idea that the events that had transpired tonight had been the straw to break their relationship apart forever.

Chapter Nineteen

The girls stayed up all night as paranoia kept them alert. They each knew the type of clout and hood prestige that Nahvid carried. The entire city was loyal to one man so if they were caught slipping by anyone it was curtains. Everyone was on his payroll and therefore they knew that they weren't wanted by one . . . they were wanted by all. A thousand unknown faces knew their faces and at any moment they could be attacked.

"We just have to get out of here. We keep moving south and when we finally get to Florida we'll figure everything out," Chanel said.

"How do you know this friend of yours will even help us?" Gucci asked.

"Because a long time ago he used to love me," Chanel whispered, her voice distant as if she was strolling down memory lane.

Raegan kept her eyes low as she thought of Nahvid. "That doesn't mean anything now does it?" she said. Her statement wasn't meant to be malicious, but she was devastated. "I was naïve to think that he would forgive me after what I did."

Gucci nor Chanel had no words that would comfort Raegan so they said nothing at all concerning Nahvid.

"What if she's right?" Gucci asked. "I don't want to get all the way down there and then be left on stuck. We have to have a backup plan. We need money and enough of it to buy our way out of the country just in case this friend of yours doesn't come through."

Chanel looked around the deserted parking lot and then turned around in her seat. "Y'all know what we have to do. There's only one way we're getting that type of money."

"At this point we have to do what we have to do. I'm all in. I have nothing left to lose," Raegan replied.

Raegan pulled up to Nahvid's storage unit and took the key off of her ring. "Everything we need is inside. He'll never know that it's missing," she said as she hopped out of the car. The other girls followed suit and their heads were on a constant swivel as they looked around to make sure that no one was watching. Raegan unlocked the padlock and slid the heavy door up, revealing the goodies that were hidden inside.

The storage unit was huge. It was like a mini warehouse, and everything from guns, cars, and cocaine was concealed inside. The unit could never be traced back to Nahvid, however. It had been rented ten years ago by an old woman on her deathbed so technically it was owned by a ghost. If it was ever discovered nothing would lead back to Nahvid's doorstep. In fact Raegan was the only other person beside himself who knew where it was located.

"Damn," Gucci exclaimed as she looked around the massive space and at the hood riches that filled it. "I need to be whipping this!" she shouted as she touched the hood of a luxury car.

"You will be," Raegan stated. "The keys are under the mat. We all will be driving something nice. If we're going to do this again . . . this time we do it right. You take the BMW, Guch, I'll take the Benz, and Chanel you take the Cadillac. We drive separate cars all the way down to Florida. We'll use the one outside to do the bank job and these three will be waiting for us to switch into. There are sets of plates registered to dummy names in each of the trunks so whenever we get hot we can always switch the plates." Raegan walked over to a large box and ripped the tape from the top. She reached inside and pulled out an automatic assault rifle. "We have everything we need to pull this off."

Gucci and Chanel looked at each other in shock. Raegan was going all in and they knew that it was because of her scorned heart. She would have never shown them one of Nahvid's spots under normal circumstances, but she was feeling crossed so now nothing was off limits. He had her son and she was going to do what she needed to do to get him back. "When we get out of the country we upload that tape and we use that as leverage to get my son back. If Nahvid doesn't send him to me, I mail the tape to the police."

"Do you think he will hurt your baby before then?" Gucci asked, sincerely worried.

"I don't know. If you had asked me yesterday I would have said no. Today I can only pray," Raegan said sadly. She was truly scarred by Nahvid. She didn't know how he could look her in the eyes and promise forgiveness one moment and then send goons for her head the next. "I can't focus on that right now. I need my head right if we are going to pull this off. We're not hitting the tellers this time . . . this time we hit the bank's safe."

"What bank?" Chanel asked.

"First National . . . downtown," Raegan replied.

"Are you crazy? Every cop in the city will be on us. It's right in the middle of every government building in D.C.," Gucci protested.

"It also has the most money and we don't have time to play. I don't want to go on another robbing spree. We need to take one bank, one time. This time we need to do it right. Everything is riding on this."

***

Reason pulled up directly behind Nahvid and hopped out of his car. He joined Nahvid, hopping into his passenger side.

"What's good, fam?" he asked as they slapped hands. He immediately noticed Raegan's son sleeping soundly in the car seat behind him and he hid his disapproval.

"I need you to find her, Reason. It's not something that I feel obligated to explain. Just find her and bring her to me, unharmed. I don't want a hair on her head out of place," Nahvid said seriously.

Reason's temperature rose, but he kept his composure. "Yeah, whatever you need, baby. I got it."

"She's into some shit. Some shit that she's not even built for. You find her for me. Put your ear to the streets until you locate her. I need her back before things get so out of hand that they can no longer be worked out," he admitted.

Reason did not understand the connection between Nahvid and Raegan. It was baffling him and mind-boggling to see Nahvid so hung up on one chick. "What is it about this broad, Nah? You really going to let the shit with the stash and your mom dukes just ride? I can't understand this shit . . . shit's crazy. You moving different."

"It's not for you to understand," Nahvid replied.

Reason sniffed and gritted his teeth as he got out of the car. "This soft-ass nigga got the game fucked up . . . I'ma find the bitch a'ight," Reason mumbled as he sauntered back to his car and pulled out into traffic recklessly. In all honesty the more weakness Nahvid showed, the more Reason wanted to make a move. It was time for new leadership and Reason was slowly becoming comfortable with the idea of wearing the new crown. All he had to do was take it.

***

"Everybody on the floor! Don't try to be a hero and I won't make you a memory! On your stomachs flat on the floor! Do it!" Raegan yelled as Gucci and Chanel followed suit. Raegan went to the tellers and immediately tied all of their hands up with plastic zip cuffs, as Gucci commanded the customers to the ground, and Raegan kept her guns fixed on the security guards. The plan was to be out in three minutes flat and as adrenaline raced through their bodies they left all inhibitions behind as they strong-armed the bank. Time was moving so quickly that none of them were actually thinking of what they were doing. The first bank job had been peaceful, but this time they were going for broke. Heels, wigs, sunglasses, and trench coats they came through the bank like they were official. They were scared shitless, but no one would have ever detected that they were amateurs.

"If you fucking move, I will blow your top off!" Gucci shouted as she walked back and forth, gun moving from customer to customer as her eyes traced over each person swiftly.

"Get to the safe! I've got it up here," Chanel yelled.

Raegan grabbed one of the tellers off the floor, roughly snatching the heavyset woman up. The woman trembled so badly that she could barely keep her composure. "Who has the power to get in the safe?" she asked.

"Oh . . . Lord . . . I . . . I . . ." The woman was nervous and Raegan's stomach knotted when she saw the stream of urine darken her pants leg.

"Listen . . . I'm not going to hurt you. We just came for the money. You don't even have to speak. Just point. Who can get inside the safe?" she asked, lowering her voice this time to make the woman feel more at ease. "Just point," Raegan coached.

The woman pointed to a young white man. "Nobody likes a snitch, Judy!" he sneered as he stood to his feet while holding his hands up.

"The safe . . . now!" Raegan instructed sternly. He guided her to the back of the bank where a large vault stood closed with a steel dial keeping it secure. "Open it."

"Okay . . . okay," he complied as he inserted his key. He began to turn the dial and Raegan slapped fire from his ass, using the handle of her AK to bust his mouth and nose open. Blood gushed everywhere.

"Don't play with me. If you don't enter the code after the key the alarm is triggered. You must not like your life," she threatened.

"Please . . . I . . ."

"Open the vault," she ordered, this time with no patience left for his attempt at heroism. She had no time for his antics. It wasn't his money that she was taking. Hitting banks was a victimless crime. The system took a loss, not an individual and because of that she felt no guilt. The bank had the sign posted directly on its doors: FDIC INSURED.

"Hurry uuupp!" Chanel shouted.

"Two minutes!" Gucci added.

The man opened the vault and Raegan was momentarily in awe at the amount of money that filled the steel walls. Raegan ordered the bank manager back to the ground and zip cuffed him to the inside of the vault so that his hands were connected to his ankles. She then opened the two large duffel bags she carried and began to stuff the neatly packaged bundles inside. The money was so new that it looked fake and the smell of the fresh paper was intoxicating. They had hit the jackpot and she was high off the lick. She stuffed money into the bags until they were dumb full. The zipper would barely close by the time she was done. Sweat dripped into her eyes as her body temperature rose from the stress of it all and she struggled to carry both bags back into the main lobby.

"Let's go!" she shouted.

They were headed for the exit when Gucci remembered the tapes. She ran back over to the same woman that Raegan had questioned and pulled her to her feet once again.

"Oh Lord. Please you have the money . . . just leave me be," she sang out as her eyes shot toward the sky.

"Where's the tape? The system that records the bank, where is it?" Gucci asked.

The lady led her to a closed wooden door and opened it to reveal an array of TV monitors and recording devices. This system was too complex. There was no physical tape. It was all digital set up to DVRs. She had no time to figure it out. She looked around the room and saw a coffee maker with a full pot of coffee sitting on a stand. She quickly took the liquid and poured it all over the expensive technology. Static immediately erupted and the monitors turned grey. The entire system was completely ruined.

"Let's get out of here!" she heard Raegan shout.

"Sit down," Gucci told the woman, aiming the gun to make her comply. Cuffing the woman's hands to the door, Gucci knew that they were in the clear. No alarms had been triggered and everyone in the bank was tied up so it would be awhile before the police even realized that anything had gone down. What she didn't know was that there was a backup system that was still recording their every move.

Gucci ran back toward the lobby and out the front door. They hopped into the getaway car.

"Oh my God! I thought I would piss on myself in there!" Chanel screamed. "How much did we get?"

Raegan shook her head and replied, "I don't know . . . I just kept stuffing the bags until they were full. Just drive, Chanel . . . Worry about the money when we are out of this area."

She kept waiting for sirens to blare in her ears, but she heard nothing. When they finally pulled up to the parking garage where they had parked the cars they had stolen from Nahvid, she breathed a sigh of relief.

They parked and Gucci began to wipe down the car, removing any possible fingerprints that they could have left behind as the other girls each took a duffel bag and headed toward their cars.

"Be careful and be smart. I'll see you bitches in two hours," Chanel said. They were all Southern bound but decided to take three different routes.

"Whoa! Wait! What about my cut?" Gucci asked before she stepped into her car.

"We'll divvy up the money when we get to the spot," Raegan said.

Gucci's face fell in insecurity. She wanted to trust her friends, but in all honesty they hadn't been friends for too long. She knew people who would snake their own mothers for the type of paper that they were dealing with. So to leave empty-handed without any assurance was hard to do. Both Chanel and Raegan saw the look of doubt in her eyes.

"You're our sister, Gucci. We would never get you," Chanel said.

Raegan held up her duffel bag. "We don't have time to split it into three right now, but here," she said as she handed her bag over to Gucci. "Take this one. I trust you, Gucci, and I hope by now that you would trust me. I'll get my cut when I see you in VA."

Gucci hugged Raegan and held her tightly for a brief moment. Raegan had just proven without a doubt that they were family. This thing ran deeper than a shallow friendship. Their backs were against the wall and the security of their friendship was all they had to keep them sane.

"See you soon," Raegan said. "Be careful, Gucci."

Gucci nodded her head and all three girls hopped into their cars and headed their separate ways.

Chapter Twenty

"Fuck is your mama doing?" Nahvid exclaimed as he sat with baby Micah cradled in the crease of his arm, while watching the scene of the bank robbery unfold before his eyes. Images of the three girls were all over every major news station. They had gotten caught slipping because they didn't realize the bank had a backup video system set up in case of a robbery and now their heist was playing on every major network. He rushed to the phone and dialed her number only to be sent directly to voice mail. "Damn it, Raegan!" His temper flared at the thought of her reckless actions. Why had she chosen this path? He had given her a clear and safe way out, but she had left his offer on the table, abandoning not only their relationship, but her son as well. *What the fuck is she thinking?* he asked himself. "She's moving all wrong," he whispered. Although the police didn't know the identities of the girls yet, Nahvid knew that it was only a matter of time before they were discovered. This wasn't some local mom-and-pop, one-chain institution they had robbed. This was the city's largest bank. There was no way the media or the Feds would let this one go unsolved. On top of that the bills that were stolen were marked so if Raegan spent even a dime of it anywhere in the United States, she would be caught. Even if the girls moved smart, the $100,000 cash reward for information leading to their capture was all the insurance the Feds needed to convince someone to come forward. Nahvid felt an overwhelming sense of fear for Raegan because if she was caught and tried to resist, court would be held in the streets. There was a strong possibility that he could lose her for good behind this and he shook his head solemnly knowing that he and baby Micah would be no good without her in their lives. The ringing of the phone blared in his ear and he answered it with urgency.

"Yeah?"

"Yo, are you watching this shit?" Reason asked. He was astonished at the measures that Raegan was taking. He had to admit that she was truly one of a kind. He had never seen anything like it. Her gangster was unrivaled by any female he had ever met. "Them bitches bolder than a lot of niggas I know."

"Look, I need you on top of this, fam. You moving too slow and every second you can't find her she's digging a hole for herself that keeps getting deeper and deeper," Nahvid said. "I need you to do me this favor, Reason."

"Yeah, yeah, I hear you, Nah. I'm all over it," Reason returned unenthusiastically.

In his mind, Reason had already made up his mind. He was tired of watching the throne. He was about to take the muthafucka, but he couldn't get rid of Nahvid until he knew exactly where he kept his work. Nahvid had never shared that information with Reason and until Reason secured his own coke connect, he would need the bricks that Nahvid had on deck. He knew that Nah was sitting on one hundred easy and he was too lazy to build his own shit up from the ground floor. He needed weight. So before he put his play down with Nahvid he needed to find Raegan. *If anyone knows where it's at she do,* Reason thought.

Chapter Twenty-one

Gucci pulled up to her mother's adult care home and got out cautiously. She knew that once she hit the highway and headed south that she wouldn't be coming back. After what they had done too much was at stake to ever step foot in D.C. again. She knew that her girls were already safely on their way, but she couldn't just dip on her mother without saying good-bye. She had to see her face and talk to her. Gucci wanted to say "I love you" before she left for good. It was risky, but it was something that had to be done. She would never forgive herself if just left her mother there without checking in on her first. Gucci parked in front of the building, nervously looking at her surroundings before she got out of the car. She popped the trunk and placed her duffel bag full of money inside. She unzipped it and took out a large stack, placing it into her purse before she headed inside. She bypassed the front desk and went straight to her mother's room.

"Hi, Mama," she said as she stepped inside and saw her mother sitting up in her bed playing with a deck of cards. She wasn't playing anything in particular; she liked the colors that made up the kings and queens. They made her smile.

"Gucci!" she shouted as her entire face lit up as she recognized her daughter. Gucci hadn't visited often. Running the streets with her girls had taken up too much of her time. Gucci had taken care of her mother all of her life, so when she met a group of friends who she actually connected with she just wanted to live. Gucci had been given the burden of responsibility at an early age, so being irresponsible and reckless felt good to her. But now looking at her mother's face she could tell that she had missed her. In a lot of ways Gucci had been the parent and it felt like she had abandoned her child. "I missed my Gucci!"

"I missed you too, Ma," Gucci whispered as she sat in the bed. She removed her shoes and put her feet up as she sat back against the headboard. "Do you like it here?" she asked.

"Yeah," her mother replied in a childlike voice.

"Are they nice to you?" Gucci asked gently as she grabbed her mother's hairbrush and began to brush her hair.

"Yeah, they are nice here, Gucci. I like it here," she responded.

Gucci sighed in relief. She was glad that her mother was being treated well. There was no doubt in her mind that her mother would tell her if something was wrong. Gucci had taught her a long time ago to always speak up if someone was hurting her.

"I have to go away for a little while, Mama," Gucci said, getting choked up. "I got into a little bit of trouble so I have to leave. You won't see me for a while."

"Can I come too?" her mother asked.

"No, Mommy, you have to stay here," Gucci explained calmly. "I just wanted to say that I love you. I wanted to see you before I left. Gucci loves Mama. Can you say it with me?" she asked.

"Gucci love Mama and Mama loves her Gucci!"

Gucci laughed as she wiped away the stray tears that fell from her eyes. "That's right . . . my girl," she said. She finished the braid that she had started and then put the brush back on the nightstand. "They are going to take really good care of you here, Mama. It will feel like a long time before you see me again, but just remember that Gucci loves you okay?"

Gucci's mother nodded her head and Gucci stood up to leave. Everything in her wanted to pack her mother up and take her along, but Gucci didn't know what the future held. She had to go alone. Taking her mother would be too risky for the both of them. Gucci paid up her mother's bills for an entire year before she left and cried her eyes out until she reached the car.

Her leg shook the entire time she drove, only stopping for gas as she headed south. She wished she could have just ridden with one of her girls, but it was best if they stayed separated until they were in another state. The farther she got away from D.C. the heavier her chest became. After what she had done she would never feel safe going back. There would be a target on her back until she was caught and stepping foot inside D.C.'s limits would be like committing suicide. She finally made it to Norfolk, Virginia and pulled up to the motel that she had agreed to meet her friends in. She didn't know if they were there yet. Neither Chanel nor Raegan had called her and as she waited inside of her room, curtains drawn, and gun fully loaded on the bed beside her, she prayed that everything was okay. Before her mind had the chance to run rampant she heard the knocking at her door that announced her friends' arrival.

Gucci ran to the door and snatched it open eagerly.

"What took you so long?" she asked, staring at Raegan.

"Traffic," Raegan said with a shrug as she hugged Gucci's neck and entered the room. "Chanel isn't here yet?" she asked, voice full of concern.

"I'm right here, bitches, and I've never been so happy to be in a crummy motel in my life," she laughed as she threw the bag of money at Raegan and stepped inside. "Let's count this shit up!"

Raegan, Gucci, and Chanel stayed up 'til 3:00 A.M. counting and recounting the money, their hands enjoying the feel of so many dead presidents passing through them. They laid the bills out in $5,000 stacks until they came to the final tally.

"That's what two million dollars look like," Gucci stated in awe when they were finally done.

"That's a lot of money. Even when we split it, it's still a lot of money," Chanel whispered. The girls couldn't fathom the fact that they had gotten away with so much cold, hard cash and they sat in a circle staring at the money . . . afraid that if they went to sleep, somehow when they awoke the money would be gone.

"Let's get some sleep," Gucci said soothingly. "We have a long drive ahead of us tomorrow. We need to be well rested if we're going to make it to Florida."

"Does your friend know that we're coming?" Raegan asked, turning to Chanel.

"No, but he won't turn us away. He owes me," Chanel confirmed. "All we have to do is get there."

Gucci smiled as the ocean came into view as she drove closer and closer toward it. "We made it," she whispered it disbelief as a huge weight lifted from her burdened chest. The drive to Florida had been a long one. Careful to steer clear of law enforcement the girls followed each other all the way down, leaving a few car lengths between them just to be safe. They didn't stop, not even to use the restroom out of fear of being caught. Although their faces weren't quite clear in the video being played on a loop on national news stations, they still wanted to move accordingly. They had to be smart because the tiniest slip-up would land them behind steel and bars. Gucci laughed out loud, releasing some of the built-up tension she felt as she banged her hand against the steering wheel in sheer happiness. "Thank you, God!" she exhaled. The odds had definitely been against them, but they all had made it through with enough money to last them a long time. The girls were about to hop on a boat to paradise and start an entirely new life. Not many people were rewarded with the chance to start over and Gucci was grateful. She was using the money that lay neatly stacked in the duffel bag beside her to purchase a new beginning. She trailed Raegan and Chanel as they drove closer and closer to the marina where Chanel's boat connection was waiting for them. They were so close . . . so close to freedom, but when she saw Chanel's car fishtail out of control her smile instantly faded. Red taillights from the car filled her vision and she slammed her brakes to avoid hitting the back of Raegan's car. They both came to an abrupt stop and Gucci hopped out of her car.

"What happened?" she yelled as she slammed her door and ran toward Raegan.

"I don't know!" Raegan replied frantically. Both girls rushed to Chanel's car and stopped dead in their tracks when they saw her leaning over the steering wheel with a dark crimson hole pierced her temple.

"Oh God!" Gucci yelled as she backpedaled away from the gruesome scene. It was then that the police made their presence known. They seemed to pop out of nowhere. They came from everywhere. Out of storefronts, on top of roofs, out of police cars. The strong gusts of wind blew their hair wildly in their

faces as Gucci and Raegan looked at one another for answers.

"What do we do?" Gucci asked.

"I don't know!" Raegan replied with tear-filled eyes.

"Put your hands up!" The words cut through the air as the lead detective warned them through his bullhorn.

Gucci and Raegan stood on the defensive, afraid to move, but more afraid to stand still and be caught.

"Fuck this!" Raegan whispered as she pulled out her gun and began firing, aiming at anyone in a black-and-white FBI jacket.

"Raegan, don't!" Gucci yelled, but she was drowned out by the street serenade of gunfire as she watched her friend be gunned down. Raegan didn't even get to empty her clip before she hit the pavement. Blood spewed out of her as bullets ripped her apart. The gunfire stopped and a silence that only death could feel filled the city block.

"No!" Gucci screamed as she ran to Raegan's side. She grieved over her bloody body, taking her into her arms while whispering, "This is so fucked up. Everything is all fucked up."

She never even felt the federal agents grab her up and put the handcuffs on her. All she saw was the news camera in her face as she heard a reporter ask, "Was it worth it?"

Gucci jumped out of her sleep in a cold sweat, the hairs on the back of her neck standing straight up as an eerie feeling came over her. Quickly reaching for the lamp she turned it on in a panic as her neck swiveled around the room. Her heart raced frantically as she breathed rapidly, feeling as though she was still in the realm of her nightmare. "It was just a bad dream," she whispered. She looked over at her girls and saw that they were still sleeping, but rest was elusive for her. Gucci kept imagining the different ways that this thing could play out and none of the endings she conjured up in her head were positive.

The room was quiet, almost too quiet as if everything had been put on a standstill. She got out of the bed and walked over to the hotel window and what she saw made her legs give out. Gucci grabbed the windowsill to stop herself from falling as her eyes bugged in horror. Red, white, and blue police lights flashed silently as she watched the police accumulate outside in the dark.

"Get up, get up, get up!" she whispered as she rushed over to Chanel and Raegan, shaking them out of their sleep. "The police are outside!"

"What?" Raegan asked as she threw the covers off. "How did they know we were here?"

"The money! The money was marked! It had to be! Gucci, you paid for the room with the money from the bank?" Chanel asked frantically.

"Yeah, it was all I had," Gucci admitted.

Chanel brushed past her and peeked out of the window. "We're fucked," she said in a low tone of despair, knowing that they had gotten themselves caught up. It wouldn't have mattered where they went; as long as they were spending marked money, they would always be at a disadvantage.

"I'm sorry . . . I didn't know!" Gucci defended.

"None of us knew, Guch . . . it's okay. Any of us could have made the same mistake," Raegan snapped. "I have to think. How are we going to get out of this?" she asked.

Chanel went to the duffel bag that she had carried and opened the zipper, revealing the weapons she had inside.

"I put them in here just in case. I figured if we ever needed them, they wouldn't do us any good inside of that trunk," she said. She began pulling them out and laid them across the bed.

"What are you doing? We just supposed to go all out? Against the police?" Raegan asked.

Gucci shook her head wishing that she were still dreaming. This wasn't supposed to happen. *How could I have been so stupid?* she thought, knowing that whatever happened from this point on her life would never be the same.

"We don't have a choice," Chanel said. "Look around you. We have three bags full of bank money in here and a bed full of illegal firearms. They'll toss football numbers at us for this. I'm not going to jail. I'll hold court right outside in that parking lot before they take me to jail."

Chanel held out a pistol for Gucci and if she had any other choice she would have never have taken it, but this was the only way out. It was do or die. As she grabbed the gun out of Chanel's hand, Raegan grabbed one from the pile and made sure that it was loaded.

"There's FBI out there. No matter where we go they are going to find us," Gucci said frantically.

"Listen . . . My friend, he has a house in the British Virgin Islands. If we make it to Florida he can get us over there. The Feds can't touch us once we're out of the country. Once we go out that door we make our way to our own cars. If you make it out of the crossfire you meet me in Fort Lauderdale at the port day after tomorrow," Chanel said, explaining thoroughly so that everyone had clear instructions.

"I love you bitches. Y'all are my family and I love you," Gucci said as if they were her final words. "If I don't make it out of this just look after my mom. Please just do me that favor."

Raegan shook her head and said, "We all are going to make it out." The three friends hugged each other, overwhelmed by emotion as Raegan began to pray.

"God, please see us through this . . . please." The quivering plea that Raegan sent up to her Maker was one of desperation. She was about to go up against the impossible and the lonely prayer was all she had left in her bag of tricks. Her voice broke from anxiety as she continued. "Watch over us and let us meet back up one day. Keep my friends safe and help us make it through this. We are all we got," Raegan said as she stood with her head pressed against the foreheads of her best friends Chanel and Gucci. The three girls stood in a circle, arms wrapped around each other's shoulders, heads bowed. It was now or never . . . all or nothing. Their freedom depended on this one moment. They had done a lot of dirt together and now it seemed as though karma had come full circle. Now they stood grasping one another, hearts racing, tears falling down their tired eyes as they thought about what they were about to do. The odds were stacked against them, but they had no choice but to fight despite how dismal the outcome appeared to be.

"If we don't make it out of this . . . forgive us, Father, for we have sinned . . . in your name we pray, amen," Raegan finished. A hard lump filled her throat as she walked over to the living room blinds and pulled them down discreetly. Red, white, and blue lights lit up the night sky as the police barricaded the city block in an attempt to thwart their escape route. Raegan could hear the pounding inside of her head as the rhythm of her racing heart blocked out all other sound. In all her years on this earth she had never been afraid of anything, but secretly she feared the altercation to come. She didn't want to step one foot outside of the motel room, but she knew that she and her girls had no choice. If they didn't come out eventually the police would come in and she would rather go out under her own terms. She was going to determine how this thing played out and she knew as long as they made the first move they would have the advantage.

"We're like sitting ducks in this bitch," Chanel whispered anxiously as she came up over Raegan's shoulder and peeked at the scene outside.

"Then let's stop sitting," Raegan said in a low, determined tone. She cocked the pump of the sawed-off double-barrel shotgun she carried with one hand and said, "Fuck it, I'll see you bitches in the Islands."

Chanel racked the automatic AK she carried as Gucci chambered the first round in her semi-automatic 9 mm as they burst out of the front door. The three of them rushed out onto the lawn, adrenaline pumping, fear pulsing through their bodies as they shot it out with the entire police department. Desperation caused them to fire their weapons endlessly and their marksman aim was enough to give the officers outside the shootout of the century.

BOOM! BOOM! BOOM!

Raegan was so swift with the shotgun that you would have never thought she had to reload her weapon. There was nothing hesitant about her trigger finger. As she came out blazing, bullets flew past her head as she inched as quickly as possible to her car.

The melody of the police sirens harmonized with the gunshots as the girls popped off, serenading the streets.

The three girls exchanged fire with the entire police force and held their own as they each tried to escape to their prospective cars. It was time to fly solo. Although their chances of escape were slim to none they knew that by splitting up they increased their chances of eluding capture and avoiding the sticky situation. The cops couldn't focus on all three of them at once, so they each took their own risk as they cleared a path for themselves, popping off recklessly. They were too hot and they needed to split up before making their way to the British Virgin Islands.

Chapter Twenty-two

"Aghh," Raegan shouted mercilessly as she fired over and over again. Hitting an officer was not her objective ... she only meant to incite fear. She was skilled enough with her aim to come dangerously close to homicide without actually committing it. Killing a cop was the last thing she needed to add to her hood resume so she was cognizant of exactly where her bullets struck. Her hair whipped wildly around her face as she turned quickly to check on the status of her girls. Her mouth fell open in horror as she noticed an officer sneaking up behind Gucci. It was as if the entire scene were playing out in slow motion before her.

"Nooo! Guch!" she shouted. Gucci turned her head toward Raegan's voice and her eyes opened in horror when she saw Raegan pull a handgun from her back waistline. With precision Raegan let off a shot that laid the officer out, dropping him where he stood before he could ever pull his trigger. In the blink of an eye things had gone from bad to worse. As a matter of fact things were already at worse ... now they were just out of fucking control. The consequences of her actions were now irreparable and tears of regret immediately surfaced in her horrified eyes.

"Oh shit!" Gucci yelled as she realized how close she had come to death. Raegan's hand shook as she looked at the smoking gun in her hand. In a split second the situation had escalated, but before she could even pro-

cess what had happened a blinding pain shot through
her as her body jerked forward. Her mouth fell open in
agony, but no sound came out. Her eyes watered as she
looked Gucci in the eyes, desperately begging for help
without uttering a word. Her hand fell over her right
shoulder as she realized she had been shot. It seemed
as if the entire police force had her in their crosshairs.
By killing one of their own, Raegan had become public
enemy number one and she crouched down to shield
herself from the bullets that were flying her way. Enraged, Gucci blazed off, aiming at the officers behind
Raegan. Regan was frantic and in shock as she pulled
a bloody hand away from her body. She grimaced in
excruciating pain. With one of their own laid out in the
dirt, the officers became even more relentless in their
pursuit.

"Raegan, go!" Gucci yelled as she continued to fire
cover shots. The automatic machine gun that Gucci
spewed was enough to give Raegan time to run. Raegan snapped out of her daze and scrambled to fire her
gun with her left hand. Her entire right side was on
fire, which hindered her shot. With her left arm, Raegan shot wildly and ran for dear life until she finally
reached her car. Gunshots shattered her rear window
and bullets riddled the body of her car as she pulled
off, her tires burning rubber as her foot pushed the gas
pedal to the floor. Her car tipped to the side until she
finally gained control of the vehicle's speed as she sped
away. As her eyes darted wildly in her rearview she saw
that Chanel was long gone and that Gucci was still going gun to gun with the cops. Everything in her wanted
to turn around and help her friend, but knew that she
couldn't. *Gucci will make it out . . . she has to,* Raegan
thought. She was bleeding profusely onto the leather
seats and she knew that she needed help, but there

was nothing she could do but keep driving. The sirens behind her indicated that the cops were following her. The logical thing to do would be to give up . . . to pull over the car and surrender, but there was no way she was going to prison. Nothing in her would allow her to surrender. She would make those crackers chase her from one coast to the other before she gave up. *I've got to shake these squad cars,* she thought as she pressed the car to the max while bobbing and weaving through traffic. The traffic light in front of her turned yellow signaling for her to slow down, but instead she sped up, flying through the intersection and causing the cars that had the right of way to hit their breaks fiercely. When the officers following her tried to follow suit they were hit with a sudden surprise as a semi truck smashed into the side of their vehicle.

SCREECH!

The sound of tires wailing as cars tried to avoid the pileup accident was all that Raegan heard as she kept it moving. "I have to get out of this car," she whispered frantically as she bent a sharp right. She drove the car for ten more miles before she finally ditched the car on a suburban street. Grabbing a jacket out of the back seat she tried to hide her injured shoulder as best she could, but the blood quickly seeped through the fabric. There was nothing inconspicuous about her appearance. She was hot and she needed to get the hell out of dodge. She grabbed her empty gun and hid it inside the jacket as she weakly walked. She was trying to put as much distance behind her as she possibly could, but she wouldn't get far on her feet. She was losing too much blood. She needed a car. Her blood speckled the pavement as she trudged along begrudgingly. As her head began to spin she stumbled slightly, beginning to feel faint. Grateful for the night's shadow, she sat down on the street curb to reserve her strength as she tried to piece together a plan in her head. *I have to stop this wound from bleeding,* she thought as she held on to her arm, applying pressure and grimacing at the same time. As she came to a corner house she noticed a man leaving his home. Black baggy jeans, a black jacket, and a matching fitted he secured his front door, never noticing Raegan as she approached. She pulled her chrome .45 from her waistline, knowing that it contained no bullets. *He doesn't know that,* she thought, deciding to use the empty pistol as leverage. She walked directly up on him and put her gun to the back of his head.

"If you move I will pull this trigger you understand?" she asked, her voice unwavering.

Surprised that the voice behind him came from a woman he nodded in shock.

"Open the door and go back inside," she instructed as she looked around anxiously.

The man did as he was told, not wanting to buck because he had too much to lose. He had no idea how he had been caught slipping, by a bitch no less. She could feel his shoulders tense as she pushed him forward into the house. She was straight pump faking, holding up the guy with an empty gun. As long as she kept control this would play out in her favor.

"Put your hands up," she said.

The guy gripped the duffel bag that he held in his hand and spoke calmly. "You don't have to do it like this," he said.

"Don't make me put your brains on your front porch. Shut up and close the door," Raegan ordered.

"Sit down," she demanded harshly as she kept her gun trained on him.

The guy was beginning to feel as if his life was on a countdown. He didn't know Raegan but he knew her type. If she had enough balls to run up on him then she had enough balls to kill him. Deciding to go for broke he spun around unexpectedly and grabbed her arm forcefully as he slammed her into the wall.

"Aghh," she yelled as she fought ferociously with him for control of the gun. With her injured arm it didn't take much effort for him to overpower her. Snatching the gun from her hand he pushed her away from him. Without hesitation he aimed at her head and pulled the trigger.

Chapter Twenty-three

CLICK!

Heaving from the altercation, he looked at the girl in exasperation. "Fuck is you doing? You robbing niggas with empty guns?" he asked in disbelief as he tossed the .45 onto the ground. Enraged he cleared the space between them and hemmed her up. He wrapped his hands tightly around her neck, choking her out as he lifted her off of the ground. "Who sent you?" he yelled through clenched teeth, his temple throbbing in rage.

"Who sent you?" he shouted. He demanded answers, but the tight hold he had on her neck prevented her from answering. She clawed at his hands as her eyes burned in desperation. She scratched and clawed violently, reaching for his face as her nails dug into his skin. She was fighting him with all of her might, but her blows and protests were in vain. He was literally squeezing the life out of her.

"Please . . ." she gasped as her face turned red and the room began to close in around her.

Her eyes pleaded with him as he scanned her, reading her, observing her. He saw that she was soaked in blood and shaking in fear. She could feel the life leaving her body as he choked her ruthlessly. Reluctantly, he loosened his grip on her.

COUGH! COUGH!

Raegan choked as she gulped in air, bending over as she welcomed the oxygen into her burning lungs. Her legs gave out under her as she slouched onto the floor.

The guy looked down at Raegan, silently wondering what events had brought her to his home that night. As Raegan struggled on the floor the guy looked at her curiously. Anger turned to sympathy when he noticed that she was in tremendous pain.

"Why are you here?" he asked, his voice skeptical and stern.

Raegan looked up at him, grimacing as her shoulder continued to bleed profusely. She didn't have a choice but to answer him. She had invaded his home . . . if he shot her dead it would be justified.

"I need help," she whispered.

"You've got a funny way of seeking help, ma," the guy replied sarcastically. A part of him wanted to slap the taste from her mouth for running upon him toting a gun, but the desperate look in her eyes told him that she was between a rock and a hard place. He didn't know the circumstances that had placed her in his presence, but for some reason he didn't feel right just putting her out and leaving her on stuck.

"I'm sorry," she replied with tear-filled eyes. "I wasn't going to shoot you. I just needed to clean up and I needed a car. Nobody sent me. I'm hurt and I couldn't make it much farther on foot."

Her voice was shaking and the fear he noticed in her was enough for the guy to let down his guard. He reached his hand out to help her up from the floor.

Wide-eyed, she stared at his hand unsurely.

"You gon' stay down there all night or what?" he asked. "You bleeding all over my Brazilian hardwoods, ma. Get up."

Raegan grabbed his hand with reluctance as her fear was replaced by her embarrassment.

"Look I'm sorry. I just need to get out of here," she said in a panic as she turned for the door.

"I don't know why you're running, but you won't get very far with that arm," he commented. "It looks like you need a doctor."

"No!" Raegan shouted in protest. "No doctors! No hospitals and no fucking doctors." She held her injury tenderly as the thought of being apprehended overwhelmed her. There was no way she could walk into a hospital without being arrested. The police knew that she had been hit and would surely have units posted at all the local hospitals, anticipating her arrival.

"Okay, okay," the guy replied. "At least clean yourself up. There's gauze and peroxide underneath the bathroom sink."

Raegan nodded her head and answered. "Where is it?"

"It's upstairs . . . first door on your left," he replied.

Raegan hesitantly walked toward the bathroom. She was sure that he would call the police on her as soon as she disappeared from sight, but she planned on being long gone before they ever got there. *I just need to get myself together first,* she thought as she entered the bathroom, frantic. She grabbed a towel from the countertop and turned on the faucet. Her bloodstained hands painted the sink as the water flowed onto her palms. She removed her shirt and the sight of the gaping hole in her shoulder made her gasp in shock. A knock at the door caused her to jump in fear. Holding her breath, she stared into the mirror's reflection, eyeing the door behind her. She just knew that the police were standing on the other side of it. Her nerves were quickly eased when the guy peeped his head inside. He immediately noticed the terror in her eyes and said, "It's just me." He stepped inside and reached beneath the sink and removed a first-aid kit. "Let me see your shoulder."

Raegan turned toward the guy and winced as he began to clean her wound.

"What's your name?" he asked.

"Raegan . . . Sunny Raegan," she replied.

"Who shot you?" he asked as he did his best to clean the crusted blood from the gaping hole in her shoulder.

"The police," she answered.

He hesitated and looked her in the eyes, his gaze revealing his disbelief. "You're running from the police?" he asked.

"My girls and I . . . we got into some trouble," she replied, not giving him too much information. "We never had anything; no one ever gave us anything. It was always a struggle . . . from day to day. We got tired of struggling . . . tired of being the have-nots."

The guy taped her shoulder and handed her a bottle of aspirin.

"Oww . . . Jesus! Can you press any harder!" she shouted in annoyance as extreme pain took over her entire body. Her skin was pale and sweat shone on her brow as she cringed.

"Look, pressure is the only thing that's going to stop this bleeding. You've got a bullet in your arm. You can let me do this or you can take your pretty ass to the hospital or you can run out of here and leave a trail of blood behind you. Choose one," he said authoritatively, speaking to her as if she were an unruly child.

She sighed knowing that she didn't have many options. "Fine, but be easy . . . it feels like I'm being shot all over again," she complained. She turned her head and closed her eyes in impatience as she anticipated the agony to come. "Who are you anyway?" she asked rudely as if he had invaded her home.

"Brelin Nolen," he answered shortly. "I would say it's nice to meet you, but considering . . ."

"Ha-ha," she said as she looked him in the eye sarcastically. For the first time she inventoried the man in front of her. His dark-as-night skin and beautifully white teeth were so attractive to her. His clean-shaven face was sculpted perfectly with the exception of a tiny scar that rested above his left eyebrow. Handsome was an understatement. He had a grown-man appeal that gave her butterflies and the stern, disapproving look that he gave her made her feel as if he was one of the few men in the world who could put her in her place.

"I'm no doctor but I did the best I could," he said. "There's a clean shirt in the master closet." He nodded toward the door and began to exit the room.

"Why are you helping me?" Raegan asked.

"I haven't figured that out yet," he replied as he walked out.

Raegan quickly dressed and returned to the living room where Brelin waited patiently. "What's next?" he asked.

"I have to get out of this city," she said surely.

"Can I give you a ride somewhere?" he asked.

She thought about saying yes, but quickly dismissed the notion. She couldn't afford any slip-ups. Brelin was just one more person who could get her caught. *I've already been in his presence for too long,* she thought as she shook her head. "No, thank you. I'll be fine."

Brelin stood to his feet and walked close to her. She could tell from the look on his face that he didn't believe her. "Well look. I'ma hit you with some paper. It'll be enough to call you a cab and get yourself a room for the night." He peeled off ten hundred-dollars bills from the stack he retrieved from his pocket and placed them in her palm.

"I can't . . . You don't even know me," she said.

"You can stick a nigga up, but you can't take a genuine offer?" he asked with a chuckle.

She smiled back and closed her hand around the money. "Thank you. I swear one day I'll pay you back."

He nodded his head to make her feel better but they both knew that they wouldn't cross paths anytime in the near future. Brelin could tell that Raegan prided herself on her independence so he didn't rob her of her dignity by refusing her. As he stared at her almond-colored face he wondered what had brought her to this point. Her beauty hid her cruel intentions, which made her a deadly threat. He knew that she had broken many hearts in her day.

"Can I use your phone?" she asked.

He grabbed his cell phone and tossed it to her, then listened as she called a cab company. As she hung up the phone she gave him a weak smile.

"I'll wait outside for my ride. You don't want to be mixed up in the mess I've gotten myself into," Raegan stated sincerely with regret in her voice as she tossed his phone back to him.

As Brelin watched her walked out of the door he couldn't help but wonder where she had come from. The old saying that looks could be deceiving was absolute . . . Raegan was the epitome of that. He felt guilty, as if he owed her more than what he had given her, and his conscience weighed heavily upon him. Everything in him told him that he was playing with fire, but he ignored his instincts and ran out of the door after her. He stopped dead in his tracks and his heart sank when he looked at his empty driveway. *Fuck,* he thought as he looked at the vacant space that his Benz used to occupy. He pulled out his phone and started to dial 911, but stopped when he saw the message that Raegan had left in an open text.

I don't ride in cabs. Thanks for letting me borrow your car.

I'll return it, I promise. . . R

Taken aback by Raegan, Brelin had to smile. He shook his head because there wasn't a nigga walking on two legs who could pull one over on him, but within a matter of minutes a beautiful woman had walked into his life and suckered him out of his whip. He had never encountered a woman so slick. He was definitely intrigued. As he walked back into his home, he dialed his insurance company as he shook his head in disbelief. *That bitch is crazy as hell,* he thought as he chuckled to himself while shaking his head. *I hope she gets away.*

Chapter Twenty-four

Raegan tried to drive the speed limit as she made her way out of town, but her nerves caused her foot to press heavily on the gas. As she passed a highway sign she noticed that she was 150 miles away from North Carolina. Once she had a few states between herself and the District of Columbia, she would be able to relax. All she had to do was make it to Florida. There was a boat and a connect with fake passports waiting there to take her and her girls to paradise . . . if they ever made it. A honking horn behind her caused her to check her rearview mirror and her heart sank into her stomach when she recognized the car. A Lincoln town car followed behind her, blowing to get her attention. She frowned in confusion. "What the fuck are you blowing for?" she complained to herself as she rolled her eyes. "Damn it . . . today is not the fucking day. It's a red light, you idiot!" she shouted. The car pulled up beside her and the back window slowly rolled down. As Raegan realized who was in her presence, she felt all of the blood drain from her face. His face was her worst nightmare . . . the last person she wanted to see and without thinking she pressed the gas pedal down to the floor.

"Fuck! How did he find me?" she asked as she instantly took off. No matter how fast she drove she couldn't shake the tinted car.

BOOM!

The driver crashed into the rear of her car causing Raegan to swerve into oncoming highway traffic. She cut the wheel to the right and barely missed a collision only to be rammed from behind again.

"Agh!" she screamed in a desperate attempt to maintain control of the car. The driver pulled up to Raegan and rolled down his window.

"Pull over!" he shouted as he lifted a pistol up to show her he was strapped.

Raegan grabbed the pistol from her passenger seat and held it up as she raised an eyebrow in rebuttal. *Nigga, you're not the only one who can pop something,* she thought angrily as she kept driving like a bat out of hell. There was no way she was stopping that car. She knew who sat in the back seat of the town car and she most definitely wasn't trying to see him. She could only imagine the type of revenge he sought and tears came to her eyes. She held on tightly to the steering wheel and then slammed the car into the driver's side door. "Get . . . away . . . from . . . me," she shouted as she rammed the car again, this time making the town car rub against the metal divider on the side of the road. Sparks flew as the metals clashed but Raegan never let up on her gas. Her eyes bugged in horror when she saw the town car recover and she knew that her escape was impossible when the driver resumed his speed. He stuck his gun out of his window and fired two shots, deflating both of her passenger side tires. The Benz fishtailed out of control as she desperately fought to maintain control of the car. The world around her was like one carousel of confusion as she spun wildly, gripping the steering wheel. The collision that stopped it all wrecked her brain on impact as her head jerked back. The foggy haze that enveloped her made it hard for her to process her thoughts. Her mind said, *run!* But her body didn't listen. She saw a figure looming over her as her car door was opened.

"No," she protested as she slapped at the hands that snatched her from her seat. She scratched and swung, clawed and fought, but her efforts were futile. The large driver picked her up, bear hugging her, as he carried her to the tinted town car. Kicking, screaming, and spitting, Raegan did all she could to free herself but she knew that there was no getting away . . . not from this. Her shoulder was on fire and she was bleeding profusely but she refused to go down without a fight. She ignored the pain as she struggled to break free. The back window of the car rolled down.

"Get in the car."

As soon as she heard his voice the fight within her left her body. The emotional dams she had built up broke as tears flowed down her cheeks.

"Don't do this," she whispered as she looked him in the eyes. She could see the resentment, the rage . . . the need for vengeance in his deadly stare.

Her plea fell upon deaf ears as she watched the tinted window roll up and she was forced into the car. As she sat, trapped in the back seat, fear filled her. She closed her eyes and cried silently as she thought about all the things she had done to bring her to this point. "Reason, please just let me speak with Nah . . . please! Let me explain."

Reason chuckled and shook his head. "Now the bitch want to explain," he mumbled to the driver sarcastically. "Yo, fam, turn that broadcast up."

The sound of a national news station filled the air.

"In the news today a group of three young women robbed the downtown branch of First National Bank today. The three unidentified suspects held it up at gunpoint. The branch manager was able to flip the alarm and alert police, which caused the ladies to flee with two million dollars. Three people were injured in the robbery and police have labeled these women as the Red Bottom Bandits due to their oddly fashionable disguises. If you have any information that will aid in the arrest of these perpetrators please contact your local police . . . who will in turn contact the federal authorities. The suspects are armed and extremely dangerous. . . ."

"What you think? You think I should contact the police, Raegan?" Reason asked her as he nodded for the driver to turn off the radio. He sat beside her menacingly as the car pulled off. He was too calm and the smirk on his face taunted her. She knew that it was over. She was caught and a murderous goon like Reason only had one fate in mind for her. "I knew you were a snake bitch the first time I laid eyes on you. You're too fucking pretty. It's the ones like you who hide ugly motives. My man trusted you . . . I never did," he said.

"I didn't know it was Nahvid's spot," she defended as tears fell down her face.

Reason cackled in her ear as he unbuckled his pants. "I'ma fuck the dog shit out of you before I blow your head off." He grabbed himself mannishly as he loomed over her. She kicked him off, letting her legs fly at full speed but he was too strong for her. He wrestled her down onto the seat and spread her legs forcefully.

"You fucking bastard," she screamed. "Stop!"

He hit her so hard that stars appeared before her eyes causing her entire body to go limp. Her heart pounded with intensity as she tried to think of a way out of this situation. A part of her wanted to jump from the moving car, but they were going too fast and she knew that she would be committing suicide if she reached for the door handle. As if he could read her mind Reason spoke up, "Put the kiddie locks on the doors back here. Don't want this bitch getting any crazy ideas." He dug his pistol into her rib cage to remind her who was in control.

"Reason, please just let me speak with Nahvid . . . I . . ."

"Close your mouth before I put something in it," he said in a low tone. Raegan could see the animosity in his eyes. This was about more than the money to him. He wasn't doing this for Nahvid . . . he was finding satisfaction in it. He was paying her back for choosing Nahvid over him. Raegan's stomach turned as fear filled her. She tried to guess his intentions but he wore his poker face so well that she didn't know what he had planned for her. She prayed that he was taking her to Nahvid, but when they pulled up to an abandoned house she knew that wasn't the case. Reason opened the door and grabbed her arm, snatching her from the car as he pushed her ahead of him toward the back of the house. Boards covered the windows and door but not even those could hide the smell of death that filled the air. This house had been used on many occasions. It was a death chamber and most who walked through its doors never walked back out of them. Raegan planted her feet firmly in the ground, lowering her body in resistance as Reason pulled her harshly toward the door.

"Get yo' ass up," he demanded through clenched teeth while forcing her to her feet. Reason looked at the driver and said, "Wait in the car." The goon didn't ask questions; he simply followed orders as Reason pulled back the wooden board and dragged Raegan inside. She held on to the wall in an attempt to stop herself from being forced into the basement, but it was no use. Reason flung her like a rag doll down the entire flight of stairs. She hit the concrete bottom hard, landing on her arm and snapping it like a twig.

"Aghh!"

The heavy thud of Ralph Lauren boots sounded off as Reason descended the steps slowly, unfastening his belt as he neared her. Like a one-winged bird she was trapped. There was nowhere for her to run and the lustful look in Reason's eyes terrified her.

"No!" Her screams fell upon deaf ears as Reason turned her around and pushed her face into the ground. Rubble dug into her cheek as she struggled to get out of his grasp. His strong hands felt like chains as he gripped her wrists painfully behind her back, handcuffing her in his tight grasp. He pulled her pants down, snatching the denim off of her and revealing her thong.

"Reason, please . . . please don't do this," she asked as she heaved helplessly. "You don't have to do this. Please."

Reason mercilessly held her down as he removed his hard ten inches. She felt as he placed it on her ass and in that moment she knew that he was about to torture her. Fire ripped through her body as Reason broke through her anus, plunging himself into her. The sound that erupted from her was inhumane. Like a wounded animal she wailed painfully as he tore through her body and damaged her soul. She clawed the concrete floor so desperately that her fingernails snapped off. Her salty tears fell into her mouth and everything moved in slow motion as she felt every excruciating inch enter her. Reason sweated profusely as he forced himself on her. His grunts of passion sickened her and deep down she had always sensed jealousy from Reason. He wanted everything that Nahvid had, including his bitch and now he was indulging in her as if he owned her. When he was done with one hole he filled up the other, not even taking the courtesy to wipe the feces off of his penis before he defiled her all over again. Raegan prayed that he would satisfy himself quickly, but unfortunately for her the thought of disrespecting her kept Reason going strong. Nothing about the rape went by fast. It was as if he was taking his time with her, doing the unthinkable and she felt every unbearable moment of it. Her legs shook violently, weakly, until she could no longer take the pain and she blacked out. Physically she was there but mentally she had checked out.

It wasn't until she felt the cold water dripping onto her forehead did she realize that she was in the basement alone. Raegan could still feel the semen dripping out of her and onto her bloodied thighs. A leaky pipe tortured her as it rained one drop at a time onto her forehead. The water rolled down her face, resembling tears so closely that they mixed with her own. Her body felt as if it had been through a war as she tried to pull herself up onto her feet. Her limbs were weak and unstable . . . bruised from the many body blows that Reason had rained upon her. Bite marks covered her inner thighs.

She wanted to scream for help but whom could she call? The only person who could save her was the very same man she had crossed. Nahvid had sent his Grim Reaper to her door and now that she was facing death, she wanted nothing more than to repent. She wasn't a gangster, a killer, or even a hood chick. She never proclaimed to be tough. She was just greedy. Money had been her motivation and she had used her quest to see her son as an excuse to do bad things. The locks to the basement door clicked and Reason descended the steps. He stood in front of her . . . his pistol aimed, ready to take her life.

"That pussy is good, ma. I see how you had my man's head gone," Reason commented as he circled her.

Raegan whimpered as she tried to pull against the thick ropes that were cutting into her wrists.

"Please, Reason, just let me go. Please just call Nahvid," she pleaded. "I can explain. He'll let me explain."

Reason shook his head and scoffed sarcastically. "You got a lot of balls, bitch. Taking all of them stash houses the way you did. There isn't a nigga in town that could get away with what you did. I'll give you that."

"Please just call him," she said as tears flowed down her face.

"Thought you were too good for a nigga when I came at you," Reason spat. The contempt in his tone was evident. "But you threw the pussy at my man. All you bitches are the same. You don't love that nigga . . . you love the money . . . the power. That nigga reaping all the rewards while the real soldiers on the field during battle . . . putting in work. Wouldn't be no dope game in D.C. without me," Reason barked. "I got the same jewels, the same whips, the same everything, bitch. My paper long but a greedy slut like you only see the number one man huh? Reason couldn't pay to sniff that pussy." He circled her maliciously and kicked her with all of his might, his heavy Ralph Lauren boots caving in her rib cage. "Shit wasn't even all that. You know how the saying goes though . . . ain't no fun if your homies . . ." Reason smiled wickedly as he let his words linger in midair as circled her.

"Aghh!" Raegan screamed at the top of her lungs. "Help me!"

Reason shook his head and wrapped his finger around the trigger of his .45. "Don't worry, bitch. I have enough of that poisonous pussy. Too much of that shit will make a nigga lose his mind," Reason stated, smirking at his own joke.

Raegan closed her eyes and imagined her child's face. It was the last thing she wanted to see before she was permanently put to sleep.

Chapter Twenty-five

Gucci sat behind the steel table, tapping her foot nervously, while she cupped her face in her hands. The sight of dried blood on her hands caused a sob to escape her. She wondered where her friends were. Had they had made it out of the shootout intact? Were they even still alive? Gucci trembled as she sat waiting impatiently for someone to walk into the room. There was no clock on display and they had taken her phone away from her so she had no idea how long she had been waiting. Her bladder felt as if it would burst at any second and her mind was on overdrive. *What's going to happen to me? What have I done?* she thought. Before meeting Raegan and Chanel, Gucci had never been involved in anything where the stakes were so high. If things didn't fall in her favor, her life would be over. All she could feel was fearful remorse as time tortuously stood still. She wasn't naïve enough to think that she could walk away from this unscathed. The first body that she had ever caught had been a cop and because of that alone she was public enemy number one. When the door finally opened a federal agent walked into the room.

"I need to use the restroom," she said urgently.

"Hold it," he replied as he pulled out a chair across from her and sat down. In his hands he held a manila folder that contained every important event that had ever happened in Gucci's life. "Gucci is it?" he asked as he opened up the file and thumbed through its contents. "I'm Federal Agent Jim Starzycki. You want to tell me what happened?"

Gucci eyed him warily. She knew enough to know that she needed to do more listening then talking. She had heard of too many hustlers who had convicted themselves just by yapping too fucking much. Loose lips had sunken a lot of ships, and she was trying to keep hers afloat as long as possible. She had expected a team of corny officers to walk through the door playing good cop/bad cop, but this man was intimidating. As she surveyed the serious expression on his face and the Brooks Brothers suit that adorned his fit exterior she knew that she was outwitted. Her heart beat wildly inside her chest. There was no keeping her composure. She wrung her fingers nervously, her eyes darted around the room, and her foot tapped against the tiled floor. Gucci was terrified and the apprehension in her timid stare caused the federal agent to smirk slightly, knowing that he had the upper hand.

"Your sheet looks really clean. No priors, no juvenile records. Good grades in high school, community involvement in your background. You even took care of your mentally disabled mother coming up . . . How did you get here? All of a sudden you're robbing banks and shooting cops?" the agent grilled.

Gucci remained silent but the tears that filled her eyes let the agent know that she was listening.

"Seems to me that you're playing out of your league," the agent said. "The bank jobs are federal. You shoulder that weight all by yourself you're looking at being locked up for a very long time, young lady. Now the state charge . . . well that's another ordeal. You shot him in Virginia, sweetness. You better hope he pulls through because as soon as he flatlines you'll be facing the death penalty."

Gucci's chest collapsed and she felt as if she couldn't breathe as she processed his words.

"I don't want to die . . . We never meant for any of this to happen," she whispered.

"Who's 'we,' Gucci? What are the names of the other two women? Where are they headed?" he asked. "We are going to eventually catch them and whoever cracks first will be the smartest one. She'll get the best deal. Protect yourself, because I guarantee when your friends get the opportunity to throw you under the bus . . . they will. Now I can't take these charges away, but I can lighten them . . . if you help us."

Faced with the consequences to her actions, Gucci felt trapped. "I want a lawyer. You have to get me a lawyer. You can't deny me that right? You can't talk to me without my attorney, right?" she stammered.

"I must say you ladies were pretty slick. We wouldn't have known your identity if you hadn't spent the marked money to pay for your mother's foster care. After that we had you . . . now you just have to help us get the other two. We don't know their names yet, but now that you're in custody it won't be long until you put the rest of the puzzle together for us—"

At that moment Starzycki's cell phone rang, loudly interrupting the interrogation. Agent Starzycki pulled the phone off of his belt and flipped it open. The news he received instantly changed the expression on his face. He ended the call and looked at Gucci. "The cop you shot was just pronounced dead."

He closed her file with a heavy sigh and stood to his feet. Starzycki came around the table that separated them, pulling her roughly to her feet.

"Get me a lawyer," Gucci protested as he dragged her out the door and through the hallways of the precinct.

"You'll get your lawyer," Starzycki shot back as he escorted her down a set of stairs. The more they walked the quieter it became and Gucci noticed that there were no officers in this part of the police station.

"Where are you taking me?" she asked, becoming panicked.

"This wing of the station is under construction . . . so there will be no one here to interrupt," Starzycki said.

"Interrupt what?" Gucci screeched as she tried to plant her heels firmly to stop him from pulling her forward.

"You know what we do to cop killers?" he asked.

Chanel drove like a madwoman, eyes burning, ass numb, but never stopping as she tried to get as far away from Virginia as she possibly could. Everything had hit the fan and nothing had gone as planned. Now she was on the run, with her girls in the wind, desperate for an escape. Gucci's arrest had been playing on a constant loop on her XM CNN radio stations and both she and Raegan were wanted. Chanel didn't know what to do. She had to get out of the car that she was in. Although she had switched the plates she was still pushing her luck. Every cop in the country probably had its description by now and she had to move smart. She got off on the next exit and pulled into a truck stop. Cautiously she looked around before getting out of the car and rushing inside. She half walked, half ran until she was safely inside. Her paranoia was in overdrive. Chanel leaned over the porcelain sink in the public restroom and everything in her stomach seemed to come up. She breathed deeply as she splashed water on her face. "

"Just calm down . . . You have to calm down. Think clearly . . . You have to get yourself out of this," she coached. At this point she couldn't worry about the team. She had to do what she had to do to make sure that she was out of harm's way. She hoped that Gucci would stand tall and figured that she hadn't cracked yet because Raegan or her own name hadn't been mentioned in any press.

As Chanel lifted her head and stared into her reflection she felt unsure. For the first time since she was a teenage girl she didn't know what to do. Overwhelmed with indecision and fearful of being caught she let her tears burst through her normally controlled façade. She quickly gained her composure when a woman came out of one of the stalls.

"Is everything okay, baby?" the mature, well-aged black woman asked, her long Southern drawl sounding genuinely concerned. The woman stared curiously at Chanel's reflection in the mirror.

Chanel wiped her face. "Everything's fine."

The old woman didn't budge as she peered at Chanel. Chanel fidgeted as she stared back inconspicuously, noticing as a hint of recognition glimmered in the woman's eyes.

"Aren't you that girl?" the woman asked as she snapped her fingers while trying to jog her memory. "You're the one with the banks on the news!" the woman shouted as she suddenly grabbed her clutch a bit tighter.

Chanel shook her head. "No, I'm sorry. I don't know what you're talking about," she said.

"I'm old but my eyes still work. Those disguises was something terrible. You wasn't hardly covering nothing! How do you think I noticed you? You're in some kind of trouble, girl," the woman said. Chanel could hear the criticism in her voice.

"I told you I don't know what you're talking about . . . mind your business," she said.

"See that's the problem with you narrow-tailed little girls. Don't know how to respect your elders. You're still wet behind the ears. I was going to ask you if you needed help, but since you want to get fly with the lip . . ."

"I didn't ask for your help," Chanel said as she stormed past the lady. "People are starting to recognize me," she mumbled while walking with her head down. As she passed a set of TVs in the rest stop lobby a picture of her and her girls flashed across the screen. *We didn't get all of the cameras,* she thought. Her mouth dropped in horror as she lifted the collar of her shirt to conceal herself as best as she could while reading the headline . . .

One suspect in custody. The others still at large.

Her world shattered when she thought of her friends. She knew that Gucci was the weakest of them all and she felt an extreme sadness sweep over her just thinking of what Gucci could be going through. Although the greedy side of her had deceived her girls, she still loved them. They were family and she had silently prayed that they would all meet down South to sail away to freedom together. Now it was clear that it wasn't going to happen. She didn't know if she would ever see any of them again and it put a painful hole in her chest knowing that they didn't even get to say good-bye.

Chanel lowered her head in hopes that no one else would point her out and hurried to the pay phones. She couldn't keep driving the car she was in, but she couldn't sit still, either. Chanel needed assistance and there was only one person she knew of who could help her. Faugner. It had been years but time didn't matter. He would come to her aid, especially considering the circumstances. Her heart fluttered at just the thought of him. *He'll help me,* she thought. *He has to.*

754-989-6000.

She had committed the number to memory without ever trying to but when she heard the operator's voice blare through the phone . . .

"This number has been changed."

Her jaw hit the floor, her ego crushed into a thousand pieces. She had never thought he would disconnect the lines of communication with her, not after all that they had been to one another. She had to go to him. He may have changed his number, but she knew where to find him. As she hung up the phone she saw the old woman walking out of the rest stop. Chanel didn't have a choice but to seek her help. She hurried after her.

"Hey! Lady!" Chanel called.

The old woman stopped and spun on her heels inquisitively as Chanel caught up to her. "I'm sorry for the way I treated you in there. I'm in a bind. I could really use a ride."

"I'm not riding with you, child. You're a wanted woman. Now you are welcome to Ms. May's car if you like," the woman offered.

"Really?" Chanel asked, taken aback by the woman's kindness. "You're going to let me take your car?"

"Who said anything about take?" the woman laughed as she scooted close to Chanel's ear. "I know you've got some of that good ol' bank money left. You can buy it; all you've got to do is drop me home, and you can be on your way. No questions asked."

"Buy it?" Chanel exclaimed as she realized that she was being hustled by the old lady. "I can buy one from a car lot!"

"Yep, sure could. You could carry yourself right on in there and put your name, number, and address right on down on the sales contract . . . but you won't and we both know why. . . ."

Chanel ice grilled the conniving old bat. She wasn't dealing with a rookie. *This old bird is something else,* Chanel thought in frustration.

"Five thousand dollars," Chanel offered.

"Fifteen thousand dollars," the lady countered.

"What?" Chanel shot back. "You done lost your damn mind!"

"Well good luck getting wherever you're going," the lady said as she sauntered off toward the parking lot without a care in the world.

Chanel wanted to slap fire from the old woman for beating her so bad. She knew that she was getting got, but at the moment she had to accept it. "Ten thousand dollars and not a dime more. And you can find your own way home!"

There was no way that Ms. May was turning that down. That was six months worth of social security checks for her. The deal was as good as done.

"Deal," the lady answered.

She led Chanel to a 1995 Buick and Chanel could have kicked herself. The old car was in good condition, but a complete downgrade from her normal vehicle flow. She was used to pushing foreign whips, but she held her tongue because beggars couldn't be choosers.

She reached in her bag and handed the woman two wads of cash worth $5,000 each.

"Nice doing business with you," the lady smirked.

Chanel rolled her eyes before getting in the car and driving off. She hit the highway, headed to Florida where she could find Faugner. He was the only one who could clean up the mess that she had created.

Chapter Twenty-six

Nahvid welcomed Reason into his home, shaking hands with his man. The dim chandelier of his massive foyer hid the blatant emotion that had taken over his face. His heart was heavy and his mood serious as he stood tall . . . firm . . . in front of his right hand.

"Did you find her?" he asked.

"Yeah, I found her," Reason replied with hesitation.

"Where is she now?" Nahvid asked. A confusing mixture of anger, disappointment, and relief consumed him all at once; fogging his head with an emotional storm.

"I had to put her to sleep," Reason said.

"I thought I asked you to bring her here first! There might have been an explanation . . . a misunderstanding," Nahvid said, his voice drifting off as he tried to speculate why Raegan had chosen to run away from instead of toward the escape he had offered her.

"I tried to do things peacefully, fam. The bitch just started spraying on sight. I told her you wanted to see her. She was on some straight fuck you shit. So I had to make a snap judgment and call it curtains, nah mean?"

Nahvid flinched at the thought of Raegan's murder but it had to be done. The robbery was something that he could have forgiven, but to lose his mother to the hands of the woman he was growing to love . . . that was punishable by death. How many times could he forgive her? He offered her reprieve and she had spit in his face. Her word was no good and Reason had done what Nahvid knew he would have never been able to. Nahvid thought that he would feel some type of retribution once Raegan was out of the picture, but losing her weighed heavily on his conscience. She had been a breath of fresh air when she entered his life and just as quickly as their love affair began . . . it fizzled and burned. Treachery and deceit had obviously been the foundation of their love. Was he a target of Raegan's all along? Did she simply see him as a mark? Was anything that they felt for one another truly real? Nahvid had so many questions, but knew that he would never get the answers.

"Was it painless?" Nahvid asked. It took everything in him not to show his cards. He was truly torn up over losing Raegan.

"One to the head, one to the heart," Reason assured.

A shrill cry cut through the air and Reason raised an eyebrow as he nodded toward the living room. "You want me to handle that?"

Nahvid shook his head and breathed a sigh of grief and confusion. Raegan's baby was still in his care and the killer in him knew what had to happen next. Baby Micah was a loose end that needed to be clipped, but his affection for Raegan was not something that was black or white. Their relationship had lived in a grey haze that was so complicated that he couldn't bring himself to eliminate Micah.

For the first time in their twenty years of friendship, Reason recognized indecision in Nahvid. "You know what has to be done," Reason said.

"One life was too much. No more blood needs to be shed," Nahvid resisted. "I'll take the kid back to his old man and let him take over from here."

Reason's jaw twitched because he wanted to intervene. It wasn't smart for Nahvid to even keep the kid breathing. *The kid and her bitch-ass baby's father need to be clipped,* Reason thought. He was a true killer, a stone-cold murderer and it was Nahvid who had taught him the game. Reason knew that Nahvid was making decisions based on emotion, but it wasn't his place to say anything. Reason was the number two in command and he could see Nahvid's gangster wavering. Raegan had become a soft spot for him and it was obvious . . . a little too obvious. There was a crack in the foundation of Nahvid's empire and Reason was about to bring the entire thing crumbling down.

"Fuck a bitch, let's get back to getting this paper," Reason said, trying to make light of the heavy situation.

The two slapped hands and Nahvid led his mans to the door to walk him out of the house.

Although Nahvid was papered up, his appetite for riches was insatiable. He couldn't let his heart knock him off his hustle. He had learned long ago to keep his emotions dormant. Growing up with a fien'in' out mother had taught him the hard way that getting caught in his feelings could ultimately cost him everything. . . .

Nahvid sat on the block inside his '85 Buick Regal watching the entire block as it went to work for him. At sixteen, he was making a name for himself, turning what once was a dead part of town into a playground for base heads. D.C. was locked down by older hustlers who had been putting in work for years. There was no room for any young boys coming up and young Nah was shunned whenever he stepped foot on someone else's turf. They looked at him as a li'l nigga . . . no competition . . . but no one took the time of day to see the hunger in his eyes. He was thirsty, a hungry young wolf who was determined to get his piece of the pie. With only his best friend Reason at his side he knew that he had neither the manpower nor firepower needed to war over turf. So instead of out gunning the old heads over city blocks that neither side owned, he outsmarted them. He settled for scraps . . . the sections of the city that no one desired. The suburbs. While the older hustlers thought they had run him off the block, he had set up shop in a less risky environment. Nahvid hustled coke. While dudes around his way were wasting time in the kitchen with baking soda boxes, Nahvid was taking his product straight to the streets. He was selling eight balls to sorority girls, accountants, and teachers. He was targeting the recreational users. The people who would never be caught dead with crack pipes, but whose runny noses and coke-eaten nostrils told the true story of their growing habits. Nahvid was selling dope in the very neighborhoods where his local police force rested their heads at night. He and Reason were slowly getting rich while flying beneath the radar.

By the time other hustlers had gotten wind of the money that was being made, Nahvid had already locked down the block. He had a crew of young, reckless niggas with nothing to lose and the world to gain. They were ruthless and ruled the neighborhoods with an iron fist, or rather their iron clips. Women, children, old ladies in church hats . . . anybody affiliated with the enemy could be a potential victim. Nahvid and his crew knew no limits so everybody was at risk. Nahvid had only been forced to make a few examples before the message was clear. He was the new king on the throne and whoever wasn't a part of his movement was moving shit. By the time he was twenty-one he had taken over the inner city and everybody was on payroll. Money was flowing like expensive champagne and everybody ate. Nahvid was getting paid. He was smart though and once the initial introduction to fast money was old news Nahvid made investments. He grew bored with fly cars and nice jewels. He quickly graduated to purchasing businesses and properties. Once he met Odom, the sky was the limit. His thirst for legitimacy grew and he was schooled on how to convert drug money into bank money. He never left the streets alone, but he became untouchable because he had the best cleaner around. His paper was clean and he had tax records to prove it. The only eyesore in his picture-perfect life was his drug-addicted mother, Nita. No matter how many rehab programs Nahvid enrolled her in or how much he spent to get her clean, Nita never let go of her pipe dreams. Crack cocaine was her drug of choice and it was the one thing she loved more than her son.

Nahvid was flawless in the way he ran D.C. He made no mistakes, but when he let his emotions influence his decisions his entire empire almost came tumbling down. When Nita's addiction began to take over her looks, Nahvid felt obligated to intervene. He moved her into his home without reservation and took a break from the streets to tend to her health. Under his watchful eye she stayed for weeks, fien'in', hurling, defecating on herself . . . as her body purged the poison from itself. She begged Nahvid, even cursed his ass out when he wouldn't feed the monkey on her back, but he never obliged her.

"Fuck you, Nahvid . . . fuck you!" she would shout.

"Fuck you too," he would reply as he kept her barricaded inside his home. He made sure that she had every comfort . . . every luxury as he weaned her naturally without any help from any man-made drug. Nahvid hired a private doctor to visit twice a week and his mother gave the poor white man hell every time. She spit, kicked, even bit the doctor because getting clean was not her decision. She was being forced to kick the habit and although she knew it was for her own good, Nita just didn't appreciate her choices being taken away.

"Your big-head ass need to remember that I'm your parent, not the other way around," she spat.

Throughout the entire process Nahvid ignored her insults and waited for his mother's true essence to reemerge. It took weeks and through it all he began to lose touch with the streets. He had put Reason in charge and although things ran smoothly, he didn't want the hood to get used to seeing a new king in rule, no matter how temporary Reason's reign was. Nahvid knew that once a man felt power and led the pack, he would never want to come in second again so when it was time to re-up Nahvid knew that he couldn't send Reason to meet his connect.

"You know you can trust me, fam. You've been focusing on your moms and I respect your love for family. You set up the meeting with your mans and I'll take care of the exchange this time," Reason stated.

"Some seeds you gotta water yourself, nah mean?" Nahvid responded.

Against his better judgment he left his mother alone for the first time in weeks. He was quick with his connect, even rude one would say, but his cocaine supplier was all knowing and all seeing. He already knew Nahvid's current circumstance. He shook his hand and wished him well, sending the young hustler on his way as soon as possible. Nahvid met up with Reason and hit him off with the product.

"Yo, stay and have a drink with me, fam. You been MIA. Let your hair down for the night," Reason said.

"Nah, I'm good. Got to take care of something," Nahvid replied. "I'ma catch up with you though. I got to shake."

The two locked hands before Nahvid headed home.

The scene that presented itself when Nahvid entered his secluded home sent him into a blind rage.

He had cooked coke enough times to recognize the disgusting smell of crack vapors in the air.

Nahvid could feel his temperature rising as he made his way to his mother's room. His home was his refuge from the world. The fact that very few people knew where he rested at night was what allowed him to sleep. Nita knew the rules and had blatantly disrespected them. He could hear the voices of his mother mixed with the baritone of a man invading his ears. He stepped into her doorway just as her luscious, full lips wrapped themselves around the glass dick. The man held the pipe up for her as his beady eyes watched as the smoke seduced him.

"You gonna give me some of that pussy, Nita?" the man asked. "Put them lips on my dick like you do that pipe?" Nita was ass naked, riding his dick while she simultaneously inhaled the drug.

Before Nahvid could stop himself he pounced on the man. "You bitch-ass nigga brought this garbage into my house? You want her to suck what?" His rage roared from his throat as he beat the man mercilessly.

"Nah, baby, wait! Baby! Stop!" his mother screamed.

Nahvid's fist slammed so hard into the man's face that he knew he had broken his own hand, but he didn't care. He couldn't stop himself. Not even the sight of the unconscious bloody figure beneath him made him stop the beating. It wasn't until he felt *hands forcefully pulling him off of the man did his senses snap back into place.*

"Nah! Chill! Chill!" Reason shouted as he restrained his best friend. Nahvid suddenly had the strength of ten men and Reason found it hard to keep him at bay. He stumbled, wrestling Nahvid into the hallway as Nita scrambled to her smoking buddy.

Reason closed the room door and watched Nahvid lose control. "I'm done with her, fam! I'm done. The bitch smoking this shit in my house after everything I do to help her!"

"You need to calm down, Nah. For real! You did some real silly shit in there, Nah. The nigga don't look like he's breathing. We've got to think," Reason said.

At that moment Nita's naked body came rushing out of the room as she attacked Nahvid. "You killed him! You didn't have to kill him!"

Nahvid couldn't stand to hear his own mother taking up for the man who had ruined all of his hard work. He had stayed in day and night trying to keep her on the up and up. Before he knew it he hauled off and slapped her. The hit sent her crashing to the ground, causing her to hit her head on the corner of the wall. Blood gushed from an open wound above her eye and it swelled instantly.

DING DONG!

KNOCK!

KNOCK!

KNOCK!

Everyone froze as the doorbell rang out followed by hard knocks. Nahvid already knew by the pattern of the pounding that it was the police.

Reason shot to the window and when he saw the flashing lights of a squad car he turned around in fear.

"It's the fucking cops," he whispered.

Nahvid knew it didn't look good for him. There was blood on his clothes . . . his hands . . . a dead body lying in the middle of his guest room floor.

Nahvid looked his mother in the eye with a hatred and disappointment that broke her heart before he turned and walked down the steps. In a daze he opened the front door. The police immediately pulled their weapons once they saw his bloodied shirt and hands.

Nahvid opened his mouth to admit his crime when his naked mother came to his side crying hysterically.

"Thank God! He raped me . . . the man upstairs raped me and my son . . . he came home . . . there was a fight . . . he tried to kill me . . . but my son . . . Oh God . . . my son saved my life!" Nita cried. She heaved and sobbed so convincingly that Nahvid thought for a brief moment that her story was based on truth.

When he finally found his voice he spoke. "We fought . . . He's upstairs. I don't think he's breathing."

The police captured Nahvid's wrists in handcuffs and stuffed him in the back of the car.

"I'm on it, Nah!" Reason yelled after him. "The lawyer's on speed dial!"

Nahvid snapped out of the bad memory as he shook his head. He had barely escaped a life sentence in prison. He had done five years after the charges had been reduced down to involuntary manslaughter. Acting off of emotion had fucked him up once before. He had lost everything and had to rebuild his empire up from the ground upon his release. His entire world had crumbled behind one irrational choice. He refused to make the same mistake twice.

There was no point in having regrets now. When Raegan betrayed him she had put her own execution order in. Her ill intent had led to her own demise and although it would take Nahvid a long time to get over her he knew that he eventually would. Raegan was a memory and now he had to refocus on the game before it swallowed him whole.

Chapter Twenty-seven

As Raegan sat in the corner of the basement, her back against the wet, concrete wall she wished that Reason had killed her. Not knowing what he had in store for her was eating her alive and as she stared through the pitch black of the basement, hopelessness set in. The sound of Reason's return caused her to shudder and terror gripped her so tightly that she could barely breathe. Staring death in the face made her realize that the life she had been living was not worth the consequences it carried. She didn't want to die. There was still so much that she hadn't done; too many places she hadn't seen; so many people she hadn't loved right. Raegan was filled with regret. Light illuminated the basement and she closed her eyes while covering her ears, not wanting to know what was to come.

"Bitch, get the fuck up," Reason said through clenched teeth, pulling her to her feet and shoving her onto an old, tattered couch.

"What do you want?" she asked.

"I want you to tell me where your boy keeps the bricks," Reason stated.

Raegan frowned in confusion, but she couldn't say that she was surprised. She had always sensed that Reason was a snake. He was filled with envy toward her man. There was no honor among thieves and now he wanted Raegan to cross Nahvid, something that she just couldn't do.

Her silence caused him to chuckle. "You killed his mother; now you wanna play like you loyal. I'ma give you a choice. You either show me where the work at or I'ma have fun killing you slow."

Fear had never pulsed so strongly through her body, but she refused to bring any more harm to Nahvid.

Seeing her strong resolve enraged Reason. He slapped her, using all of his strength, immediately bursting her lip. His handprint embedded in red upon her face as he pounced on her. Reason didn't give two fucks that she was a woman. He manhandled her, punching her so hard that he broke her nose.

"Aghhh!" she screamed. The sound of her bone cracking and the taste of the blood fountain spewing from her nose was torture. "Please stop!"

"Where's the bricks?" he asked again, standing up heaving in frustration and exertion.

"I don't know!" she yelled, clearly lying. They both knew that Nahvid had been a little bit too trusting of her. Reason knew that she knew where he kept his work and he came prepared to squeeze the information or the life out of Raegan . . . whichever came first.

"Okay, bitch . . . you want to play stupid," he said as he nodded his head and went to the top of the stairs to retrieve a bag of tools. "Let's see if this will help you remember." He removed duct tape and rope from the bag and snatched her up by the hair.

"No!" she protested as she squirmed and fought against him, but he easily overpowered her. She used everything she had, letting fists and feet fly, biting, twisting, turning, but nothing worked. Eventually he had her bound and was pulling his infamous torture tools out of his goodie bag.

"You know I see what he saw in you, Raegan . . . I do. You're a pretty mu'fucka," he said as he grabbed a cigarette and lit it. He took a toke and leaned directly in her face as he blew the smoke out in her face. "It's kind of a shame that you won't be so pretty after this," he said. Reason put the cigarette out on her face, burning a small circular hole right on her forehead. Raegan whined painfully as she bucked in the chair, but Reason held her still as he lit the cigarette numerous times, using her face to snuff out the amber glow. When he was done with her face he spread her legs and put matching burns on the pink flesh of her vagina. He was like a surgeon in his torture chamber and he didn't even flinch as he pulled out her fingernails with a pair of rusty pliers one by one.

"Agh!"

"You can stop this at anytime. All you have to do is tell me what I want to know," he said calmly. He was sadistic with it as he watched her pass in and out of consciousness. Seeing her in so much agony made his dick hard. He was so close to taking over the streets of D.C. and there was no way he was letting a conniving bitch like Raegan stop him. "Where the bricks at?"

"I don't know! Please, Reason! I would tell you anything to stop this, but I really don't know," she wailed, snot and blood mixing and dripping down her face. Raegan was feigning ignorance because she needed Nahvid in a position of power. As long as he was number one then her son might have a chance, but she knew for sure that Reason would kill her baby without a second thought. Raegan didn't want to see harm come to Nahvid or her child. She would die first.

Reason kicked her chair over causing her head to hit the cement with a loud thud. White light shot through her mind and it felt like a lightning bolt was tearing her brain apart. Reason pulled out the wooden handle from a plunger and shoved it up her anus.

"Aghh! Reason, please please please!" she yelled. "Help! Somebody help me. ..." she sobbed.

"Bitch, tell me!" he shouted.

Reason had done his fair share of torturing niggas and none had ever lasted as long as Raegan had. He was sweating profusely and exhausted as he cut her from the chair. He hoisted her bound hands up onto a metal hook hanging her up like a piece of meat as he grabbed a steel pole. Using her for batting practice he beat her almost to death, swinging full force, cracking ribs, breaking bones . . . whatever he could think to do to inflict pain he did and she still didn't break. He had no idea how strong a mother's love was. She wasn't taking this beating for Nahvid. She was taking it for her son, the one person she would die for. She was past the point of tears. Raegan could barely breathe her body hurt so badly. Her lungs felt as if they didn't work anymore as she gasped desperately for air.

Reason wiped his brow as he stared coldly at Raegan, who hung limply from the ceiling. "Okay, bitch, you don't want to tell me. I'ma show you hell on earth," Reason said. He poured gasoline on a filthy rag and stuffed it in her mouth like a gag. She was in too much pain to even protest, but when she smelled the rancid scent of gasoline in her nose her eyes bulged in horror.

He's going to burn me alive, she thought as she began to kick her feet.

"Hmm! Hmmm!" she shouted as she watched him flick a lighter and bring it close to the soaked rag. "*Hmmmmm! Hmmmmm!*"

"What's that? You want to talk now? You got something to tell me?" he asked.

He removed the rag from her mouth and looked her square in the face.

"Where does Nah keep the bricks?" he asked. Raegan saw nothing but evil in Reason's face. He was the devil and there wasn't a doubt in her mind that he would watch her burn slow. There was only so much she could take before she broke.

"The storage unit . . . It's in a storage unit right outside the city," she grunted. "Please just stop it. I gave you what you wanted."

It was the last thing she said before she saw black.

Gucci gagged, coughed, fought, and spit as she tried to stop the water from going down her throat. She couldn't breathe and she jerked like a fish out of water as she fought against the police officers as they had their way with her. A thin cloth lay over her face as one man held her feet and another held her arms down, while she lay flat on a wooden interrogation table. A third cop poured water directly over her face. The waterboarding form of torture was drowning Gucci on dry land and after hours of holding strong she couldn't take it anymore. The man removed the rag from Gucci's face and watched sternly as she choked furiously. The federal officers didn't care that they were using illegal interrogation practices. A good cop had been lost and they were determined to not only punish Gucci but to get information out of her that would lead to the arrest of her accomplices. Just as they were about to start the process again, Gucci screamed out.

"Wait! I can't take anymore. I'll talk," she screamed, while still gasping for air.

"Who are the other two women?" the man above her head asked.

Gucci's heart ached because she never pictured herself turning on her girls. She was far from a snitch, but what they were putting her through was unbearable. Gucci had held out for hours and she had to ask herself if Raegan or Chanel would have held out even that long. Her mind raced as she put the pieces of her story in place. She opened her mouth to speak and lowered her head as she told them what she knew. . . .

Chapter Twenty-eight

Chanel was shaking from paranoia and fatigue by the time she made it to Faugner's doorstep and she rang the bell as nervous butterflies filled her stomach. It had been so long since she had seen him. She had no clue how he would receive the unexpected visit. The door was opened by an older gentleman who wore a butler's uniform. He frowned when he saw Chanel. Her appearance was less than satisfactory. She had been driving for days and had no time for cosmetics or even a shower. She looked like she had rolled in off the streets, as if she didn't even deserve to drive down the prestigious block.

"May I help you?" he asked.

"I'm here for Faugner Scott. Please tell him Chanel would like to speak with him. I'm an old friend," she explained.

The butler escorted her inside and Chanel was in awe at how beautiful the house was. Faugner had always come from money, but it seemed as though he was doing exceptionally well these days. Everything about the house screamed wealth. From the invisible staircase leading upstairs, to the imported Austrian tiled floor. The finishes were so elegant and extravagant that she knew that they had been professionally appointed. Chanel was so busy looking around that her head was in the clouds when Faugner entered the room.

Faugner Scott stood in the entryway to the great room admiring Chanel. So much time had passed, but the way that he felt for her hadn't changed. She was such a grown woman now . . . such a lady. Despite the fact that she looked worn from travel, the way that she held her shoulders back in perfect posture, and the way that she stood one foot behind the other in a pageant pose were all things that he had taught her. Class. She was gorgeous and Faugner had to clear his throat before she even knew that he was behind her.

"It must be my lucky day for I am blessed with the presence of a queen," he complimented with a charming smile as he stood with one hand in his Ferragamo slacks.

"Faugner," she crooned as she ran to him. He welcomed her with open arms just as she had hoped and his embrace felt so safe that she finally felt secure enough to break down.

"Shhh! It's okay! Let it out," he whispered as he caressed her head while he allowed her to pour all of the sadness into him. He didn't know what had caused her to run to him after so many years of staying away but he was glad that she had come. He had thought of her often. After leaving his D.C. firm to a promising young lawyer he relocated to Florida to begin more lucrative business ventures.

"I'm in trouble, Faugner. I need your help!" she wailed as she looked up at him desperately. He cradled her face between his hands and wiped her tears away with his thumbs.

"Why don't we let Jennings make us some tea and we'll discuss it on the veranda," Faugner said soothingly as he nodded for his butler to give them some privacy. He escorted her out of a set of French doors that gave way to a gorgeously landscaped estate. The home was magnificent with its own swimming pool, sauna, and tennis courts. They sat under the covered deck as Faugner looked at Chanel with stars in his eyes. Before he was looking at her through a guilty lens because of the baggage that he carried from his marriage to her mother and the fact that she was underage, but now as he looked he could see clearly. He could see a woman who was more beautiful than an evening sunset. He sat and listened to her speak of the things that she had done and the crimes that she had committed. As she spoke he came up with legal game plans in his mind on how to get her out of trouble. There was no way that he was losing her to the system when she had just reappeared in his life. Chanel spoke with regret in her tone, uninterrupted as she tried to convince him to help her out of the bind. Little did she know, the moment she stepped across his threshold she had him as an ally, but he listened anyway. He knew that she needed to get these things off her chest.

When she was done she looked at him with a mixture of concern and hope. "Will you help me?" she asked.

Faugner nodded his head and took her hand in his. "Of course I will. I don't want you to worry yourself over this, Chanel. I will fix it. I don't know why you didn't come to me when you were in trouble, before you ever started robbing banks or stash houses and everything else. You know if you needed anything I would have provided it," he said.

"I didn't want to face my past. I've felt guilty about what we did for a long time. I haven't spoken to my mother in years. I don't even know where she is. Loving you I lost myself. I was just trying to find myself, Faugner, and now I feel like I'm even more screwed up," she admitted. "And my friends . . . God, I'm the one who messed everything up by getting greedy. One of them is in custody and I haven't even heard from Raegan . . ."

"Don't worry," he said. "Just let me make a few calls so that I can wrap my head around the legal side of things. You're welcome to anything in this home. And Jennings will provide you with anything you ask for."

"Thank you," Chanel said, genuinely grateful.

"Always, love," he replied before disappearing inside.

Chapter Twenty-nine

Reason dragged Raegan inside of the storage unit roughly. She could barely stand she was so badly beaten, but he wanted to make sure she had told him the correct location. "If you're lying, I'm not playing any more games with you. I'm gonna dead your ass right here and then I'm going over to Nahvid's and murking your kid. You understand?" he asked.

Raegan nodded. "This is it."

She let him inside and he dragged her behind him as he made his way to the boxes she had described. Just looking around he could tell that she wasn't lying. He had hit the jackpot. This was a gangster's paradise. Everything he would need to enforce the streets was conveniently tucked away inside. He went to the plush leather couch that was stored inside and pulled out a pocketknife to split the cushions. He cut into raw cocaine as he punctured one of the many kilos that were hidden inside. He practically salivated over all of the coke. Right now he was only getting 30 percent while Nahvid was taking home the big dough. Reason was eating, but Nahvid was sitting back getting rich. It was time for the tables to turn. Nahvid had too much love in D.C. It didn't matter what hood niggas were from, Nah had goons from every borough. In order for them to jump ship and hustle under Reason's regime, Nahvid had to go. He didn't want to have to murk his mans, but it was a part of the game. Every hustler's reign eventually had to end and it was time for Nah to be removed from his position of power. A new era was about arrive. Reason turned toward Raegan and pulled out his pistol.

Raegan couldn't even lift her head to plead for her life. She was out of it and knew that if she didn't get help soon she would die anyway. He had beaten her just that badly and a part of her was praying for it all to end.

Reason clicked off his safety. He no longer needed her and it was time for him to snuff her lights out.

"God, please protect my child," Raegan whispered, fully prepared to meet her Maker. There wasn't a reason for her to hope until . . .

"FBI! Put the weapon down now!"

After running from the very same organization, it was ironic that they were the ones to save her life.

"Mr. Grimes! Lower your weapon!" Starzycki said as he cut through the agents and made his way to the front of the armed crowd. "We will shoot you! Last warning. Lower your weapon!"

Reason thought about dying like a real nigga. Movie scenes where gangsters went out in hails of glory flashed through his mind, but at the end of the day Reason had never been a thoroughbred. He didn't have the balls to hold court in the street. He was just trying to live grand. His greed had placed him in the wrong place at the wrong time, putting himself in a compromising position to be caught with enough bricks to build his own jail. On top of that Raegan lay at his feet broken and bloodied. Today was definitely not his lucky day. He tossed his weapon to the side while shaking his head in disgrace as he went to his knees. "Fuck," Reason mumbled as he agents swarmed on him like bees to honey, quickly cuffing him and reciting his rights as they escorted him to the car.

Starzycki went to Raegan's side and didn't realize that she was another suspect in the bank robberies until he looked down and saw her face. She was busted up like he had never seen before but he had been investigating perpetrators long enough to ID her with his eyes closed. He shook his head, fearing that she may die before he ever got a chance to question her. "Get her a bus," he mumbled. "Put an officer on her door. I want to be the first one to question her."

Faugner Scott walked into his old firm, briefcase in hand, as the associates who remembered him welcomed him warmly. After learning of the details surrounding Gucci's arrest he realized that she had never given up Chanel or Raegan. In her official statement to the police she had claimed that Reese "Reason" Grimes, recruited three girls who were unacquainted, and blackmailed them into robbing the banks. She said that he threatened their families and even kidnapped one of their children in order to keep them in compliance. She then gave up the location of Reason's stash house giving her room for negotiating a deal with the DA. Both Gucci and Raegan were in federal custody, but because Chanel's identity was never discovered she was in the clear. Faugner had to admit that he was surprised at the loyalty between the three girls. He had been in the profession long enough to know that snitching was all too common, but these ladies had held each other down in the most dismal of circumstances. He walked up to his old office and smiled as he greeted Rose, the woman who used to be his assistant.

"Well I can't say that I was expecting to see you, Mr. Scott, but it sure did make my day!" she exclaimed, recognizing him instantly.

"It's been a long time, Rose. How are you?" he asked as he gave her a hug.

"I'm great," she responded.

"And Dawson and the boys?" he asked.

"They are all doing very well . . . thank you for asking. If you're Mr. Nolen's ten o'clock, he is ready for you," she said as she opened the door and motioned for him to walk past.

Faugner walked inside and was greeted by his protégé, Brelin Nolen. He was the youngest partner at the firm and owned a majority stake in it thanks to Faugner. When Faugner had left town he left everything at the firm in Brelin's hands and as he looked around he felt confident that he had made the correct choice.

"Faugner, it's good to see you, my man," Brelin greeted with a smile. He gave him a firm shake and then removed his Prada suit jacket and hung it on the back of his chair before he sat down behind his large executive desk.

"Good to see you too, son; looks like things are running smoothly here," Faugner said.

"Definitely, definitely. I reviewed the information you sent me on the two women involved in the bank robberies. I take it you have a personal interest in this?" he asked.

"Let's just say I need you to do all that you can to help them, Brelin. It's imperative that they come out of this unscathed. Now Gucci Stewart gave quite the convincing story to the federal bureau. They're buying it hard because the fish that she gave up is a much bigger catch then three women bank robbers. He has a rap sheet a mile long and was on the DEA radar anyway. This thing can play out nicely for these ladies if we steer it in the right direction. Sunny Raegan was picked up . . ."

The name immediately caught Brelin's attention. He had been thinking of her since she stuck him up and stole his car, leaving him with a higher insurance premium. "Sunny Raegan?"

"You know her?" Faugner asked.

"No, not really . . . no," he concluded, knowing that it would be a conflict of interest to take on the case if he answered otherwise. "Does Ms. Raegan know the story that Gucci is telling the Feds?" he asked. "It's important that they are saying the same thing. One little inconsistency and it's a wrap."

"No, not yet. Raegan is unconscious at Washington Medical Center. Reese Grimes beat her almost to death. She was taken into custody when they captured Grimes at the location where he kept his drugs," Faugner informed. "I need you to take this on for me."

"I'm already on it. This case will be my top priority," Brelin assured as he stood to his feet and quickly put on his jacket. "I don't mean to run, but I need to get down to both the jail and the hospital to make sure the Feds know that I'm the representing both girls."

"Thank you," Faugner said, confident that Chanel's friends were in good hands. "And when you meet with these ladies be sure to inform them that Chanel sent you."

"Not a problem. After I get them off you owe me a drink. I take it the retainer will be wired first thing in the morning?" Brelin inquired.

"It's already in the account," Faugner confirmed. He walked out of the office and stepped into the back of the limousine. He was sure that Chanel would have many questions, but he had secured the best defense attorney in the tri-state area to help her friends of out of their predicament. His main concern was ensuring that Chanel's name didn't ever come across the desk of Agent

Starzycki because once she was mentioned it would be much harder to keep her safe. So if Gucci and Raegan got off, then Chanel would be in the clear for good.

Chapter Thirty

Brelin couldn't believe that he and Raegan had crossed paths in this manner. He knew that she was in trouble the night that he had met her, but he could never imagine the web that she had woven for herself. He was intrigued by Raegan and as he made his way to the hospital he was eager to see her again. He hadn't prepared himself for what he saw when he walked through the door. Her eyes were swollen shut and her nose was covered in bandages. Her entire face was black and blue; there were bruises everywhere. Every part of Raegan looked as if it were injured.

"No one is allowed in here, sir," the nurse said once she realized that he had entered the room.

"I'm her attorney," he announced with authority. "Is she going to be okay?"

"The doctors think so. It'll just take some time. She's beat up real bad. Somebody really did a number on her," the nurse replied.

"Will she wake up?" he asked.

"Yeah, she'll come to. She's up one minute and sleeping the next. She has been asleep for a while so she may wake up for you soon," the nurse informed.

Brelin sat down in the chair across the room and watched Raegan sleep. He could not imagine what had brought her to this point. She did not look anything like the vivacious, challenging con artist he had met before. Her fragile state of being now evoked sympathy from him. It did not matter what she had done. No woman deserved to be beaten so mercilessly. He used his time to inform the Feds that he was taking over Gucci and Raegan's case, then he reviewed everything that he had on the two ladies. Neither had serious priors so he was sure that he could resolve this amicably. The girls might have to do short stints in prison, but compared to the life sentences that they could face without him, a year or two was nothing. Raegan began to moan in her sleep causing Brelin to put up his files and stand near her bedside. Her eyes opened slowly as she stared up at Brelin in confusion.

"Chanel sent me. I'm an attorney, Raegan. I'm going to get you out of this mess," he said.

"I'm sorry about your car," she said, barely audible. She immediately recognized him. A face that handsome was hard to erase from memory. The pain medication the doctors had coursing through her veins had her so high she barely felt like moving her lips to speak.

He chuckled. "We'll talk about that after we beat this case. I'm not going to bother you much until you are out of the hospital, but I do need to fill you in on the story that your friend Gucci is telling so that you will give the same version when you give your statement to the detectives that will interview you."

He filled her in on all the lies that Gucci told to cover their tracks. What he was doing was completely immoral, but it was all a part of the crooked system of the law. His only concern was his clients and he had no problem bending the rules. Raegan was grateful that Gucci didn't pin everything on Nahvid. Reason was the perfect person to take the fall for their misdeeds. Karma was a bitch and she hoped that he received a thousand years for what he had done to her.

After she got her story together she looked at Brelin and said, "Please don't let them take my life from me. I have a child to get back, too. I don't want to spend the rest of my days in prison."

"You won't," Brelin assured. "I'll make sure of it."

Chapter Thirty-one

Nahvid received word of Reason's arrest when it flashed across the evening news. The fact that he had been caught in his storage warehouse let Nahvid know that Reason was a snake. Rumors swirled through the hood of Reason turning state's evidence, but Nahvid wasn't worried. He had played the game by the rules and had moved smartly from day one. There was no way that Reason could give the Feds anything. In fact, all of Nahvid's money was washed and cleaned. He was as legal as a Wall Street broker. The Feds' investigation into his finances would dry up quickly. Nah wasn't worried. He wanted to see Raegan, but she was in federal custody and no matter whose pockets he laced, they refused to let him see her. So he did the only thing he could do and decided to blow town for a while. He wanted to let things cool off before he returned to D.C. He had a quarter million on Reason's head and knew that one of his prison goons would catch Reason slipping one day during rec time. Somebody would want to make that money. Every nigga locked up had family on the outside struggling to get by. As soon as Reason had a tag on his toe, Nahvid would pay up. Nahvid was going to make a good example out of his so-called right-hand man. One hand was supposed to wash the other, but Reason had forgotten that along the way and now Nahvid was about to show niggas how he got down. His best friend's disloyalty wasn't the only reason why

Nahvid wanted him knocked off. Nahvid knew that any man facing fed time would fold under pressure. That's why he never let Reason know too much. He was putting in the execution order because of the torture Reason had taken Raegan through. Finding out she was still alive had felt like the luckiest day of his life, but not being able to see her was agonizing. Hearing of how she had been injured made Nahvid's heart bleed in strife. That was one woman he loved dearly. He had so many things to tell her. At this point he didn't care about their past, he just wanted to fix the present and look forward to the future with her. Unfortunately for Nahvid, her future was so uncertain. Baby Micah was growing each and every day. Nahvid hated that she was missing so much of his life. Raegan didn't deserve any of this. Life had beaten her up and a lot of poor choices had caused them to separate and go down different paths. Nahvid couldn't help but to feel as if this was his fault. Raegan was his woman. He should have protected her better. He held himself accountable for the things she had endured, especially her encounters with Reason. Feeling the pressure from the streets, Nahvid didn't like all of the attention. Even his connect was concerned about the situation. A drug dealer in the limelight was a drug dealer who wanted to get caught and Nahvid wanted neither. So he concluded that it was time to get out of town. He tried to contact Raegan's attorney to send word to her through him, but he was unable to connect with D.C.'s most prestigious criminal defense lawyer. Even the check he had sent to cover Raegan's legal fees was sent back to him. Nahvid felt hopeless as he packed up his life and planned his getaway. If he was in federal crosshairs, by the time they counterfeited a case on him, he would be in the wind. He put baby Micah in his car seat then drove to return him to

his real father. He didn't have the right to run away
with Raegan's son. He desperately wished that Micah
was his own, maybe then his and Raegan's love would
have reached its full potential, but the reality was baby
Micah wasn't his blood. He knocked on Micah's door
and waited until Micah answered. Micah's expression
didn't change when he saw his son in Nahvid's arms.

"Fuck do you want?" Micah asked.

Nahvid ignored Micah's rudeness and stayed focused on what he had come there to do. "I know you
know what's going on with Raegan. I'm shaking town
for a bit. I came to return your son to you. He doesn't
have his mother so he at least needs his father right
now," Nahvid said.

"I don't want shit to do with that bitch or her bastard
son. She's probably been fucking around with you. The
little nigga probably ain't even my kid. You wanted to
play daddy nigga, so keep on playing," Micah spewed,
full of hate and resentment. He was so stubborn that he
no longer had an interest in his own child because he
knew that he could never provide him with the things
that Nahvid could. He was jealous and angry that
Raegan had moved on. So he was snubbing their son,
punishing him instead of taking accountability for the
things he had done to end their relationship.

Nahvid just scoffed in complete disbelief, but he
wasn't going to ask again. He didn't want Raegan's son
left with a fuck boy like Micah anyway.

"I guess it's me and you, li'l homie," he said as he
put the baby and his belongings back in the car. "If you
don't have anyone else in the world you've got Nah."

He headed toward the private airstrip that he had
rented. An extreme emptiness filled him because he
knew that he was leaving his soul mate behind, but it
was something he had to do. If he got locked up too he

would be no good to her. He had to let the dust settle and get his own life in order before he could be of any assistance to her. Two lovers in two different federal jails would be a tragedy. He had to stay free so that he could work on her freedom. He boarded the plane and settled in with baby Micah sleeping on his chest as they waited for the departure. He picked up his phone and dialed Raegan's number, knowing that she couldn't answer. Her voice mail picked up and he spoke, "Hey, beautiful. I'm sorry that you are going through all of this, ma. I wish that I could be there for you but every time I try to see you, I'm turned away. Look a lot of heat is coming down on me so I have to shake for a while. Your son is safe. He is with me and I will look after him as if he is my own. I love you, Raegan. I will always be fighting for you; until the day you're free I'ma ride this out with you. Take care of yourself and stay hopeful. You're the love of my life and I'll get you out of there if it's the last thing that I do on this earth."

Chapter Thirty-two

When Raegan walked into the correctional facility she felt as if her entire world had been taken away. In an attempt to put up a hard front, her face was cold, but if you looked closely you could see the tears she was stifling as they accumulated in her eyes. She had been through so much. From the day her son was born her life had spiraled out of control. Baby Micah was the only bright spot in her dim existence and she had managed to screw that up as well. It had taken her three months to recover from the trauma Reason had put on her. She still wasn't at her full strength but the Feds were tired of waiting to prosecute her. They pulled her out of the hospital as soon as they possibly could. Brelin had been a blessing in disguise. He focused all of his attention on her, taking a personal interest in her situation. They spent almost ten hours a day together for her entire hospital stay, and their conversation was surrounded around so much more than just legal matters. He wanted to know everything. Where was her son? Where was her man? Why was he not by her side? What did she like? Dislike? He wanted to know her and the fact that she found herself curious about him surprised her. She did not think that she would ever find someone who piqued her interest like Nahvid, but Brelin Nolen did. After receiving Nahvid's devastating phone call Raegan had fallen into a horrible depression. She was grateful that Nahvid had promised to look after her baby, but with both of them gone who was going to look after her? When Brelin stepped up to the plate, his sincere actions surprised her. His handsome, grown-man persona was like a magnet and he was able to make her smile. She loved how he nursed her back to health and stayed by her side. Client or not, he was putting in way too much overtime for a man who wasn't interested. Although Brelin had assured her that he was working with the federal DA to reduce the charges, it felt as if she would be in jail forever. She had been questioned, processed, then transferred directly to the city jail. She corroborated Gucci's story almost word for word so the Feds had to take it as truth. When they asked her about her son, she told them she had convinced Reason to spare her son and to take her life instead.

She was blocked off from the world and the only person who she had seen in the past few months was Brelin and she was grateful for him. Without him constantly supporting and reassuring her that everything would be all right she would have gone insane.

She entered her temporary holding cell and her heart melted when she saw Gucci sitting inside.

"Guch!" she exclaimed as they rushed toward each other hugging and crying. "Oh my God, Gucci!"

"I'm so glad to see you," Gucci said as they touched each other's faces. "I'm so sorry. I heard about what Reason did to you, Raegan."

"It's okay. In a lot of ways I feel like I deserved it. If it wasn't for you though, Guch, I would be dead right now. Your little story saved my life. I would not be here if the Feds hadn't showed up when they did. He was going to kill me," Raegan admitted. She lowered her voice and continued. "Thank you for not dragging Nah into this."

"I would never. I know how you feel about him," Gucci replied.

"I have to get my life together, Guch. We've been living so wrong. I just want to be a mother to my son and just get right you know? What if I would have died? Would I have gone to heaven? After all that I've done I honestly can't answer yes. I have never been so afraid in all my life, Gucci. I don't want to be afraid to die. I want to know that I have done good things in this world. If I ever get out of here my main priority will be my son. It has to be. Money isn't a good enough excuse to go around living the way that we did. I hurt so many people," she said as tears fell while she thought of Nahvid and her child.

"Look at you. You've really changed," Gucci said.

"Almost dying will do that to you," Raegan said with an emotional laugh. "Brelin and I talked a lot about the things that I've done . . ."

"Brelin huh?" Gucci asked in shock, knowing that she addressed their lawyer as Mr. Nolen.

Raegan smiled and shook her head. "Stop it, Guch . . . He's a friend. He's been by my side nursing me back to health," Raegan explained, trying to convince herself that their relationship was strictly platonic. She couldn't ignore the butterflies she felt when his name came up, however. She was confused as to how she could have growing feelings for Brelin when her love for Nahvid was very much alive. Raegan was neither in the place nor mental space to figure her feelings out, however. The only thing she had time to focus on was survival in the atmosphere she had been thrown into. "I'm serious though, Gucci. We both have to do better. We were selling ourselves short. I mean we out here risking our lives, robbing niggas, banks, basically whoever had it . . . but why couldn't we go out and get it ourselves? There is a world of opportunities out there. Why couldn't we just dream bigger?" Raegan asked sincerely. She was tired of hustling, scheming, and screwing her way through life. Raegan wanted to live with a guilt-free conscience and a love-filled heart. She didn't know what would happen, but it didn't matter. Innocent or guilty, imprisoned or free, she was going to start to live better and focus on the things that mattered most.

As the driver pulled up to the tall glass building Chanel gripped Faugner's hand tightly.

"Everything is okay. You're not at risk, Chanel. The Feds have no clue who the third female accomplice was. Gucci and Raegan have kept their mouths closed regarding you," he assured as he helped her out of the car and escorted her up to Brelin's office.

She hadn't felt completely free in months. Part of her felt guilty for being the one who got away. She made sure that she kept their commissaries stacked and that their legal fees were all taken care of. She couldn't take the risk of writing them, but Brelin always delivered messages to them on her behalf. Those girls were her sisters and it was killing her that they were locked up. The federal DA was dragging his ass on allowing them to cop pleas because he was hoping that the time in jail would cause Gucci or Raegan to crack. He felt that there was more to the story, but little did he know that they would never turn on one another. So he was waiting for nothing.

They entered the office and Chanel was immediately surprised at how young Brelin was. He couldn't have been a day over thirty-five. She had to smile because

she knew her girls and knew that both Gucci and Raegan were enjoying the eye candy.

"You must be Chanel," Brelin greeted.

"And you must be the miracle lawyer who is going to
get my friends off," she answered with a friendly smile.

"The three of you together, I could only imagine you
all being nothing but trouble," he said, noticing that
all three girls were drop-dead gorgeous. He would
have imagined them on the arms of important men,
not strong-arming banks and hustlers. Chanel was
back on top and the queen in Faugner's castle. She was
designer clad and her hair and makeup were flawless.
Brelin shook his head knowing that looks could be deceiving and the Red Bottom Bandits were living proof.

"I need them out like yesterday," Chanel said as she
sat back in her chair.

"I've tried to explain that the legal system takes
time," Faugner said.

"But I'm tired of waiting. I need them out. With them
locked up two-thirds of my heart is locked down. What
is the DA saying?"

"They have offered Raegan two years and five years
probation," Brelin revealed.

"Two years!" Chanel exclaimed.

"That's not bad considering that the charges con-
stitute twenty years to life in prison," Faugner interrupted.

Brelin stood to his feet and walked in a back and
forth path behind his desk. "It's Gucci who concerns
me. The DA is being lenient on Raegan because she was
a clear captive of Reese Grimes and they understood
her need to protect her son. Gucci killed a cop. They
want to give her fifteen years," he said. "I've been arguing them down for months, but they're not budging.
Gucci is the one who might have to do the time."

"She's the one who can't do the time! Gucci is too soft for prison. She can't spend that much time behind her bars, especially without Raegan or me in there with her," Chanel said.

"What amount of money would make this disappear?" Faugner asked.

"If I was having this conversation, which I'm not," Brelin replied seriously. "About three million dollars. That would be enough to fake a death, get the warden and the DA to confirm it. But she would have to start completely over. She couldn't ever contact anyone from her past life, including her mother."

"And Raegan would do two to three years," Chanel confirmed.

"That's not enough time to pull anything fishy. With good behavior she'll be out in a year and a half and if you count time served that knocks it down to a year. Raegan will be fine," Brelin assured. He had grown extremely fond of her so it was in his best interest for her to come home as soon as possible. He was ready to get to know her on an intimate level. He was intrigued by her and wanted her to gain her freedom more than anyone knew.

Chanel looked at Faugner and she nodded her head.

"Just to make sure that you and I are on the same page . . ." Brelin began.

"This conversation never happened," Chanel confirmed as she put on her oversized Burberry sunglasses and walked out of the room.

Chapter Thirty-three

It was the middle of the night when Gucci was snatched from her bed. Before she could protest her mouth was gagged with chloroform, putting her lights out temporarily. Raegan lay still listening to the commotion as tears fell down her cheeks. She had known that the guards would come for her. Brelin had snuck in a letter from Chanel explaining both of their fates. Directly after reading it Brelin destroyed the incriminating note. The selfish part of her was jealous that Gucci got to go home, but she understood the reasoning behind the decision. It still didn't make it hurt any less because now she was facing jail alone.

The next morning she woke up and immediately felt the absence of Gucci's presence. It seemed as though the other inmates noticed too, because bitches who had never messed with Raegan before were trying her now . . . pushing her buttons . . . testing her limits. Brelin came for a legal visit first thing in the morning.

"Can I speak with her in private, my man?" he asked with authority.

The guard left the room, leaving them with complete privacy.

"I feel lost without my friend," Raegan said. "I'm scared, Brelin. I don't have anybody."

He took her in his arms and held her tightly. "You have me and you have two great friends who are waiting for you on the outside. They need you to hold strong, Raegan. I need you to be strong. I don't know what it is about you, but you've had my attention from day one, shorty," he admitted. "And I'd like to explore that once you're free. Once things are settled and I'm driving you home."

"You don't want me, Brelin. Trust me. I hurt everyone who tries to get close to me," she admitted. "I'm only pretty on the outside."

"Oh I want you, ma," he whispered as he stepped closer to her, putting his lips to her ear. "I want to kiss you, and taste you, and make you cum, I want you and I'm going to have you. We just have to handle this first. You have to stay positive and let this time go by. I'm going to be campaigning the DA for your early release every day until he agrees. You won't do any more than a year. I promise you that. That's my word."

Brelin's pledge made Raegan moist between her thighs. There was definitely a mutual attraction, but she was ridden with guilt because of it. There was not a doubt in her mind that she loved Nahvid, but here she was having strong feelings for the man in front of her.

"I have a lot of baggage, Brelin," she whispered. "I have a boyfriend."

"I don't want to be your boyfriend. I'm a man and I'm not interested in being friends, Raegan," he answered. "I want to pursue the real thing with you."

There had been so much treachery between her and Nahvid that the idea of starting over felt refreshing, but she couldn't do anything in her current circumstance.

"I like you, Brelin. I care a lot about you. You were the only face I saw when I needed someone the most," she said. "But I need time. Time to fix myself, time to pay my debt to society, and time to learn how to be a good mother. I have to figure out what I want and I can't get involved with you when I'm clearly involved with someone else right now. Not to mention that Nahvid has my son in his care. If you're still around after all of that, then we can explore these feelings that we're having, but I can't promise you anything because there is someone else tugging at the other side of my heart," she said. The last thing she wanted to do was push him away, but she needed to be honest with him. Her love had a lot of limitations these days and he deserved to know upfront.

The guard reentered the room at that time and Brelin changed the conversation and took a step back to put space between them. "I respect that and I'll wait for your decision. I'll see you soon," he said before walking out of the door.

Gucci awoke with the worst headache she had ever experienced and in complete exasperation as she looked around the room she was in. She climbed out of bed and cautiously peeked out of the bedroom door, looking up and down the empty hallway of the fancy house. "Where the hell am I?" she asked herself as she crept with the stealth of a cat, making no noise as she walked along the plush, carpeted floor. The last thing she remembered was going to sleep in a prison cell. How had she ended up here? *Am I dreaming?* she thought. She saw the front door at the bottom of the steps and thought about making a run for it, until Chanel stepped into her line of sight.

"Chanel?" she whispered.

Chanel stopped mid-step and looked up the staircase to find Gucci staring incredulously. "Hi, Guch," she greeted warmly as she stood staring happily at her friend. She ascended the stairs and hugged Gucci so tightly that they both began crying.

"Did you break me out?" Gucci asked, still astounded by the sudden freedom that she possessed. "Am I dreaming?"

Chanel laughed as she wiped her tears. "No, Guch, it's real. I paid for you to have a new life. They were trying to give you fifteen years, Gucci. So Faugner helped me set it up so that you could fake your death," Chanel answered. "I couldn't tell you. Raegan knew, but we didn't want you to turn down the opportunity to start over so we didn't tell you. You can never go back, Guch. Gucci Stewart is dead. Your mother will be taken care of. I will make sure that her bills are paid monthly, but in order for you to stay free you have to change who you are and cut off all old ties to D.C."

Gucci's eyes burned at the pain of letting go of her mother, but it was too late to decide otherwise. Chanel had made an executive decision, one that Gucci appreciated, but one that hurt nonetheless.

"Do you understand?" Chanel asked, seriously.

Gucci nodded her head and replied, "What about Raegan? Is she here?"

"Raegan is still in prison. She has two to three years. Brelin Nolen says she will be out sooner if she behaves. The day that she is released we are flying her down here. We made it out of D.C., Gucci, and now we don't ever have to go back."

Final Chapter

One Year Later

Raegan, I think about you all the time, ma. Life here in London doesn't feel right without you. I know that our history is complicated. I hurt you and you hurt me. We did a lot of that to each other, but through it all you are still the greatest love I've ever known. I'm addicted to you. You're my Sunny Rae. I show baby Micah your picture every day. He's getting up there now. He's not the little baby who you remember. He can't wait to see you and I don't mean to add pressure but neither can I. I need to be with you, Raegan. Even if we can't pick up where we left off, I yearn for your friendship. You complete me. Having you in my life makes me whole so please allow me that. I know you won't write me back so I'm done begging, lol. But just remember that you have two people out here that's missing you and thinking about you every day that you're away. You're a real woman, Raegan . . . be my real woman.

Nah

Raegan closed the note and wiped away a stray tear as she put it inside the prison-issued laundry bag. It didn't contain much and in all honesty she wanted to say to hell with her things and leave all the bullshit behind. She was getting out today and she was so anxious that her stomach hurt. Brelin had kept his promise and had stuck it out with her until the very end. She only ended up serving thirteen months, but to her it felt like forever. Without a crew in prison she didn't have the easiest time adjusting. Bitches tested her every day, but as she prepared to leave her cell she felt so proud of herself because no matter what they couldn't break her. She was the one on her way home while the bum bitches were stuck behind bars. Tired of living in captivity she was ready to breathe free air. It was funny because out of all the things that she had gone without it was the simple freedoms that she had come to miss. She valued the little things now, but more importantly she had become a person of value while being locked up. Her time hadn't been served in vain; she was wiser and a better person. She was walking out of prison and never coming back again. She came out of her cell with the laundry bag slung over her shoulder and she looked back at the tiny space that had been her home for the past year. Turning up her nose she shook her head and bowed her head as she whispered, "Thank you, God, for seeing me through this. Now please take me to my son."

A part of her feared that Micah wouldn't recognize her, but she knew that when she laid him on her chest the synchronized beats of their hearts would remind him of who she was. She was his mother and no time, distance, space, person, or place could ever keep them apart. Their bond was unbreakable and she would never jeopardize her role as his mother again. Prison

had given her time for self-reflection and she had realized that she had put herself in this position. For so
long she had pointed the finger at her child's father.
Using excuses and scapegoats to justify her getting in
the game, but at the end of the day it was her actions
and her bad decisions that had ultimately sent her life
spiraling out of control.

She saw Brelin waiting at the end of her cell block
and she waved excitedly. He gave her a wink and she
headed toward him. She never saw the sneak attack
coming her way. She was merely steps away from freedom when Bianca, the leader of a lesbian girl gang, and
her crew came out of nowhere. They had tried to bully
Raegan into submission her entire bid, but she had
steered clear of them until now. Her face dropped in
horror when she felt the blade plunge into her abdomen as Bianca stabbed her up.

Raegan saw red as she flew into a rage as a stabbing
pain filled her stomach. She lunged toward Bianca in
defense mode, pushing the girl off of her. She couldn't
focus on all three chicks but she could focus on one.
She knew the rules of the street. Take out the head and
the body will fall so she planned to beat the fucking
brakes off of Bianca. Raegan grabbed Bianca's hand
and fought her for the homemade shank knife. She
knew that the fight was unbalanced as long Bianca
was carrying and she wasn't. Raegan bit into her wrist
until she tasted blood, forcing Bianca to drop it to
the ground. Then she worked the big bitch. Throwing
blows relentlessly and shoving the girl forcefully as the
two tussled. Raegan was taking out all of her aggres-
sion. She pushed Bianca with all of her might causing
the girl to break the weak railing that separated the
highest cellblock from the concrete floor below. Bianca's face instantly transfixed in horror as she felt her

body going over the edge and she grabbed Raegan's clothes, sending them both flying over the edge.

"Agh!" Raegan screamed as she grabbed for the hanging metal and held on with all of her might. Bianca desperately hung on to Raegan's leg as the two girls held on for dear life. "Brelin!" Raegan called out as she heard the commotion of guards rushing to help them above her head. Her hands were sweating and her abdomen piercing with excruciating pain as she tried to hold on.

"Don't you let go of that rail!" Bianca yelled in a shrill voice. "I can't get a grip. I'm slipping! Help . . . please hurry!"

Bianca tried to climb up Raegan's body, causing Raegan grip to loosen. "Stop it . . . stop."

Raegan twisted her body, causing Bianca to completely lose her grip and go plummeting to the floor below.

The sickening sound as Bianca's body completed the fifty-foot drop made Raegan close her eyes as Brelin and the guards finally approached her. Brelin rushed past the guards and reached his arm down to pull Raegan up.

"Grab my hand!" he shouted. Raegan reached up and when their hands connected she knew that he wouldn't let her go. He pulled her up onto the tier and she collapsed into him, sobbing hysterically.

"Raegan, on the ground!" one of the COs yelled.

"What?" she asked as she was snatched out of Brelin's arms. Like a deer in headlights Raegan protested. "No! Wait! Brelin! Help me! Please . . . it was a mistake," she said. She looked over the edge and saw a pool of blood circling around Bianca's body. "Please don't let them do this!" she yelled at Brelin, who was stressfully yelling at the head correctional officer.

He turned to Raegan and yelled, "Stop resisting, Raegan! I'll get you out of here! I promise! I'll take care of it."

Within the blink of an eye she had caught a body and contributed to a murder that would stop her from tasting the freedom she so desperately yearned for. It seemed no matter how hard Raegan searched for redemption, it eluded her. Now she was certain that her life was over and she could forget about ever reuniting with the loves of her life. They were going to hit her with more charges and lock her away for the rest of her life. She was about to lose everything for a second time. Just when Nahvid and her son would forget about her for good. . . .

THE END

The highly anticipated *Prada Plan 3* is coming soon!

Follow us on twitter @novelista & @realjaquavis or visit www.ashleyjaquavis.com

#TEAMA&J . . . GETADDICTED!

Notes

Notes

Notes

ORDER FORM
URBAN BOOKS, LLC
78 E. Industry Ct
Deer Park, NY 11729

Name:(please print):_____

Address: _____

City/State: _____

Zip: _____

QTY	TITLES	PRICE
	16 On The Block	$14.95
	A Girl From Flint	$14.95
	A Pimp's Life	$14.95
	Baltimore Chronicles	$14.95
	Baltimore Chronicles 2	$14.95
	Betrayal	$14.95
	Black Diamond	$14.95
	Black Diamond 2	$14.95
	Black Friday	$14.95
	Both Sides Of The Fence	$14.95
	Both Sides Of The Fence 2	$14.95
	California Connection	$14.95

Shipping and handling-add $3.50 for 1st book, then $1.75 for each additional book.

Please send a check payable to:

Urban Books, LLC

Please allow 4-6 weeks for delivery

ORDER FORM
URBAN BOOKS, LLC
78 E. Industry Ct
Deer Park, NY 11729

Name:(please print):_____

Address: _____

City/State: _____

Zip: _____

QTY	TITLES	PRICE
	California Connection 2	$14.95
	Cheesecake And Teardrops	$14.95
	Congratulations	$14.95
	Crazy In Love	$14.95
	Cyber Case	$14.95
	Denim Diaries	$14.95
	Diary Of A Mad First Lady	$14.95
	Diary Of A Stalker	$14.95
	Diary Of A Street Diva	$14.95
	Diary Of A Young Girl	$14.95
	Dirty Money	$14.95
	Dirty To The Grave	$14.95

Shipping and handling-add $3.50 for 1st book, then $1.75 for each additional book.

Please send a check payable to:

Urban Books, LLC

Please allow 4-6 weeks for delivery

ORDER FORM
URBAN BOOKS, LLC
78 E. Industry Ct
Deer Park, NY 11729

Name:(please print):_____

Address: _____

City/State: _____

Zip: _____

QTY	TITLES	PRICE
	Gunz And Roses	$14.95
	Happily Ever Now	$14.95
	Hell Has No Fury	$14.95
	Hush	$14.95
	If It Isn't love	$14.95
	Kiss Kiss Bang Bang	$14.95
	Last Breath	$14.95
	Little Black Girl Lost	$14.95
	Little Black Girl Lost 2	$14.95
	Little Black Girl Lost 3	$14.95
	Little Black Girl Lost 4	$14.95
	Little Black Girl Lost 5	$14.95

Shipping and handling-add $3.50 for 1st book, then $1.75 for each additional book.

Please send a check payable to:

Urban Books, LLC

Please allow 4-6 weeks for delivery

ORDER FORM
URBAN BOOKS, LLC
78 E. Industry Ct
Deer Park, NY 11729

Name: (please print):_____

Address: _____

City/State: _____

Zip: _____

QTY	TITLES	PRICE
	Loving Dasia	$14.95
	Material Girl	$14.95
	Moth To A Flame	$14.95
	Mr. High Maintenance	$14.95
	My Little Secret	$14.95
	Naughty	$14.95
	Naughty 2	$14.95
	Naughty 3	$14.95
	Queen Bee	$14.95
	Say It Ain't So	$14.95
	Snapped	$14.95
	Snow White	$14.95

Shipping and handling-add $3.50 for 1st book, then $1.75 for each additional book.

Please send a check payable to:

Urban Books, LLC

Please allow 4-6 weeks for delivery